1966- To [illegible]
Grandpa

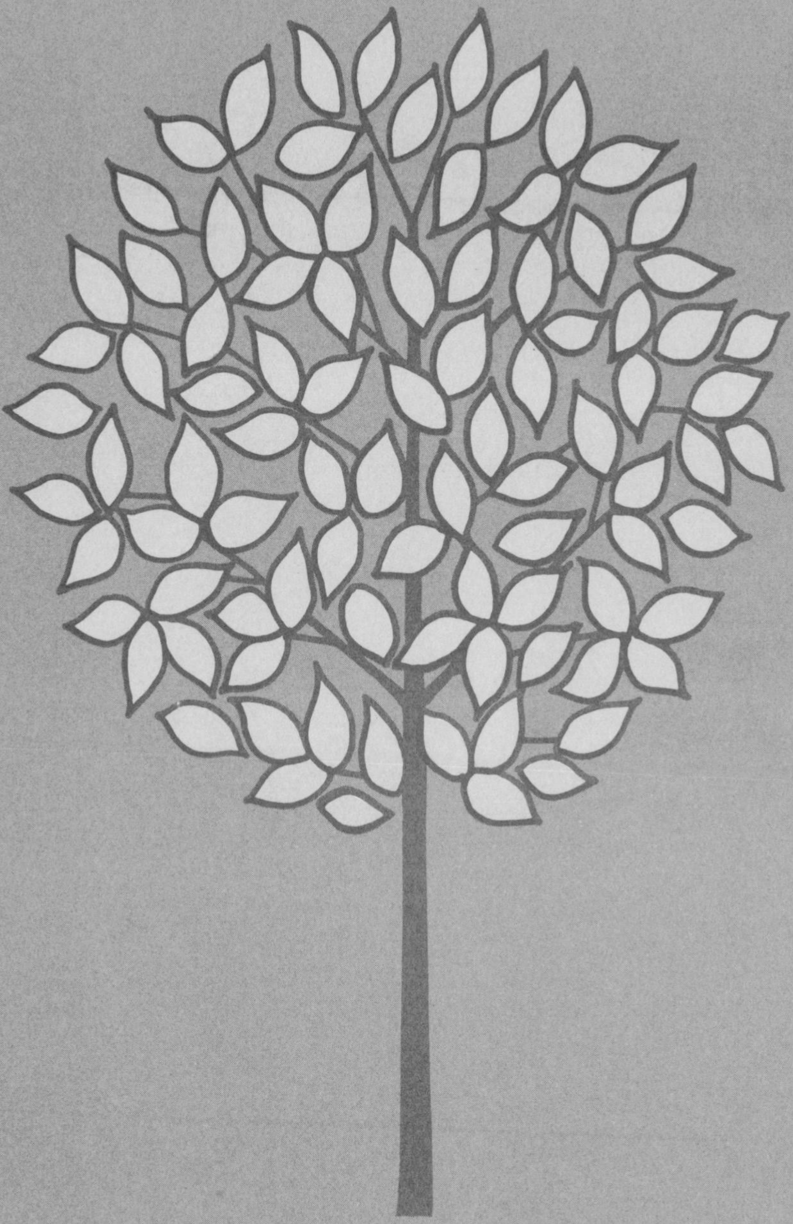

BEST BOOK OF
HORSE STORIES

Salute

Blood Royal

Misty of
Chincoteague

Ruy Houlihan

BEST BOOK

OF

HORSE STORIES

Edited by

PAULINE RUSH EVANS

Color Illustrations by

RAY HOULIHAN

Line Illustrations by

DAN NOONAN

Doubleday & Company, Inc., Garden City, New York

Preface

I have watched the *Best Book Series* in the making—and over and over again I have wished that such books had been available when my children were growing up. It seems to me that arranging stories by subject matter will be most appealing to children. And certainly there is something here for every child. . . . Each volume contains weeks and months of fine reading.

What I particularly like is that this is a series of books for *reading*—not for looking. Every book is illustrated, and handsomely illustrated, but the emphasis is where it should be—on the stories themselves. Today, as always, children want and need reading that they can really get their teeth into.

The child who has this series to grow on is fortunate indeed. It comes too late for my own children, but my younger grandchildren will be able to enjoy the *Best Book Series*—every one of them.

SIDONIE M. GRUENBERG
Former Director, Child Study Association of America

The Best Book Series

BEST BOOK OF ADVENTURE STORIES

BEST BOOK OF ANIMAL STORIES

BEST BOOK OF DOG STORIES

BEST BOOK OF FUN AND NONSENSE

BEST BOOK OF HEROES AND HEROINES

BEST BOOK OF HORSE STORIES

ACKNOWLEDGMENTS

Thanks are due to the following authors, publishers, publications and agents for permission to use the material indicated.

Paul Annixter for "Champion of the Peaks," copyright 1948 by Paul Annixter, originally published in *Story Parade*. Montgomery A. Atwater for "Blood Royal" by Montgomery A. Atwater. Reprinted by permission of the author and his agent, August Lenniger. Adele De Leeuw for "If Wishes Were Horses," copyright 1955 by Adele De Leeuw. Harcourt, Brace and Company, Inc., for "A Miserable Merry Christmas" and "I Get a Colt to Break In" from BOY ON HORSEBACK by Lincoln Steffens, copyright 1931, 1935, by Harcourt, Brace and Company, Inc.; "Elimination Race" and "Final Race" from RED HORSE HILL by Stephen W. Meader, copyright 1930 by Harcourt, Brace and Company, Inc.; renewed by Stephen W. Meader. Helen Train Hilles for "The Potato Race." Reprinted by permission of the author and her agents, McIntosh and Otis. Gladys Lewis for "The Black Stallion and the Red Mare," copyright 1945 by Gladys Lewis. Reprinted by permission of the author and Copp Clark, Ltd., Toronto. The Macmillan Company for "Learning to Ride Together" from SALUTE by C. W. Anderson, copyright 1940 by The Macmillan Company. The McGraw-Hill Book Co., Inc. for "The Sorrel That Turned on a Dime," from MOUNTAIN PONY by Henry V. Larom, copyright 1946 by Henry V. Larom; "The Pony Race" from WINDY FOOT AT THE COUNTY FAIR by Frances Frost, published by Whittlesey House, copyright 1947 by The McGraw-Hill Book Co., Inc. David McKay Company, Inc., for "Fortune Frowns" and "Fortune Smiles" from KENTUCKY DERBY WINNER by Isabel McLennan McMeekin, copyright 1949 by Isabel McLennan McMeekin. Julian Messner, Inc., for "Horse Trading" from THE MAGNIFICENT BARB by Dana Faralla; copyright date May 1, 1947 by Dana Faralla. Rand McNally & Company for "Pony Penning Day," "She Can't Turn Back" and "Caught in the Whirlpool" from MISTY OF CHINCOTEAGUE by Marguerite Henry, copyright 1947 by Rand McNally & Company. *Story Parade* for "Can a Horse Know Too Much?" by Genevieve Torrey Eames, copyright 1945 by Story Parade, Inc. Henry Z. Walck, Inc., for "Bucephalus" from EACH IN HIS OWN WAY by Alice Gall and Fleming Crew, © copyright 1937 by Henry Z. Walck, Inc., Willis Kingsley Wing for "No Sum Too Small" by Murray Hoyt, copyright 1947 by Murray Hoyt.

The editor and publisher have made diligent efforts to trace the ownership of all copyrighted material in this volume, and believe that all necessary permissions have been secured. If any errors have inadvertently been made, proper corrections will gladly be made in future editions.

Introduction

IF ONE fine Christmas Santa Claus should be able to fill all of the requests he received, one thing is certain. There would be very few homes in America without a horse—or at least a pony. For at some time in his or her life, almost everybody dreams of owning a horse.

Don't ask me why. It doesn't do any good to talk about the history of the horse—how the little five-toed animal (no bigger than a good-sized dog) developed into the magnificent creature he is today, one of man's closest and most useful friends. It's an interesting story, but it certainly doesn't explain why a twelve-year-old girl living in the heart of a big city would gladly give up all of her friends just to possess a horse of her own. But she would—in hundreds of thousands of cases. I don't know why, and, if you asked her, I don't think she could tell you either. All that she knows is that to own a horse would be the greatest thing in the world—and, for her, perhaps it would be.

But everybody who wants a horse can't have one. There just aren't that many horses, for one thing. So if you can't *have* a horse, perhaps the next best thing is to read about them. That's the reason for this book.

There are thousands of horse stories—very old ones and new ones, real and imaginary, funny and sad—and if you are really crazy about horses, I suppose that you would read any of them. But among them are some truly fine stories, a few of them—like Seton's *The Pacing Mustang*—really great. Here are twenty-odd of the best I've found. I know that you will enjoy them.

But still—I hope you do get that horse.

Danbury, Conn.   P. R. E.

Contents

NO SUM TOO SMALL   13
  by Murray Hoyt

CAN A HORSE KNOW TOO MUCH?   30
  by Genevieve Torrey Eames

BLOOD ROYAL   42
  by Montgomery M. Atwater

MISTY OF CHINCOTEAGUE   54
  PONY PENNING DAY
  SHE CAN'T TURN BACK
  CAUGHT IN THE WHIRLPOOL
  by Marguerite Henry

CHAMPION OF THE PEAKS   69
  by Paul Annixter

SALUTE   88
  LEARNING TO RIDE TOGETHER
  by C. W. Anderson

THE POTATO RACE   98
  by Helen Train Hilles

RED HORSE HILL   110
  ELIMINATION RACE
  FINAL RACE
  by Stephen W. Meader

BLACK BEAUTY 124
A FAIR START
A JOB HORSE AND HIS DRIVERS
POOR GINGER
HARD TIMES
MY LAST HOME
by Anna Sewell

ELLEN RIDES AGAIN 144
by Beverly Cleary

THE BLACK STALLION AND THE RED MARE 158
by Gladys F. Lewis

BOY ON HORSEBACK 167
A MISERABLE MERRY CHRISTMAS
I GET A COLT TO BREAK IN
by Lincoln Steffens

IF WISHES WERE HORSES 184
by Adele De Leeuw

MOUNTAIN PONY 195
THE SORREL THAT TURNED ON A DIME
by Henry V. Larom

WINDY FOOT AT THE COUNTY FAIR 208
THE PONY RACE
by Frances Frost

BUCEPHALUS, A KING'S HORSE 219
by Alice C. Gall and Fleming Crew

KENTUCKY DERBY WINNER 231
FORTUNE FROWNS
FORTUNE SMILES
by Isabel McLennan McMeekin

THE MAGNIFICENT BARB 247
HORSE TRADING
by Dana Faralla

THE PACING MUSTANG 255
by Ernest Thompson Seton

BEST BOOK OF HORSE STORIES

No Sum Too Small

MURRAY HOYT

The whole thing took place in two weeks during the year Jeanie Williams was fifteen years old. For her they were two hard weeks. By the end of those two weeks, when the letter came saying that the thing Jeanie had hoped for was to be given to someone else, she was changed. You did not see the change; she was the same quiet, polite, serious person. But you felt the change. She wasn't a little girl any more after that letter came; she was older, more mature. She was a small adult.

The first day of that two weeks I met her in front of my house. Her face was serious as always, trying to hide the way she felt, but her eyes danced and her step was so light it was almost as if she were dancing.

She said, "Look, Uncle Red—look at this."

She handed me a little magazine called Horsemanship. She pointed to an ad which said that a woman in Massachusetts wanted to find a home for a hunter she wanted to retire, where it would be cared for well and treated with kindness and affection. The woman could not keep it because she did not have stable room and had acquired a younger horse to take its place. She did not want to sell it because she wanted the right to check carefully on the character of the person who got it, and to receive reports on how it was being treated. She also wanted to control absolutely any later transfer of ownership.

Jeanie had been reading the ad as I read it and she said very softly, almost reverently, "It says 'kindness and affection.'" Then she looked full at me and she added a little louder, "It sounds almost as if she was describing me. It seems almost as if I'm the one she's talking about."

I said, "Are you going to apply, Jeanie?"

She said, nodding eagerly, "Oh, yes. Dad and Mother say I can. It's the first time they've ever agreed to anything like that. I told them that if I got it, the money I've saved toward a horse could go for tack, for shipping the horse up here and for the expense of taking care of him. A year from now I'll be old enough to get a summer job that will give me the money to keep a horse another whole year."

I watched her walking away primly, on her way to school. Under the primness I could sense that terrific excitement that made me expect that at any second her walk might become a dance.

I watched her and I thought that probably Joe and Mildred Williams, her parents, couldn't very well have said anything but yes.

But I knew that it was a mistake. I knew the terrific hurt that was coming to Jeanie when the horse was given to someone else. That magazine was read in horse circles all over the United States. It wasn't reasonable to suppose, even before the letter came, that Jeanie would be the chosen one. . . .

Kids long for things inexplicable to an adult. In Jeanie's case it was a horse. Literally, more than anything else in the world, Jeanie wanted a horse. It wasn't the "Daddy, buy me a pony," sort of thing that all kids go through; it started when she was very small, when Mr. Brown used to put her on old Duffer's back to ride from the barn to the pasture gate, and it grew and grew.

She believed that if you wanted a thing badly enough and worked hard enough for it, you'd get it. And she never lost faith that sometime the good break would come. She was a religious little kid, as much as any kid fifteen years old is religious, and she believed that God would not let her down in this matter because He alone could know how much it meant to her.

We who lived near her were rooting for her because she was a nice kid, friendly in spite of being a little on the quiet side, and because I suppose Americans always root for the underdog.

We were practical and we'd seen an awful lot of people with a faith as clear and shining as Jeanie's taste the deep bitterness of disillusion.

She asked for a horse her sixth Christmas when she made out her list for Santa Claus. It was the only item on the list.

Joe and Mildred explained to her that a horse was a very expensive present, that Santa Claus probably knew they had no place to keep a horse, and nothing to feed one. They suggested that she ask for other things in case Santa Claus should feel it best to substitute.

She said, "But he won't do that, because a horse is the only thing I want."

There were some grand presents on Christmas Day. Jeanie was very polite and appreciative. But she grew quieter and quieter all the time they were giving out presents. When they were all through, she disappeared and they knew she had gone somewhere alone to cry.

Joe felt horrible. If there'd been any way in the world he could have swung a pony for her, he'd have done it then. But he was a college professor in the little Vermont college at Mead. During the depression, college professors took a cut and he just didn't have the money to swing it. In addition Mildred had had a lot of hospital expenses when the second child was born, and they were expecting another baby. Joe was paying for his house. And to add to everything else, that house was in a development restricted to household pets. It didn't help much to know that all those things were true when he also knew that Jeanie was somewhere alone bawling her eyes out.

She never asked for a horse again. In fact beginning about then she developed the habit of not asking for anything she wasn't positive she'd receive. She'd go to amazing lengths to hint around and find out whether the answer would be yes before she actually asked. She seemed to dread being refused. That first time must have been very bad.

Joe and Mildred sat back after that and waited for Jeanie to forget the horse business, and they thought this was happening until the tin box appeared on her bureau. It had a piece of brown sticker tape pasted on the cover and on that was printed HORS MUNNE. Inside were her two bank-books, started by the two grandmothers when she was born, a dollar her grandfather had given her for Christmas, the quarter which comprised her last week's allowance, and a penny which she had found in the big chair after the insurance man had called.

Mildred called Joe in and showed it to him. He looked at it thoughtfully. He asked about the penny and she told him.

He said, "No sum too small."

And Mildred said, "But, Joe, the amount is pitiful and absurd compared to what a horse would cost. She's so ignorant of what she's up against. She's going to be so bitterly disappointed.

A tin box appeared on her bureau.

We've got to make her see just how impossible it would be for a little girl to save that much money."

They waited until the time was right, and then Mildred had a long talk with Jeanie. She explained that Jeanie could not buy a horse for much less than a hundred and fifty dollars. She tried to make her understand how many one-dollar-and-twenty-six-centses it would take to make a hundred and fifty dollars.

Jeanie listened to her and seemed to understand, but the box remained on the bureau, and the next time Mildred looked there was more money in it.

They didn't always know where Jeanie got the money, unless they asked her. But we neighbors knew. It became noised around that Jeanie would, at fifteen cents an hour, do practically anything after school and Saturdays within her strength and ability. And there were a surprising number of errands to be run, trips to the store, hickory nuts to be shucked—things like that. She'd take the nickle or dime, and she'd thank you primly and then she'd start to walk away. Only after a few steps it would be too much for her and she'd run, as if she could hardly wait to reach that tin box.

Mildred saw her put the money in, once. There was really a little ceremony to it. First she opened the box and stirred the contents a little with her hand. Then she held the new piece of money a foot or so above the box to make it clink satisfyingly when it dropped in. After she dropped it, she carefully closed the lid again.

She loved every horse within a mile of home, and some a lot farther away than that. This included several specimens of flea bait definitely not worth loving by any but Jeanie's all-embracing standards.

And all the horses loved her. When she was a little kid still, I used to watch her from my window make a beeline for old Duffer's pasture fence. And he'd trot right over and put his head down to be petted. She'd stroke him and lay her face against him, feel his soft nose. And when he grew tired of this, she'd follow him around and squat beside him to watch him eat.

You'd see her lips moving and you knew she was carrying on a one-sided, animated conversation with him. When she was called back to the house, he would follow her to the pasture fence and stand looking after her as she made for home with that sturdy businesslike walk which is peculiar to small children. Duffer never paid any attention to anyone else who came near his pasture.

As the time passed between her sixth and thirteenth years, her character began to take shape. I believed, and Joe and Mildred agreed, that wanting this one thing as much as she did probably had a considerable effect in forming it. She was a gentle kid, never cruel. She was quiet, and while she had a grand smile and you knew when she was happy, she was never boisterous in happiness. In fact all emotion, especially hurt, she hid very successfully from grownups, seeming to prefer to fight it out all alone.

She had a lot of friends but no very close companion as most girls that age seem to have. She was extremely affectionate. She was perhaps more affectionate toward her parents than the average child, and the rest spilled out lavishly among the horses she knew, and among all other animals of her acquaintance indiscriminately.

The Fergusons' horse, Perry, Jeanie rode a lot and fussed with a lot. Mary Ferguson was afraid of it, and Perry was not always completely sold on Mr. Ferguson. The result was that occasionally they could not catch their animal and had to come to Jeanie for help.

Jeanie would walk out there into the pasture and she would call with that serious, grown-up manner of hers, "Perry, you've been a very bad boy. Now you come here this instant."

And Perry would come. He'd trot over with a happy little whinny and docilely allow the halter to be slipped over his head, though a few minutes before he had been galloping from one end of the pasture to the other with a great show of heels when anyone tried to approach him. This I saw with my own eyes.

He'd trot over with a happy little whinny.

Why it was so, I don't know, unless a horse has some way of knowing who loves him and who doesn't.

She began going out to Helen Blair's when she was ten. Helen Blair lived a couple of miles outside town and owned a stable of riding horses. In the summer she furnished both horses and instruction to a girls' camp on the other side of the state. The rest of the year she gave lessons there at home. Trust Jeanie to find out about a setup like that. The couple of times I'd been out there the place had seemed to be infested with little girls, feeding, currying, saddling horses, and riding endlessly around a ring. And looking at me with polite condescension when I asked what "tack" was and what "posting" meant.

I gathered from Jeanie that, to the little girls who liked riding and horses, it was like a club out there. And they adored Helen. When they didn't have money for a lesson, they hung around anyway.

Jeanie spent most of her time out there. Helen said she used to spend hours just standing in the stalls brushing the horses; sometimes just talking to them.

She took to getting up early and doing her hour of piano practice before school. She'd do her room work at noon, then after school she'd ride out to Helen's on her bicycle. In the evening she'd study and go to bed early so that she could get up for the practicing the next morning.

I saw her out there once and complimented her on her riding. She thanked me carefully. But I watched her eyes. They were looking past me at two girls from the town below who owned their own little Morgans. If I ever read loneliness and longing in anyone's eyes it was in hers then.

When I turned away I knew that with her, the riding, the lessons, the having other people's horses come to her, was all very well. But there was a big, lonely void that only having her own horse to love and fuss over, could ever fill.

I used to ask her once in a while how the horse fund was coming along. Sometimes she'd say, "Oh, pretty good." But sometimes she would tell me something definite and I would

She used to spend hours in the stalls brushing the horses.

know that she wanted to talk to someone about it. That was
the way it was during the war when she gave the five dollars to
the Red Cross.

She said, "It didn't seem right that I should be keeping all this
money when the Red Cross was giving plasma and things to
soldiers. It didn't seem right."

Yet you could sense the sacrifice it had been, the major set-
back to her hopes. She gave to the Red Cross three times and
she bought war-savings stamps. But the stamps could go into the
tin box, which was very heavy now. It was the same box that
she had used right along, but now the HORS MUNNE had been
crossed out and over it written, in a little girl's hand, HORSE
MORNEY.

By the time she was thirteen she was official baby tender for
the neighborhood. The money always went into the tin box.

In a way it was too bad she liked ice cream and all kinds of sweets as much as she did because if she hadn't, saving would have been a lot easier. There must have been some pretty hard-fought battles behind that serious little face.

But always the tin box won out. There were only two things that she would spend money on; one was movies which had horses in them (and she saw all of those) and riding lessons at Helen's. Mostly she was able to get her dad or her mother to pay for the riding lessons but sometimes she could not, and then she very reluctantly tapped the fund. By that year when she was thirteen, she had almost one hundred dollars.

That was the year she began to grow tall. She had been a chubby little thing earlier, but suddenly she began to shoot up and all her hems were let out in a desperate effort to keep her properly clothed. I had expected she would be displeased at this sudden shooting upward, but I found her philosophical.

"It's much easier to mount now, Uncle Red."

The fourteenth year was when the pin-up boy appeared on her wall.

"It made me feel old," Joe said. "Here was my daughter starting to put up boys' pictures. It made me feel darned peculiar. So when the time was right I said to her, 'I was in your room today, Jeanie, and I noticed that Roy Rogers is your pin-up boy.' And she said, 'Oh, Daddy, that isn't Roy Rogers' picture. That's a picture of Trigger, his horse.'"

That was the year she found out about an old Morgan that could be had for one hundred and twenty-five dollars and she hinted around to find out whether Joe and Mildred would lend her the extra twenty-five dollars to buy it.

That was a fairly tough decision on all concerned. Joe could have stood the twenty-five without any trouble, but the upkeep he just wasn't financially able to handle. By that time inflation in the United States was a healthy urchin, and people with fixed salaries were pinched unmercifully under such conditions. Joe got out a pencil and a piece of paper and he began to write down the things they would need. Jeanie had an old catalogue and they looked up saddle, bridle, and probably other items which I know nothing about. Then he wrote down the every-day expenses that owning a horse would entail. There was stable rental, hay, oats, bran, shavings for bedding, pasture rental; a lot of other items like that. He said that as he wrote, Jeanie's face grew more and more expressionless. The animation drained from it and it became stoical.

They came to the conclusion that they would need at least seventy-five dollars for equipment (which Jeanie called tack) and that it would cost about one hundred dollars a year—at a conservative estimate—to take care of the horse.

Jeanie saw how impossible it was once the figures were down on paper. She thanked Joe for going over it with her, and excused herself. She didn't appear for a long time. They knew where she was, well enough, and Joe says he and Mildred both felt horrible. Jeanie was older now and very seldom went away by herself any more, the way she used to. It had to be something out of the ordinary to make her do that now.

I saw her a few days later and I asked her how the fund was coming. That was one of the times she told me something def-inite.

She explained about the cost of upkeep and of tack and everything. She said a little wistfully, "Sometimes, Uncle Red, I get very discouraged. I guess I'm going to be an old lady before I get my horse. I guess it will be so late it won't do me much good."

I said, "But you aren't going to give up, are you?"

And she said, "No, I'm not going to give up." Her jaw seemed to stick out a little when she said it, though that might have been my imagination.

That was the way things stood when the advertisement ap-peared in Horsemanship. As I have said, by that time everybody knew about Jeanie and her horse, and all of us were rooting for her. Two different people brought her the ad.

Jeanie applied. It was a nice straightforward letter with only a few misspelled words. Spelling had never been Jeanie's forte.

The weakness in the letter lay in the fact that Jeanie could not describe either the stable or the pasture, but had to say that if the horse were given to her she would have to look around and hire each of these items.

After the letter went off, everyone concerned sat back and waited. I'd see Jeanie walking to school and back and I could sense the tremendous excitement in her. She tried as always to hide any emotion she felt, but this was something out of the ordinary so that I could see it in the way she skipped along, in the way her eyes sparkled, in every move she made.

And my heart went out to her because I knew she couldn't win; I knew she couldn't because I was practical and figured the odds; they were many times a hundred to one against her.

She began to get together tack. She bought a pail to water the horse. She went down to the feed store and found out about oats and bran. She canvassed the street nearest our development for a stable. She poked into old barns, carriage houses, stalls. Everything is new in our development, but on Middle Street, which is next to ours, the houses have been there, many of them, for over a hundred years. Some of them have large barns and stables. She finally landed one of these. Then she went looking for a pasture. She spent two or three days on this. She had trouble finding one near enough to the stable, but she stuck to it in her grave, polite little way and finally she succeeded. You went into her room and you found lists of horsy things she'd have to buy. The mail contained at least one catalogue for her every day.

You watched the excitement in her and your heart went out to her because you knew that she was building up to a disappointment which would shake her through and through, which would hurt her worse than she had ever been hurt in her life. You sensed that. You wished there were some way you could protect her, you could help her—yet you knew of nothing anyone could do.

When people talked to me downtown I found myself sticking up for her. One man said to me, "That is the luckiest thing

I ever heard of. Sitting back and having a horse turned over to you."

I said, "I don't call it luck. In the first place it hasn't been turned over to her and probably won't be. But if it should be, it still isn't lucky. She's fought for it for years. She's had some tough breaks. A good break should be about due her. If she doesn't get this particular horse in this particular way, she'll get another one in a year or so because she's working for it all the time. It's the same sort of luck you might accuse a prospector of having when he's studied and worked for months, even years, and finally finds the gold a little quicker than he expected. It's one of those breaks you make yourself."

The guy looked at me surprised. He said, "Okay. You don't have to get so vehement about it. If you say so, it isn't luck."

Maybe I was touchy because I hated to see it happen to her. Sure she would get a horse in another year or so. To an adult a year is not very long. To a child it stretches away endlessly. When you're fifteen, a year is a long, long time. I wanted her to have the horse now.

It was during this period that Joe heard her praying. He went in to tuck her in for the night and open her window, and before he stepped off the carpet he heard her talking. Her eyes were tight shut and she was asking God to help her, to guide her. She had done everything she could do; now she needed help. He tiptoed back downstairs without going into the room.

She didn't say much about the mail but she went down to the post office every time a train came in, if she was free. And when she came home from school her eyes always went to the table where Joe and Mildred left the incoming letters.

At the end of two weeks the letter came. It was a short letter. It thanked her for her application but it said that under the circumstances, since she had neither stable nor pasture, the horse couldn't very well be turned over to her.

You didn't have to ask her what was in the letter. She drew into herself, and before she finished reading, her face was a mask. She stood there with the letter in her hand for a little while and once Joe thought she was going to drop it. But then she very quietly handed it to him. She wouldn't let them see her eyes.

She said, and her voice was thin and high-pitched, "Well, I'll have all these things ready anyway, when I do get one." Her voice didn't sound very natural. She was around for the next few minutes but after that they couldn't find her for a long, long time.

I guess Joe felt almost as badly as she did. He came over to see me, ostensibly to get any ideas I could give him, but I guess in reality he needed to get it off his chest. He told me that Mildred had phoned Helen for the same reason.

After Joe went back home I sat in the living room thinking about it. I thought about the hours of baby-tending and the running errands, I thought about the money gradually growing in the tin box on the bureau. I thought about Duffer following her across the pasture. I thought about her catching Perry when nobody else could lay a hand on him. I thought about her first pin-up boy, about her seeing National Velvet five complete times and parts of two others. She was just a little girl who wanted a horse very badly. And pretty soon I didn't feel very good inside. This had been her big chance. She had had faith, and having faith she had dropped her guard. Now she was hurt as she might never be hurt again. For my money it was a shame and if nobody could do anything about it at least a try could be made.

I picked up the telephone. I put in a person-to-person call to the lady in Massachusetts. The operator said, "I am sorry, sir, there will be a delay. That same call has just been put in by another party."

So I sat around and waited and I began to feel no better fast. I knew Jeanie would be away somewhere alone by that time, and little pictures of Jeanie in the past five years kept passing before my eyes.

After a while the phone rang and they told me that they had my party.

I told the lady who I was, and then I started in. I told her about Jeanie; what she looked like, all the things I knew about her. I told her about those first rides on Duffer, about that first Christmas, about Duffer following her around, about Perry, about the way she mothered all animals, about the tin box and its slow, slow accumulations, about the money to the Red Cross, about the capacity to love some horse, pet it, make over it, more than any horse was ever loved or made over before.

I said, "You want care and affection for your horse; you can never find them in such quantity anywhere again." I told her everything. She didn't interrupt me much. When I got through her voice sounded a little different. She thanked me for calling and then she told me something about the horse. His name was Topper. He was a grandson of Man o' War—by Thunderer out of a range mare. He was thirteen years old but still very sound. The only strings attached to her offer were that he must not be hunted, or ridden for hire, and must never be sold. If the person who got him could no longer keep him he must be returned. She said that Topper liked to be petted and would stand for hours and be curried. If he liked you he would follow you around. I gathered that Topper was lonesome, now that his place had been taken by another horse.

I said to her, "They're two of a kind. Jeanie has been lonely for a long time, for a horse to love. And Topper is lonely for a mistress to love him."

After that I hung up. When I got the bill later, the call cost me eight dollars and thirty-five cents. I figured I never spent eight dollars and thirty-five cents that I begrudged any less.

I found out afterward that Helen had called just ahead of me. That Massachusetts woman must have learned an awful lot about Jeanie in an awfully short time; though maybe we duplicated to some extent. If I had known about Helen's call I wouldn't have put in mine because I would have felt that as one horse woman to another, she could probably swing more weight than I could. I was just a guy who wanted to see a little girl get her horse.

Joe said that Jeanie was very quiet all evening. In the middle of the evening the phone rang and it was a telegram for her. It said: TOPPER IS YOURS. AM STARTING HIM OFF BY VAN YOUR EXPENSE EARLY TOMORROW MORNING. MAY I COME UP SOMETIME AND RIDE WITH YOU? And it was signed by the lady in Massachusetts.

Jeanie didn't mean to show how she felt any more when she knew the horse was hers than she had when she had thought it never would be. But she came tearing into the living room, her

She got out there and walked into the stall.

eyes big. Her whole face shone. Her whole body was light, as if she were hardly touching the ground.

They called me over and she had calmed down by then; but I have never seen anyone look so quietly radiant as she did. Joe said that all the next morning she whistled and sang. He said she was so happy that it was all around her like a halo. It wasn't that she had ever been unhappy; she had always been a happy kid. It was just that she had wanted something very, very badly and now she had it and she was so happy she couldn't begin to contain it.

It had to show itself somehow and so she hummed and sang and whistled all day.

At ten thirty that night Helen called and said that the horse was there and was grand; big and lovable. The next morning I took them out before breakfast, because Joe's car wouldn't start.

She got out there and she walked into the stall and up to his head, and he whinnied a little, softly, and nuzzled her with his velvety nose.

And she stroked him and held her cheek against him.

Can a Horse
Know Too Much?

GENEVIEVE TORREY EAMES

N<small>O, SIR</small>, it's like I always said, it ain't good for a horse to know too much. A horse can be too smart—and that goes double for ponies. Ponies are generally smarter than horses to begin with."

John shook his grizzled head and wiped an imaginary speck of dirt from the little Welsh mare's glossy black neck. Ten-year-old Peter, standing beside the old man, flung a glance across the stable yard to the big stone house in the distance. He wanted to be sure that his father wasn't coming along to hear these doubts about the new pony. As for her, she tossed her head and laid back her ears.

"See that, now?" John went on. "She acts as if she heard what I said and felt unfriendly. I'm afraid Lightfoot is gonna make trouble."

Peter looked up anxiously at the man's face. "Oh, John, I think she's beautiful. And you said yourself it was time we turned Mousie over to Susan and got a bigger pony for me to ride. Don't you like her?"

"Never said I didn't like her," the old man grumbled. "Only I'm glad your Dad got her on trial, so we can see how she acts. She's a good-looking pony, all right, and she sure can jump. If she had plain pony brains, I dunno where you could find a better pony, now you've outgrown old Mousie." He stopped for a moment and kicked at the soft ground with the toe of his worn riding boot. "But that's just it," he went on more slowly. "She ain't got pony brains; she's got brains like a human, and that's not right. It's not—well, natural."

"What do you mean?"

"Well, the other day when she first came, I turned her out in the paddock to get a drink and she came right back into the barn. She unhooked the grain room door with her nose and walked in and started to help herself to the oats. And that ain't all. I know she's not the first horse ever to get a door open, and maybe she's had experience with that kind of hook before. That's smart, but not too smart. But wait, I'll show you. It's time to feed her, anyway."

He led Lightfoot back to her stall and tied her up. Peter followed, keeping at a respectful distance from the pony's heels.

John brought a forkful of hay and put it in the low manger in front of the pony. Peter sat, chin on hands, and kept his eyes on the pony. Lightfoot pulled at the hay, tossing her head restlessly. She soon had the hay on the floor and started to eat, pawing constantly with one forefoot as she did so.

"Why does she do that?" Peter asked.

"Dunno," John replied. "It's a habit. Lots of horses paw while they eat. Seems to show they're enjoying their food."

"But look, John, she's pawed most of the hay so far back she can't reach it."

"Just you watch now, and you'll see what I'm talking about."

Lightfoot reached back as far as the halter rope would let her and nibbled at the few remaining wisps that she could reach. Then, as if by accident, she slid her right forefoot a few inches forward, bringing with it a small bunch of hay. When she had eaten that, she stepped back a little and again shuffled her feet forward until another mouthful of hay was within reach of her twitching nose.

"But, John," Peter asked in excitement, "does she do that on purpose?"

"She sure does. I been watching her three evenings in a row. And just look at this now." He picked up the fork and put a morsel of hay over at one side of the stall. Lightfoot stretched out her neck, but the rope was too short.

"Oh, John," cried Peter. "You're teasing her. That's mean!"

John held his finger to his lips. "Wait," he whispered.

Lightfoot reached across with her left forefoot and dragged the tempting mouthful in front of her right hoof and then slid it along the floor to her nose, as before.

"Gee, she *is* smart," said Peter. "Smart as any horse in the circus, I betcha."

The old man shook his head. "Now that's what I say is against nature. A horse paws for excitement or because he feels good, and his legs just naturally paw from front to back. He can't help it. But when he starts pawing the other way, bringing back the hay he can't reach, and using two feet almost like a pair of hands, that's thinking, and not horse thinking either. It's *human* thinking!"

Peter sighed. "I just love her, John. Don't you think she'll be all right after she gets used to me? I mean, it would be just grand to have a pony as smart as that."

John hung up the fork and started for the grain room. "I dunno," he said. "You're a pretty good rider for your age and you can manage any ordinary pony that's not downright vicious. But this one, any time she starts to think up tricks, they won't be ordinary pony tricks. You don't know enough to out-smart a pony that don't think like a pony. Still, you be down here bright and early tomorrow and we'll see how she behaves."

He turned and looked sharply at the boy. "No oversleeping now. That's for city folks. If you can't get in your morning ride before school, guess we'll have to give it up—give up school, I mean."

But Peter did not ride the next morning. He was up extra early and ran to the stable to help John. "That's right," said John. "You give Lightfoot a drink while I finish cleaning the stalls."

Peter led the pony out to the paddock and turned her loose to drink. Highboy, the hunter, was dipping his muzzle in the clear, cold water in the concrete tank. Mousie had finished drinking and was rolling happily in the dust.

Lightfoot did not go near the water. Paying no attention to the other horses, she walked to the paddock fence. Her head was high, ears forward, nostrils sniffing the sharp air. She seemed to be looking at the wooded hill across the road and she started pacing restlessly back and forth along the fence, keeping her head toward the hill as she walked. For a moment she stopped to scratch her neck against the top rail of the bar-way that led to the road. The rail loosened and one end clattered to the ground. In a flash Lightfoot jumped the lower bars and started for the road at a high trot. John came to the stable door just as Highboy and Mousie followed her lead, tails and heads high, hoofs flying.

"That pesky pony!" exclaimed John. "Making trouble already, just like I said. Here, Peter, take this rope and follow them. I'll get some oats."

Just as Highboy and Mousie followed her lead.

The three horses crossed the road and dashed gaily up the grassy slope beyond. By the time John had joined Peter, Highboy and Mousie had settled down quietly to graze. Lightfoot, however, had not stopped for so much as a nibble of the rich grass. At a fast, steady trot she headed for the woods and disappeared in the fringe of young birches along the edge of the field.

John's face wore a puzzled look. "I can't figger that out," he said. "Can't see why she'd take to the woods and leave all this good feed. It ain't natural."

"Shall we follow her?" asked Peter anxiously.

John shook his head. "Got to get the other two in, first. Can't have them roaming all over the country. Chances are Lightfoot will come back when she finds the others haven't followed her. Horses usually stick together."

He gave a clear, long whistle and began shaking the oats in the measure he was carrying. Highboy and Mousie raised their heads and trotted obediently across the grass to John. He gave them each a handful of oats, and Peter snapped the rope on Highboy's halter. John left Peter to watch for Lightfoot, while he led the hunter back to the stable, with Mousie following behind.

There was still no sign of Lightfoot when John came back. Inside the woods there was no chance of tracking the pony, and not a sound could be heard except the faint rustling of leaves in the treetops. Presently John gave up.

"Looks like the ground swallowed her," he said to Peter. "Anyway, she wouldn't go straight over the mountain unless something was chasing her. She'll most likely take it easy along the side of the hill and gradually work down into the open."

"What do we do now?" asked Peter.

"Guess you'll have to run along to school. I'll take Highboy, later, and go looking in the clearings along the base of the hill. Most likely I'll have her back by the time you get home."

But Lightfoot was still missing that afternoon, and John was grumbling about his wasted day. "That pony's more trouble than she's worth," he said. "If your Dad takes my advice, he'll take her right back where she came from. That is, if we ever do find her."

Peter could eat hardly any supper that evening. Nobody had a good word to say for Lightfoot, and he knew his father was annoyed and worried. His mother had telephoned an advertisement to the paper and had notified the police and the State Troopers. Yet no word had come in about a stray black pony.

The next day was Saturday. There was no school for Peter, and his father stayed home from the office to help with the search.

"It's hard to know where to look," he said to John. "I can't imagine any horse going over that steep ridge if she didn't have to, and you say you've looked in all the likely places on this side."

"That's right, Mr. Davis," John answered. "There's hundreds of acres of woods along that ridge, but she wouldn't stay in the woods, and I've scoured the clearings and meadows all the way to Edgehill Station."

"You know what I think?" asked Peter suddenly. "I think she went straight over the mountain. She was headed that way and she was going fast. I don't think she'd stop for anything. She acted as if she had something on her mind."

The two men turned to look at Peter. "Could be you're right, at that," said John. "We've been trying to figger what an ordinary horse would do, and she's not ordinary. Yes, sir, I'll bet she had something on her mind—some deviltry no ordinary horse could think of."

Mr. Davis nodded. "Then the thing to do is to take the river road and start searching the farms on the other side. Whose place is directly opposite here? Jackson's, isn't it?"

The men jumped into the pick-up truck and took Peter on the seat between them. In a short time they were rolling along the river road on the far side of the ridge. John stopped the truck at a neat-looking farmhouse with the name Jackson on the mailbox.

A tall man in overalls was coming out of the barn. He grinned broadly when Mr. Davis mentioned the word pony. "A black pony, did you say? Yes, I guess I have seen her, and I'll be glad to see the last of her." He led the way around the barn to a pasture gate, and there on the other side was Lightfoot, licking steadily at something that looked like a large white brick.

"Salt!" John exclaimed. "Acts like she's been salt-starved for months."

"But our horses all have salt, don't they?" asked Peter's father.

"Yes, I keep a block in each stall," John answered. "But I hadn't any for Lightfoot when she came, and when I ordered some, the feed company was all out. Said they'd send some in a few days. I never thought she'd be that crazy for it."

"How do you suppose she knew where to come for the salt?" Mr. Davis asked.

John shook his head. "It beats me. I know a horse can smell water quite a distance and I suppose he can smell salt, but this is almost too far away. Looks like she just wanted salt and set out to find it."

"I think that's smart of her," Peter broke in, and he knew at once that it was the wrong thing to say.

"Smart, yes, too smart. That's what I've been saying was the matter with this pony. A horse should depend on his master and not start out on his own every time he wants something."

"I don't know how she got into my pasture," Mr. Jackson said. "She spent most of yesterday hanging around that salt. That was all right with me, even when she drove the cows away and wouldn't let them have any. I knew somebody'd come looking for her sooner or later.

"But after I took the cows in last night, the trouble really began. She crashed the pasture gate, nosed around the pig pen until she let all the pigs out, got into the cow stable and upset a pail of milk, and then pushed the cover off the barrel of oats and helped herself. I was afraid to leave her in the pasture after that, and I haven't any extra stalls, so I had to put my work-team out in the pasture overnight and tie her up in the stable."

"Well," said Mr. Davis, "I'm glad we've found her. What do I owe you for all the damage?"

"Oh, nothing at all. Only I hope she doesn't get away again. She sure can get into a lot of mischief. I guess she'd wreck the place completely in three days."

They loaded Lightfoot into the truck and Peter rode in back with her on the way home. He could not hear what the men were saying, but he was sure they were talking about the pony. He was afraid they would decide to send her back, maybe today, before he'd even had a chance to ride her.

Unhappily, he pressed his face against the pony's heavy mane. "Oh, Lightfoot," he whispered. "Why can't you be good? If you just wouldn't make any more trouble, and if you'd only, *only* just like me a little bit, we could have neat fun together."

Lightfoot cocked her ears forward. Then she gave Peter a little nudge with her nose. "Oh," he sighed happily. "I believe you are beginning to like me, after all."

Mr. Davis looked thoughtful when they reached home. "Peter," he said, "I hate to disappoint you about Lightfoot, but it does look as if she's going to be too troublesome. So don't get your heart set on her. If she's going to be too independent, we'll have to send her back and get another pony—one that thinks like a pony, as John says. But since she's here, you can try her out a few days longer."

In spite of John's doubts, the pony behaved well with her new rider, and for several days all went smoothly. John had nailed up the bar-way and fastened all the gates securely, and Light-foot had no chance to escape.

Every morning Peter and John took a ride before breakfast. Peter loved the little mare and he was proud of her. He looked back on the days when he had ridden Mousie as if they had been ages ago. Mousie was all right for his little sister; she was only five. He saw nothing out of the way in Lightfoot's knowing more than most horses. It was what he expected of her.

Peter was learning to jump. When he and John took their morning rides they sometimes rode across the fields, jumping the stone walls and fences whenever they came to a low place. Peter was not quite sure of himself. It was fun and thrilling and just a little scary, too.

One morning they had started earlier than usual and were riding over strange country. It was near the end of the week and nothing more had been said about sending Lightfoot back. Peter was beginning to hope his father would decide to keep her.

There was a touch of frost in the air and the horses danced and fretted with eagerness. Peter's eyes were shining and his cheeks were red from the cold air. He was gaining confidence every day. "Race you across the field!" he cried, and was yards away before John could answer.

John touched his heels to the old hunter's sides and galloped easily after the pony. They slowed up as they came to the edge of the field. There was a low wall between them and a hilly pasture lot on the other side. The pony popped over and the hunter took it in his stride.

John pulled up a little. "That's enough," he called. "It's bad going here—got to take it easy." But Peter was away again, faster than ever. Maybe he hadn't heard, or perhaps, as was more likely, Lightfoot had decided things for herself.

John hesitated. His horse could overtake the pony easily on the flat, but the pony had the advantage on this rocky hillside. If it were a runaway, it would only make her run faster to hear the hunter galloping behind. He pulled Highboy to a slow trot and watched anxiously. It was too late now to catch up with them. He could only follow at a distance, hoping and praying.

Peter did not seem to be trying to stop, and Lightfoot ran as if she intended to go on for miles. They came to the edge of the pasture at last, where a low wall ran along the top of a steep bank. Below was an old lane, unused except for bringing cattle in from pasture. Lightfoot went over the wall and dropped out of sight in the lane.

Into the heap which she could not see until it was too late.

John, riding faster now, caught sight of her a few seconds later as he reached the wall. He slid from the big horse and left him standing with reins dangling. He scrambled down the bank on the other side, his knees trembling and his voice shaking with fear. "You stay right there, Peter," he called. "Don't you move. I'll get you out. I'll get you out."

Someone had been pulling down the old barbed wire from the pasture fences and had left it—a great, wicked, jagged heap —in the lane, to be picked up and hauled away by a truck. Into the heap, which she could not see until it was too late to stop, Lightfoot had jumped. The long, snake-like coils wound around her legs and over her back. The barbs bit into her skin.

Peter, thoroughly frightened, clung to her mane. He would be in the midst of the wire if he got off. He was in just as much danger if he stayed on and the pony should begin to struggle.

John was at the edge of the wire, pulling at it with his bare hands, trying to loosen some of the strands so he could get near enough to lift Peter down.

"Don't you move, little pony," he said. "Don't you start threshing around—not yet. Just give us a chance here." His trembling fingers tore at the wire. Like something alive, it fastened its teeth in his clothes and held him.

Lightfoot looked at the old man with her wide-set, intelligent eyes. Then she turned her head and looked about her, on each side and behind her. Then she did a surprising thing. Slowly and carefully she picked up one foot, found it free of the wire, and put it down in a clear spot a few inches to the rear. One after another she moved each of her feet, inching slowly backward, pausing to see her way. Once she seemed to step deliberately on a strand of wire, holding it down while she moved her other foot.

John stopped wrestling with the wire and held his breath to watch. Then he called softly, "Put your head down against her neck, Peter." Peter obeyed and shut his eyes, clasping his arms about her neck.

At last the pony's hind legs were free, but still John did not move. The wire was still snarled about her knees. There was a chance that she might start to jump and struggle, horse-fashion, and throw herself and Peter into its coils. But Lightfoot took another careful backward step and another, and they were clear.

Breathing a deep sigh of relief, John pulled his clothes loose from the wire and went around to Lightfoot's head. When he had led her out into the lane, well away from the wire, he looked Peter over carefully. A slight scratch on one hand was all he could find. Lightfoot had a few cuts about her legs but nothing serious.

Highboy had gone home but John did not mind. Peter would not ride while John walked, so together they led Lightfoot slowly back across the hills, talking as they went. The pony's ears twitched back and forth as if she understood what they were saying about her.

"I reckon," John was saying, "I reckon a horse can't know too much, after all. Any other horse I ever saw would have threshed around till she had herself, and you, too, all torn to bits. But this pony, she's different. She don't think like a pony, she thinks like a human."

"Sure thing," said Peter. "I knew it all the time." And he laughed aloud. For now he knew that Lightfoot was his for good.

Blood Royal

MONTGOMERY M. ATWATER

O N A famous horse-farm in the famous horse-raising State of
Kentucky, a colt had his first birthday. His name was Kentucky
Roamer, but they called him Tuckee for short. On this birthday morning he stood restless but obedient at the end of a hal-
ter-rope, while the owner and the trainer looked critically at him
from every angle. The colt looked back at them out of great
soft eyes, then moved closer to his mother. Perhaps he sensed
that the men were not entirely pleased with him.

"Isn't he a beauty?" said the owner. "Look at that coat and
that head."

"Yes, Mr. Harkness," answered the trainer, "he's all of that;
but what are we going to do with him? He'll never make a race
horse."

"I suppose not, he's too stocky," Mr. Harkness agreed. He
looked at Tuckee with puzzled eyes. "Where do you suppose he
got that build? We haven't had a horse like him that I can remember."

"He's what the scientific fellow would call a 'reversion to
type,'" replied the trainer. "This youngster goes back a couple
of hundred years to the true Arab horse. Look at that chest
and those shoulders, those solid bones and round feet. That's
the real Arab for you, sir. There's a horse to stick by you and
bring you through anything—a wonderful breed!"

Tuckee watched the two men attentively. The trainer's long

speech meant nothing to him, and he did wish they would let him go.

"You're right," said the owner. "He's the ideal horse—but he just doesn't fit into our horse-farm. You'd better train him for my daughter. If he's all you say, he ought to find his place on her ranch."

"I'm glad, sir," said the trainer simply. "He'll be the grandest horse the West has seen since the Spaniards landed in old Mexico."

Four more birthdays passed. Kentucky Roamer was a full-grown horse. Under his gorgeous red skin the long muscles rippled like water, but his mistress seldom took him out for a ride. Tuckee wondered about this, and nickered wistfully every time anyone passed. How was he to know that he had grown into too big a horse for a woman, and that his mistress was afraid of his high spirit?

One day there was a great rushing about on the ranch; doors banging, horses and cattle being taken away, trucks driving off with heavy loads. The ranch had been sold. Presently Tuckee himself was put into a big van and driven off to the railroad station.

At the end of a day and a night of rattling and bumping, he was led into a strange stall. He smelled dozens of strange horses near by. Day after day he was taken into a big yard where people he did not know came and stared at him, felt his legs, and looked into his mouth. Sometimes they rode him around the big yard. But always they went away saying regretfully, "Mighty fine horse, but I'd be afraid for my daughter to ride him. Too high-strung." Poor Tuckee! He had only pranced a little, just to show how much he would like to go for a real ride!

But one day there came a man who was different from the others. He wore a Stetson hat and a gray-green uniform, with a little bronze badge on which was engraved a pine tree and the words "U. S. Forest Service."

This man did not feel Tuckee's legs and look into his mouth. He gave the red horse a pat and then just stood and looked, with a light in his eyes that even a horse could read. Kentucky Roamer had found his master!

"A registered thoroughbred?" said the man at last.

"Yep. I can show you his papers," answered the person in overalls who had taken Tuckee out of his stall. "They don't take much stock in these Kentucky horses out in this country. Can't stand the hardship. We'd make you a nice price on this horse just to get him out of the way."

The gray-green man was trembling with excitement as he took a little slip of paper out of his pocket and began to write. . . . Tuckee nudged his master, as they went out through the gate, by way of making friends. His master whispered, "You beauty! Maybe you were born in Kentucky, but you're no Kentucky horse—you're an Arab, a real Arab. They must be blind in there."

That day Tuckee had his long ride. But before they started, his master took him to a blacksmith shop. Tuckee loved that. He stood like a statue and lifted each foot as soon as the blacksmith touched it. His new shoes, instead of being flat, had cleats on the front and back. He stubbed his toes once or twice before he could get used to them. Each time he did it his master laughed at him and said, "Pick 'em up, old fellow! Where we're going, you need those non-skid tires."

They stopped next at a building out of which the gray-green man brought a saddle and bridle. Tuckee could hardly stand still while they were being put on. The saddle was big and broad, not the postage-stamp of leather he had been used to. Then, almost before he knew it, the rider was in the saddle. It was good not to have to get down on one knee, as he had been taught to do for his mistress. He pranced sideways.

A touch on the reins turned him down the street, and soon they had left the pavement and the houses behind. Looming in front of them was a range of tall mountains, green with forest on the sides, white with snow on the peaks. "See those, you old crow-bait?" asked the man. "That's where we're going; so slide along, red horse, slide along."

Tuckee lengthened his stride into a running walk that flowed over the ground like water. Up, up into the mountains, where wind sang in the trees and water sang among the rocks. Up into the smell of pine and sage that made the horse want to run like a startled deer.

It was early in a June evening when Kentucky Roamer brought his master home to the forest ranger's cabin. A golden carpet of sunlight still lay on the peaks, although the canyon was in half shadow, when the gray-green man sidled the horse up to a pasture gate and unlatched it without dismounting. Tuckee had never seen that done before, and he filed his part in the trick away in his memory. Though he had covered a full forty miles since they had left the stable yard, he still walked lightly, easily, as only an Arab can walk at the end of a long day.

But now he smelled other horses and whinnied eagerly, for, like all his kind, he loved company. His call was answered. There was the thump of trotting feet, and four horses came toward him out of a thicket of pine trees. The newcomer arched his neck and pranced toward them.

"That's right, make friends," laughed the gray-green man. "You're going to see lots of each other."

One of the horses, evidently the leader of the band, laid his ears back and snapped at Tuckee's neck. "Here, you," cried the gray-green man, pushing him away with one booted foot, "none of that. I guess, red horse, you'll have to learn to scrap, or old Tony will boss you all over the place."

It was the next day before Tuckee really made the acquaintance of his future companions. After a night in the barn, the gray-green man put him in the corral with the other horses and then sat down on the top rail to watch. Again Tony, the leader, came up with his ears laid back and teeth bared. But this was a game two could play. Instinctively Tuckee flattened his own small ears and struck at his tormentor with both front feet. Tony jumped back with an expression of surprise and respect, while the gray-green master laughed. Once more Tony approached, but this time his ears were pointed forward. Just like a pair of strange dogs, they sniffed noses. Horse-fashion, they were shaking hands.

Now that Tony had accepted Tuckee, the other horses came up and went through exactly the same performance. Finding that the newcomer was willing and able to stand up for himself, they decided to make friends. In ten minutes they were all standing in a close group, switching flies as if they had known one another for years.

This was the beginning of happy, crowded months for Kentucky Roamer. He no longer stood for days in a stall, wishing that someone would take him out for a ride. He was a forest ranger's horse, and it was a poor day when he did not carry his master over twenty or thirty miles of steep mountain trails.

Over miles of steep mountain trails.

Many a time he watched the other horses come in with drooping heads and sweat-streaked sides—something he could not understand, for he had never yet been really tired. He could scramble through the mountains from dawn till dark and reach home tugging at the bit. That was the legacy of his blood —the gift of his Arab forefathers—endurance and courage.

There were dozens of things for Kentucky Roamer to learn in this new life. Most of them he picked up by copying the other horses: to come at his master's whistle or the rattle of the oats can against the barn door; to follow a trail no matter how faint and dim; to remember the way home no matter how tangled had been the course; never to wander more than a few yards when his reins were dropped on the ground. He overcame his instinctive fear of a swamp where he sank to his knees in the mud. He learned to pick his way through a maze of fallen logs without stumbling; to wriggle among close-set trees without scraping his rider's legs. He could run full speed down a rock-strewn slope without stumbling or breaking his stride. This was life as it should be lived!

Until this year Tuckee had never known much about winter, for he had spent the cold months in his stall, with a blanket to keep him warm. But now the other horses taught him to eat snow when the stream in the pasture froze solid. They taught him how to paw the feathery covering of snow away from the grass when he grew tired of hay. He grew his first long winter coat, and soon became more expert in deep snow than any of his companions. Perhaps the reason for this was that he had absolute confidence in his master. If the gray-green man told him by voice and rein that he must plunge through a deep drift, he would do it, no matter how terrifying it was to lose the feel of solid ground under his feet.

But winters are long in the mountains, and Kentucky Roamer was heartily tired of this one before spring.

Warm weather came at last, and all the horses were wild with joy. They ran from one end of the pasture to the other, kicking and snorting like colts. Their winter coats began to itch and fall out. They rolled and rolled on the soft spring earth, leaving great patches of hair. Never had Tuckee's coat glistened as it did after he had rubbed away the winter wool. Never had he felt such power in his legs as he did after the green grass came.

As spring turned to summer, he learned two new words: "forest fire." He heard them so many times each day that they came to have a meaning to him. They meant hot, scorching weather that seemed to suck the energy out of him. They meant a dark pall of smoke hanging over the mountains, filling his nostrils with a pungent, terrifying smell.

Unlike the summer before this year, there were always many people at the cabin of the gray-green man. Trucks came laboring up the canyon at all hours, piled high with boxes and bales, or crammed with men. The pasture was crowded with strange horses, whose milling feet ground the earth to dry powder and whose teeth ripped up every blade of grass. Each day a part of this wilderness army would be swallowed up in the forest, to be replaced before dark. Less often a part of it would return, the men blackened, exhausted, and discouraged, the horses hobbling on sore feet and flinching from saddle-sores. Even Tuckee's high spirits felt the drag of anxiety and fear, for he was in the midst of a time of terrible danger to the wilderness, a forest-fire year.

One by one the other horses belonging to the gray-green man gave up under the pressure of desperate work. They grew so thin that each separate rib showed through the skin, and they stood in the barn with hanging heads. At last even Tony could do no more. The gray-green man led him into the barn one night, limping so badly that he could hardly move. Only Kentucky Roamer was left, and he was sick with weariness—Kentucky Roamer, who had never been tired in his life. On the night the ranger tied Tony up for good, Tuckee could not eat the dry hay in his manger. Even oats tasted like ashes.

Very early the next morning the gray-green man came into his stall with saddle and bridle.

Tuckee did not arch his neck and prance when the cinch tightened around his body; there was no pleasure now in the thought of another day on the trail. But his head was still high as the ranger led him out of the barn. In the light of dawn drops of water could be seen running down the cheeks of his master.

"I'm sorry, old fellow," said the man in a crooning voice. "I know you're just about all in. But we're soldiers, and we've got to go. If it would only rain—if it would only rain!"

They rode far that day, thirty miles over the steep mountains. The forest ranger drooped in the saddle, for the man, too, was weary almost beyond his strength.

Suddenly the ranger stiffened. A new forest fire was eating its way savagely through the trees. It was still small, but under the urge of the wind the flames were spreading rapidly. Like one in a dream the gray-green man unstrapped his tools and gave battle. In the path of the fire he began to dig a long trench down through the forest litter to the bare, uninflammable earth. When the flames reached this trench they stopped for lack of fuel. But again and again the wind blew sparks and bits of flaming wood across, so that the fire gained new foothold. The gray-green man was staggering. All that long afternoon Tuckee watched while the fire forced his master back and back, gaining headway with each victory. To the horse it seemed that his master had gone out of his mind. He was gasping, smoke-blackened, wet with perspiration. His efforts had ceased to be systematic. He ran back and forth, lashing at the flames with his ax. The struggle had long ago become hopeless, but he would not retreat.

The forest ranger was chopping frantically at a tree with its lower branches afire. In his haste he did not notice another tree, dead and with its roots rotted away, leaning against it. At the second jarring blow of the ax, the dead tree shook itself loose and came crashing down upon him, knocking him headlong and coming to rest across his legs. The gray-green man gave a single cry, and then lay still.

Tuckee's first impulse, when the tree fell, was to run away. He started back, snorting with fear. But something stopped him— his reins dangling on the ground. Those trailing bits of leather were a sign that his master wanted him to stay where he was—and he stayed, with the sting of the smoke in his eyes and the fear of fire in his heart.

The flames had put out two long arms on either side of them, and the circle was almost closed when the gray-green man regained consciousness. Tuckee was glad to see him move. Now they would go away from this place. But his master did not get up. He strained at the tree, tried to dig away the earth with his fingers. But it was no use. Next he pushed himself as high as he could on his arms and looked at the fire. It was coming closer and closer, with fierce snaps and crackles as it consumed the dry underbrush in its path. To the ranger, and to the horse as well, it was bringing a horrible death, if they did not escape those long arms of creeping, flame-joined hands.

"Get up, Tuckee," called the man. "Get out of here!" He seized a small stick and threw it.

The horse did not understand. Was his master trying to tell him to leave? He could not, he would not, until those reins lay against his neck and a man's weight was in the saddle. Again the ranger looked at the fire. Only a few yards away now. After a moment he gave the whistle that Tuckee recognized. It always meant, "Come here."

Tuckee did not want to go closer to the creeping monster of flame, but he obeyed. The man looked up and said quietly, "It's up to you now, thoroughbred. If you won't go without me, you'll have to pull me free." As he spoke, he laid hold of the stirrup hanging above his head. Then he ordered sharply, "Now, Tuckee, let's go!"

Kentucky Roamer responded. He felt the drag at the stirrup, and a sickening wrench. He continued to move away from the fire, step by step, sidling so as to avoid stepping on the weight that hung beside him. After several yards he stopped and looked around questioningly.

The forest ranger still clung to the stirrup, his face as gray as dust. As Tuckee stood waiting, the dead tree from whose grasp he had pulled his master burst into flames along its entire length.

The red horse snorted. It was so hot that he felt dizzy. The fire was all around them now, pressing closer. Why did his master delay?

The ranger was stirring, trying to pull himself into the saddle. But both his ankles were broken, and his arms were not equal to the task. He managed to pull himself half-way up, and there he hung, with his useless legs brushing Tuckee's knee.

Kentucky Roamer stood dead-still, while his memory went back and back, to a woman who used to scramble at his side in just this way. The picture was dim, but that touch on the leg meant something. He had it now! It meant "Get down on one knee." At once he dropped down so that his back was only half as high as before. He heard a gasp of surprise from the man and felt him struggle into the saddle. Like a statue he held his position, as he had been taught, until his rider was firmly seated.

The gray-green man had expended the last of his energy. He simply clung now to the horse's back. But in some way Tuckee knew, as a good horse always knows, that the man was helpless, dependent upon him for his very life. He looked around, seeking a way through the ring of fire. There was only one chance and Tuckee took it. At a quick trot he charged the wall of flame, plunged through it! For a moment it was in his nostrils, burning the hair on his legs, singeing him as high as the mane. But he broke through and plunged away, galloping past the gaunt, smoking trees, kicking up little puffs of ash, fine and gray as dust, at each step.

He must go home, that was the idea firmly in his mind. He must carry his master away from the fire monster, to the only place of peace and happiness he knew. But it was a long way for weary, scorched legs to go—all those miles of rocky hillsides and fallen logs.

On and on he struggled. He knew at last the agony of complete exhaustion. The fire monster was far behind. Why not just stop and let that dead weight he balanced so carefully on his back slide off? But the royal blood in his veins, the blood that never surrenders, drove him on.

The world grew dark and a new wind began to blow. Was that night already? Tuckee snuffled the wind without pausing. It was

There was only one chance and Tuckee took it.

a cool, wet breeze, and the horse knew, though he did not care, that it would rain.

But the cold air was soothing to his parched lungs, and he pushed on a little faster. The ranger seemed to feel it too, for he began to babble and moan. "Rain, Tuckee," he cried. "We've won, we've beaten it!" He sang it over in a cracked, harsh voice: "We've won!"

It was midnight when Kentucky Roamer, sweat-soaked and shaking all over, reached the pasture gate. He swung sideways to the gate so that his rider could slip the latch. He had to wait a long time, but at last a shaky hand pushed the latch free and Tuckee lurched through.

In front of the cabin he stopped. Voices sounded inside, there was a shout, the door opened, and men came running to lift down the gray-green man. Tuckee heard him mumble, "Take care of my horse—saved me."

But no one else heard, and there was no one to watch while Tuckee's head dropped lower and lower and his legs gradually buckled. With a great sigh he rolled over on his side. The rain struck his body with refreshing coolness.

All night he lay motionless, with the rain beating down on him. But in the gray morning he got to his feet and stumbled off toward the barn to find some hay. The rain made him feel hungry. An Arabian doesn't die easily!

FROM

Misty of Chincoteague

MARGUERITE HENRY

*The story of Misty is part of the true story about the wild
horses of Assateague. Hundreds of years ago a Spanish gal-
leon sank near the Virginia coast and its cargo of 15 ponies
swam to Assateague Island where they adapted themselves
to the primitive life and became large bands of wild free
creatures. Every year at harvest time, the folks on Chincoteague would cross over to Assateague and round up wild
ponies for sport. Today the most famous of them is the
Phantom, a swift and mysterious mare who has outsmarted
everyone. Paul and his sister Maureen have set their hearts
on owning her. Paul feels that now there is a chance of his
dream coming true because, for the first time, he has been
invited to join the men in the roundup.*

Pony Penning Day

Pony Penning Day always comes on the last Thursday in July.
For weeks before, every member of the Volunteer Fire Depart-
ment is busy getting the grounds in readiness, and the boys are
allowed to help.

"I'll do your chores at home, Paul," offered Maureen, "so's
you can see that the pony pens are good and stout."

Paul spent long days at the pony penning grounds. Yet he
could not have told how or by whom the tents were rigged up.
He hardly noticed when the chutes for the bronco busting were

built. He did not know who pounded the race track into condition. All he knew was that the pens for the wild ponies must be made fast. Once the Phantom was captured, she must not escape. Nothing else mattered.

The night before the roundup, he and Maureen made last-minute plans in Phantom's stall. "First thing in the morning," Paul told Maureen, "you lay a clean bed of dried sea grass. Then fill the manger with plenty of marsh grass to make Phantom feel at home."

"Oh, I will, Paul. And I've got some ear corn and some 'lasses to coax her appetite, and Grandma gave me a bunch of tiny new carrots and some rutabagas, and I've been saving up sugar until I have a little sackful."

In the midst of their talk, Grandpa, looking as if he had a surprise, joined them.

"I hain't rode on a roundup to Assateague for two year," he smiled, hiding one hand behind his back, "but I recommember we allus had a chaw and a goody after the ponies was rounded up and afore we swimmed 'em across the channel. Here, Paul," he said, with a strange huskiness, "here's a choclit bar fer ye to take along." And he pressed the slightly squashed candy into Paul's hand.

It was dark and still when Paul awoke the next morning. He lay quiet a moment, trying to gather his wits. Suddenly he shot out of bed.

Today was Pony Penning Day!

His clothes lay on the chair beside his bed. Hurriedly he pulled on his shirt and pants and thudded barefoot down to the kitchen where Grandma stood over the stove, fying ham and making coffee for him as if he were man-grown!

He flung out his chest, sniffing the rich smells, bursting with excitement.

Grandma glanced around proudly. "I picked the first ripe figs of the year fer ye," she exclaimed. "They're chuckful of goodness. Now sit down, Paul, and eat a breakfast fit for a roundup man!"

Paul sat on the edge of his chair. With one eye on the clock he tried to eat the delicious figs and ham, but the food seemed to lump in his throat. Luckily Grandpa and Maureen came downstairs just then and helped clean his plate when Grandma was busy testing her cornbread in the oven with a long wisp of straw.

"I got to go now," Paul swallowed, as he ran out the door. He mounted Watch Eyes, a dependable pony that Grandpa had never been able to sell because of his white eyes. Locking his bare feet around the pony's sides, he jogged out of the yard.

Maureen came running to see him off.

"Whatever happens," Paul called back over his shoulder, "you be at Old Dominion Point at ten o'clock on a fresh pony."

"I'll be there, Paul!"

"And you, Paul!" yelled Grandpa. "Obey yer leader. No matter what!"

Day was breaking. A light golden mist came up out of the sea. It touched the prim white houses and the white picket fences with an unearthly light. Paul loped along slowly to save his mount's strength. He studied each house with a new interest. Here lived the woman who paid Maureen three dollars for hoeing her potato patch. There lived Kim Horsepepper, the clamdigger they had worked for. Mr. Horsepepper was riding out of his lane now, catching up with Paul. All along the road, men were turning out of their gates.

"Where do you reckon you'll do most good, Bub?" taunted a lean sapling of a man who, on other days, was an oysterman. He guffawed loudly, then winked at the rest of the group.

Paul's hand tightened on the reins. "Reckon I'll do most good where the leader tells me to go," he said, blushing hotly.

The day promised to be sultry. The marsh grass that usually billowed and waved stood motionless. The water of Assateague Channel glared like quicksilver.

Now the cavalcade was thundering over a small bridge that linked Chincoteague Island to little Piney Island. At the far end of the bridge a scow with a rail fence around it stood at anchor.

In spite of light talk, the faces of the men were drawn tight with excitement as they led their mounts onto the scow. The horses felt the excitement, too. Their nostrils quivered, and their ears swiveled this way and that, listening to the throb of the motor. Now the scow began to nose its way across the narrow channel. Paul watched the White Hills of Assateague loom near. He watched the old lighthouse grow sharp and sharper against the sky. In a few minutes the ride was over. The gangway was being lowered. The horses were clattering down, each man taking his own.

All eyes were on Wyle Maddox, the leader.

"Split in three bunches," Wyle clipped out the directions loud and sharp. "North, south, and east. Me and Kim and the Beebe boy will head east, Wimbrow and Quillen goes north, and Harvey and Rodgers south. We'll all meet at Tom's Point."

At the first sound of Wyle's steam-whistle voice, the sea birds rose with a wild clatter.

"They're like scouts," Paul said to himself. "They're going to warn the wild ponies that the enemy has landed."

"Gee-up!" shouted Wyle as he whirled his horse and motioned Kim and Paul to follow.

Paul touched his bare heels into Watch Eye's side. *They were off!* The boy's eyes were fastened on Wyle Maddox. He and Kim Horsepepper were following their leader like the wake of a ship.

As they rode on, Paul could feel the soft sand give way to hard meadowland, then to pine-laden trails. There were no paths to follow, only openings to skin through—openings that led to water holes or to grazing grounds. The three horses thrashed through underbrush, jumped fallen trees, waded brackish pools and narrow, winding streams.

Suddenly Paul saw Wyle Maddox' horse rear into the air. He heard him neigh loudly as a band of wild ponies darted into an open grazing stretch some twenty yards ahead, then vanished among the black tree trunks.

Each man took his own horse across the gangway.

The woods came alive with thundering hooves and frantic horse calls. Through bush and brier and bog and hard marshland the wild ponies flew. Behind them galloped the three riders, whooping at the top of their lungs. For whole seconds at a time the wild band would be swallowed up by the forest gloom. Then it would reappear far ahead—nothing but a flash of flying tails and manes.

Suddenly Wyle Maddox was waving Paul to ride close. "A straggler!" he shouted, pointing off to the left. "He went that-a-way! Git him!" And with a burst of speed Wyle Maddox and Kim Horsepepper were after the band.

Paul was alone. His face reddened with anger. They wanted to

Behind them galloped the three riders.

be rid of him. That's what they wanted. Sent after a straggler! He was not interested in rounding up a straggler that couldn't even keep up with the herd! He wanted the Phantom. Then

Grandpa's words flashed across his mind. "Obey yer leader. No matter what!"

He wheeled his pony and headed blindly in the direction Wyle had indicated. He rode deeper into the pine thicket, trying to avoid snapping twigs, yet watching ahead for the slightest motion of leaf or bush. He'd show the men, if it took him all day! His thin shirt clung to him damply and his body was wet with sweat. A cobweb veiled itself across his face. With one hand he tried to wipe it off, but suddenly he was almost unseated. Watch Eyes was dancing on his hind legs, his nose high in the air. Paul stared into the sun-dappled forest until his eyes burned in his head. At last, far away and deep in the shadow of the pines, he saw a blur of motion. With the distance that lay between them, it might have been anything. A deer. Or even a squirrel. Whatever it was, he was after it!

Watch Eyes plunged on. There was a kind of glory in pursuit that made Paul and the horse one. They were trailing nothing but swaying bushes. They were giving chase to a mirage. Always it moved on and on, showing itself only in quivering leaves or moving shadows.

What was that? In the clump of myrtle bushes just ahead? Paul reined in. He could scarcely breathe for the wild beating of his heart. There it was again! A silver flash. It looked like mist with the sun on it. And just beyond the mist, he caught sight of a long tail of mingled copper and silver.

He gazed awestruck. "It could be the Phantom's tail," he breathed. "It is! It is! It is! And the silver flash—it's not mist at all, but a brand-new colt, too little to keep up with the band."

The blood pounded in his ears. No wonder the Phantom was a straggler! No wonder she let herself be caught. "She's got a baby colt!" he murmured.

He glanced about him helplessly. If only he could think! How could he drive the Phantom and her colt to Tom's Point?

Warily he approached the myrtle thicket, then stopped as a hot wave of guilt swept over him. Phantom and her colt did not want to be rounded up by men. He could set them free. No one had brought the Phantom in before. No one need ever know.

Just then the colt let out a high, frightened whinny. In that little second Paul knew that he wanted more than anything in the world to keep the mother and the colt together. Shivers of joy raced up and down his spine. His breath came faster. He made a firm resolution. "I'll buy you both!" he promised.

But how far had he come? Was it ten miles to Tom's Point or two? Would it be best to drive them down the beach? Or through the woods? As if in answer a loud bugle rang through the woods. It was the Pied Piper! And unmistakably his voice came from the direction of Tom's Point.

The Phantom pricked her ears. She wheeled around and almost collided with Watch Eyes in her haste to find the band. She wanted the Pied Piper for protection. Behind her trotted the foal, all shining and clean with its newness.

Paul laughed weakly. *He* was not driving the Phantom after all! She and her colt were leading him. They were leading him to Tom's Point!

She Can't Turn Back

Tom's Point was a protected piece of land where the marsh was hard and the grass especially sweet. About seventy wild ponies, exhausted by their morning's run, stood browsing quietly, as if they were in a corral. Only occasionally they looked up at their captors. The good meadow and their own weariness kept them peaceful prisoners.

At a watchful distance the roundup men rested their mounts and relaxed. It was like the lull in the midst of a storm. All was quiet on the surface. Yet there was an undercurrent of tension. You could tell it in the narrowed eyes of the men, their subdued voices and their too easy laughter.

Suddenly the laughter stilled. Mouths gaped in disbelief. Eyes rounded. For a few seconds no one spoke at all. Then a shout that was half wonder and half admiration went up from the men. Paul Beebe was bringing in *the Phantom and a colt!*

Even the wild herds grew excited. As one horse, they stopped grazing. Every head jerked high, to see and to smell the new-comer. The Pied Piper whirled out and gathered the mare and her colt into his band. He sniffed them all over as if to make sure that nothing had harmed them. Then he snorted at Phantom, as much as to say, "You cause me more trouble than all the rest of my mares put together!"

The roundup men were swarming around Paul, buzzing with questions.

"How'd you *do* it, Paul?" Wyle Maddox called over the excited hubbub.

"Where'd you find 'em?" shouted Kim Horsepepper.

Paul made no answer. The questions floated around and above him like voices in a dream. He went hot and cold by turns. Did he do the right thing by bringing the Phantom and her foal in? Miserably he watched the Phantom's head droop. There was no wild sweep to her mane and her tail now. The free wild thing was caught like a butterfly in a net. She was webbed in by men, yelling and laughing.

"Beats all!" he heard someone say. "For two years we been trying to round up the Phantom and along comes a spindling youngster to show us up."

" 'Twas the little colt that hindered her."

" 'Course it was."

"It's the newest colt in the bunch; may not stand the swim."

"If we lose only one colt, it'll still be a good day's work."

"Jumpin' Jupiter, but it's hot!"

The men accepted Paul as one of them now—a real round-up man. They were clapping him on the shoulder and offering him candy bars. Suddenly he remembered the bar Grandpa had pressed into his hand. He took off the wrapper and ate—not be-cause he was hungry, but because he wanted to seem one of the men. They were trying to get him to talk. "Ain't they a shaggy-lookin' bunch?" Kim Horsepepper asked.

"Except for Misty," Paul said, pointing toward the Phantom's colt. "Her coat is silky." The mere thought of touching it sent shivers through him. "Misty," he thought to himself wonderingly. "Why, I've named her!"

The little foal was nursing greedily. Paul's eyes never strayed from the two of them. It was as if they might disappear into the mist of the morning, leaving only the sorrels and the bays and the blacks behind.

Only once he looked out across the water. Two lines of boats were forming a pony-way across the channel. He saw the cluster of people and the mounts waiting on the shores of Chincoteague and he knew that somewhere among them was Maureen. It was like a relay race. Soon she would carry on.

"Could I swim my mount across the channel alongside the Phantom?" Paul asked Wyle Maddox anxiously.

Wyle shook his head. "Watch Eyes is all tuckered out," he said. "Besides, there's a kind of tradition in the way things is handled on Pony Penning Day. There's mounted men for the round-up and there's boatmen to herd 'em across the channel," he explained.

"Tide's out!" he called in clipped tones. "Current is slack. Time for the ponies to be swimmed across. Let's go!"

Suddenly the beach was wild with commotion. From three sides the roundup men came rushing at the ponies, their hoarse cries whipping the animals into action. They plunged into the water, the stallions leading, the mares following, neighing encouragement to their colts.

"They're off!" shouted Wyle Maddox, and everyone felt the relief and triumph in his words.

Kim thumped Paul on the back as they boarded the scow for the ride back. "Don't fret about yer prize," he said brusquely. "You've got the Phantom sure this time. Once in the water she can't turn back."

But he was wrong!

Caught in the Whirlpool

On the shores of Chincoteague the people pressed forward, their faces strained to stiffness, as they watched Assateague Beach.

"Here they come!" the cry broke out from every throat.

Maureen, wedged in between Grandpa Beebe on one side and a volunteer fireman on the other, stood on her mount's back. Her arms paddled the air as if she were swimming and struggling with the wild ponies.

Suddenly a fisherman, looking through binoculars, began shouting in a hoarse voice, "A new-borned colt is afeared to swim! It's knee-deep in the water, and won't go no further."

The crowds yelled their advice. "What's the matter with the roundup men?" "Why don't they heft it into deep water—it'll swim all right!" "Why don't they hist it on the scow?"

The fisherman was trying to get a better view. He was crawling out over the water on a wall of piling. It seemed a long time before he put his binoculars to his eyes again. The people waited breathlessly. A small boy began crying.

"Sh!" quieted his mother. "Listen to the man with the four eyes."

"The colt's too little to swim," the fisherman bawled out. "Wait! A wild pony is breaking out from the mob. Swimming around the mob! Escaping!"

An awed murmur stirred the crowds. Maureen dug her toes in her mount's back. She strained her eyes to see the fugitive, but all she could make out was a milling mass of dark blobs on the water.

The fisherman leaned far out over the water. He made a megaphone of one hand. "Them addle-brained boatmen can't stop the pony," his voice rasped. "It's outsmarting 'em all."

Maureen's mind raced back to other Pony Pennings. The Phantom upsetting a boat. The Phantom fleeing through the woods.

Always escaping. Always free. She clutched the neck of her blouse. She felt gaspy, like a fish flapping about on dry land. Why was the man with the binoculars so slow? Why didn't he say, "It's the Phantom!" Who else could it be?

Now he was waving one arm wildly. He looked like a straw in the wind. He teetered. He lost his balance. He almost fell into the water in his excitement.

"It's the Phantom!" he screamed at last. "I can see the white map on her shoulders!"

The people took up the cry, echoing it over and over. "It's the Phantom! She's escaped again!"

Maureen felt tears on her cheek, and impatiently brushed them away.

Again the fisherman was waving for quiet.

"Hush!" bellowed Grandpa Beebe.

The people fell silent. They were like listeners around a microphone. "It's the *Phantom's* colt that won't swim!" he called out in a voice so hoarse it cracked. "The Phantom got separated from a bran'-fire new colt. She's gone back to get it!"

The people whooped and hollered at the news. "The Phantom's got a colt," they sang out. "The Phantom's got a new colt!"

Again the fisherman was waving for silence.

"She's reached her colt!" he crowed. "But the roundup men are closing in on her! They're making her shove the colt in the water. She's makin' it swim!"

Grandpa Beebe cupped his hands around his mouth. "Can the little feller make it?" he boomed.

The crowd stilled, waiting for the hoarse voice. For long seconds no answer came. The fisherman remained as fixed as the piling he stood on. Wave after wave of fear swept over Maureen. She felt as if she were drowning. And just when she could stand the silence no longer, the fisherman began reporting in short, nervous sentences.

"They're half-ways across. Jumpin' Jupiter! The colt! It's bein' sucked down in a whirlpool. I can't see it now. My soul and body! A boy's jumped off the scow. He's swimming out to help the colt."

The onlookers did not need the fisherman with the binoculars any more. They could see for themselves. A boy swimming against the current. A boy holding a colt's head above the swirling water.

Maureen gulped great lungfuls of air. "It's Paul!" she screamed. "It's Paul!"

On all sides the shouts went up. "Why, it's Paul!"

"Paul Beebe!"

Grandpa leaped up on his mount's back as nimbly as a boy. He stood with his arms upraised, his fists clenched.

"God help ye, Paul!" his words carried out over the water. "Yer almost home!"

Grandpa's voice was as strong as a tow rope. Paul was swimming steadily toward it, holding the small silver face of the colt above the water. He was almost there. He *was* there!

Maureen slid down from her mount, clutching a handful of mane. "You made it, Paul! You made it!" she cried.

The air was wild with whinnies and snorts as the ponies touched the hard sand, then scrambled up the shore, their wet bodies gleaming in the sun. Paul half-carried the little colt up the steep bank; then suddenly it found its own legs.

Shouts between triumph and relief escaped every throat as the little filly tottered up the bank. Almost to the top, her feet went scooting out from under her and she was down on the sand, her sides heaving.

Maureen felt a new stab of fear.

If only the big ponies would not crush her! That tender white body among all those thrashing hooves. What chance had she? What chance with the wild wind for a mother?

But all the wildness seemed to have ebbed out of the Phantom. She picked her forefeet high. Then she carefully straddled her colt, and fenced in the small white body with her own slender legs.

"God help ye, Paul! Yer almost home!"

For a brief second Paul's and Maureen's eyes met above the crowds. It was as if they and the mare and her foal were the only creatures on the island. They were unaware of the great jostling and fighting as the stallions sorted out their own mares and colts. They were unaware of everything but a sharp ecstasy. Soon the Phantom and her colt would belong to them. Never to be sold.

The Pied Piper wheeled around Paul. He peered at the dripping boy from under his matted forelock. Then he trumpeted as if to say: "This sopping creature is no mare of mine!" And he pushed Paul out of the way while the crowds laughed hysterically.

Dodging horses and people, Grandpa Beebe made his way over to Paul.

"Paul, boy," he said, his voice unsteady, "I swimmed the hull way with you. Yer the most wonderful and the craziest young'un in the world. Now git home right smart quick," he added, trying to sound very stern. "Yer about done up, and Grandma's expectin' ye. Maureen and I'll see to it that the Phantom and her colt reach the pony pens."

Champion of the Peaks

PAUL ANNIXTER

SLIPPY himself was primarily to blame for what happened that fall day. He had always been a bit too independent for his own good, and since his friendship with old Sounder, the ranch dog, had sprung up, he'd been a constant worry to Jesse Hunnicutt.

Slipstream, he was called—Slippy for short—and he'd been named for his speed. His hide was the color of running bronze. When in action, with flying mane and wild of eye and nostril, his head might have been that of Pegasus the winged. He was only a two-year-old, but already the pride of High Ranch. Some day, Jesse Hunnicutt believed, Slippy would be as good as any of the champion polo ponies he had raised.

There was nothing really bad about Slippy. He was just too full of ideas and pranks which walled him off from serious training. Sometimes in his wide-browed skull a cunning brain seemed bent on mischief—at least, so Jake Marden, the ranch foreman, claimed. Let a day dawn when a visiting buyer was to appear and Slippy would disappear up the mountain. As High Ranch was fenceless open range there was little to be done about this, unless someone remembered to lock Slippy in the barn.

It was old Sounder who had really gotten Slippy into the habit of these disappearances. He was the special property of young Jesse, who was fifteen, and old Jesse's only son. Part Walker, with an admixture of mastiff in his blood, Sounder had a seamed and melancholy face, big bones, great lubberly paws, and the heart of a lion. No respecter of bounds or barriers was

Sounder, but a privileged character who spent a great share of his days on the heights, tracking rabbit, fox, or wild cat.

Slippy had met Sounder one day in spring far up among the piñon pines. They had smelled noses and each had belonged specially to the other from there on in. They had met often after that, up there in the peaks, far from the sounds and scents of the ranch. Sometimes the pair would remain away for two days and two nights running, dependent upon one another for company and moral support; Slippy feeding and rolling in some cup between the peaks where the grass grew lush all summer, Sounder digging for marmots on a near-by slope or tracking rabbits in the brush, till darkness brought them close together. Great days for them both.

Alone, Slippy would never have had the initiative for such forays, but with Sounder to lead the way, the long wanderings among the crags were an endless adventure. At such times, with all the animals' wild instincts uppermost, not even young Jesse or old Jesse himself could get near the two when they happened to sight them among the peaks.

So it was on the November day in question. For some time knife-edged blasts of wind had warned of bad weather close at hand, but Jesse Hunnicutt had elected to stay at High Ranch till snow actually fell. Then one morning the ranch hands awoke at dawn with a norther sobbing through the cracks and chinks of the bunkhouse and a sting of sleet in the air. Dun clouds hung low over the peaks and the valleys were lost in a smudgy haze. There was not an hour to spare if they expected to get stock and equipment to the lowlands in time to escape the oncoming blizzard.

Slippy and Sounder were missing again. Both had been away overnight, and old Jesse muttered profanely as he scanned the high trails. Within an hour gear and stock were ready to move, and still no sign of the runaways. Grudgingly Jesse gave the order to leave, but he himself rode up-trail a way for one last look for Slipstream. Young Jesse followed on Uncle, a solid, sure-footed piebald.

The two searched and called into the teeth of the wind.

For nearly an hour the two searched and called into the teeth of the wind, but to no avail. Slippy and Sounder were far up the mountain at the time, taking refuge in the lee of a rock ledge. Old Jesse hated to abandon the search, not the least of his reasons being the loss of one of the most promising horses ever raised on High Ranch. For when he turned his mount down-trail that day he never expected to see Slipstream alive again, though he hid the fact from his son.

"We'll come back when the weather breaks and look for them again, son," he placated. "Old Sounder'll come through, never fear. But we've got to go now, or we'll never get down the mountain."

When the storm broke shortly before dawn, Slipstream was sheltered in a high spruce grove where he had spent a chilly and restless night. Sounder was afar, engaged in his endless game of digging out mountain marmots, and now and then coursing after snowshoe rabbits. Slippy could hear him from time to time, sounding his hoarse bell-like hunting cry.

By the time the sleet had turned to driving snow, Sounder gave up his splendid game and sought his friend among the trees. When morning came with the storm increasing, uneasiness began to ride the pair. What feeding there was had already been covered with snow. Slippy's thoughts turned to the warmth and security of the great barns at High Ranch. He had had enough for a time of this fodderless freedom. So, too, had Sounder. But when their steps turned down-trail and they emerged from the shelter of the spruce, they were almost swept from their feet by the sheer force of the gale. In places the snow was already belly-deep on Sounder, and everything familiar about the landscape had been obliterated.

Sounder and Slipstream pressed on, heads bent to the blast. Trails were gone. Only their sure feet and their wild instincts kept them to the right way. On the steep slopes they slipped and scrambled precariously, then picked a slow and dextrous course along a mile of shelving rock ledges that pinched off into space.

Later it was an even greater battle bucking through the drifts of the sheltered places.

It was far past midday when they sighted the ranch buildings and Slippy experienced one of his first great shocks. The ranch was deserted. Not a trace of smoke rose from the ranch-house chimneys, and there were not even any fresh tracks to show which way the men had gone.

Behind the summer lean-to the two took refuge and there Slippy found a few wisps of hay and straw in the long feed trough. Still others he uncovered by pawing the snowy ground beneath. Somewhat heartened by these mementos of man he settled down, eyes half closed, sensitive ears a-twitch, to await the ranchers' return. But Sounder had no such illusions. He prowled forlornly, whining with a growing unrest.

All that day the storm continued. Slippy finished every last sprig of hay in the lean-to. As the darkness of another night, hostile and smothering, descended on the mountain wilderness, he lifted his voice in sharp, imperative neighs. But no one came.

Through the dark hours the two runaways huddled together for warmth. When another day dawned with no lessening of the storm, loneliness and growing fear gripped Slippy. All that day the two waited and shivered in a world filled with storm, cold, and misery. But no one came, and through a second stormy night they pressed together for very life's sake, their coats covered with a thickening layer of frost and snow.

By noon of the third day the storm had subsided. Sounder set off down the mountain, whither he knew the ranch hands had gone. Slippy fell in behind him. The snow by now had piled belly-high on the horse and in two hours the pair progressed scarcely a mile, with the going harder every yard. Twice Slippy almost pitched into oblivion over the sheer cliffs; at last he turned back up the trail. Sounder followed him, for each was bound to the other now by ties as deep as life.

When hunger drove them forth from the lean-to again, it was up the mountain instead of down, for on the heights the snow was far less deep. In places the ridges were swept almost bare by the force of the wind. Up along the sparse spruce valleys they plodded, Slippy finding here and there some uncovered forage, and chewing many evergreen twigs for good measure. Sounder ran rabbits through the thickets.

Later that afternoon Slippy came upon a small herd of deer banded together in a winter "yard." Moved by an urge for com-

Slippy came upon a small herd of deer.

panionship, he moved forward eagerly to join them, but the two leading bucks of the herd shook menacing heads.

Slippy was too forlorn and miserable to care what the deer thought of him. Even ill feeling was preferable to the empty loneliness of the peaks. He waited meekly, some fifty paces away, to see what would happen.

The snow roundabout was too deep for the deer to flee their yard, so the bucks contented themselves with stampings and repeated challenges. But Slippy had a disarming way of his own.

He ruckled softly in his chest, and after an hour or so his quiet presence broke down resistance. The deer resumed their sketchy feeding, nibbling at the hanging branches of the trees and pawing down to the sparse feeding beneath the snow.

Later, when Sounder came in from a successful hunt, the deer were thrown into fresh panic. In fall or summer the deer would have fled like shadows and Sounder would have given chase in wild abandon. Now he came up meek and silent as Slippy himself and dropped panting beside his friend. Before long even his presence was accepted by the deer, for a magic truce had descended upon all.

By the time darkness came, horse and dog were learning the shelter and warmth that lies in snow when one is wise enough to burrow into it.

Each of the next four days they visited the ranch house, returning to the heights in the afternoon. Then on the fourth day they returned to find their wild friends had moved. The feeding had given out in the vicinity of the yard, and the deer had left to seek a better sanctuary.

Slippy followed along their trail, laboring slowly through the deep snow. He came upon the herd again a half mile away, tramping out a new yard which was to become a tragic prison for all of them. A thaw the next day was followed by another snowstorm. The high walls of the deer yard froze to the hardness of concrete, forming a prison from which there was no escape until another thaw.

Only Slippy's restlessness and his persistent urge to find his human friends saved him from sharing the fate of the deer. He was keeping vigil again at the ranch house when the freeze came. When he labored back to the deer yard he was unable to join his friends as usual. An iron crust had formed over the snow, and the pony stood nearly seven feet above the yard, looking dejectedly down on his imprisoned friends.

After four days, the feeding in the yard was consumed and the deer grew leaner and leaner, until the does and younglings were so weak they could hardly stand. Still no thaw came to liberate them.

The slow drama ended in tragedy one night when a mountain lion discovered the starving herd.

What followed was swifter and more merciful than starvation. Death came to them all, in their prison of ice.

Slippy, growing woodswise and wary, was warned of the menace that threatened on the lean dawn wind. A faint rank smell had come creeping into his consciousness, the musty reek of mountain lion. He knew it though he had never scented it before, and even to his peaceful intelligence that taint meant death. It sent him scrambling wildly out of the woods and onto a cleared slope just above.

Two days later Slippy and Sounder returned to find what was left of their friends, the deer. At the sight of the frozen and half-devoured carcasses, they did not wait for any chance encounter with the cougar. Keeping close together, they left that part of the mountain far behind and climbed toward the frozen peaks of the Divide. Now, because of the cougar, they avoided the dense timber for the rest of that day and therefore went hungry. And to add to their misery, another snowstorm started toward nightfall.

It was morning of the third day, with Sounder hunting far below, when Slippy rounded an outcrop of rock high above timber line and had the surprise of his life. A dozen or more fleecy hummocks of snow suddenly came to life about a hundred feet ahead of him.

Slippy was staring at his first band of mountain goats. One of them, the biggest, with pale fierce eyes, had a long, frosted white beard and black horns curling above his head. He snoofed explosively in challenge while the others melted away behind him.

The goats, fifteen of them, fled up over the rims as Slippy moved forward, but they could not go far because of the drifted snow. Slippy pressed on, disregarding the loud snoofing challenges of the old leader, who sought to engage Slippy in combat. But it takes two to make any sort of battle. Finding nothing to

vent his wrath upon, the old Billy subsided at last into an occasional angry snorting and stamping.

When Sounder approached in search of his friend, the whole
goat band disappeared like magic beyond a seemingly unscalable
peak, and Slippy thought he had lost them for good. But next
morning he found them again.

When the band moved, Slippy followed silently in their wake,
edging closer by degrees. When they uncovered the short cured
grass of the heights and ate, he also ate and found it good. The
goats began to look upon him as a friendly, harmless creature.
By the third day Slippy was suffered to feed and bed at will on
the edge of the band during the daytime hours when Sounder
was hunting afar. But the dog they would not accept.

At night old Sounder always found Slippy, and the two slept
together in some cranny out of the wind. But by day Slippy
continued to follow the goats. He found their feeding lean fare,
but it kept life in his body.

In the second week the goat leader led the band along a series
of narrow, precipitous ledges to the distant peaks. Slippy's small,
trim hoofs were becoming almost as sure as those of the goats
themselves. Acrobatic feats, however, were a bit beyond him.
The narrow ledge the band had been following pinched sharply
off into space. But ten feet below it a two-foot nubbin of rock
protruded from the face of the cliff. The old goat leaped for it,
balanced a moment, then dropped to another still farther on,
and thence to another narrow ledge beyond. One by one the rest
of the goats followed suit.

Slippy stood at the end of the ledge looking miserably after
them. He could not follow, or even turn around. Misery seized
upon him and he lifted his voice in a protesting neigh. The goats,
however, paid no heed. Already they were out of sight.

There was but one thing to do. Cautiously, feeling for each
foothold, Slippy began backing along the ledge down which he
had come. There were four hundred yards of that before he
reached a spot where he could turn. Up over the rims he went
by a roundabout way, but the goats were nowhere in sight.

Slippy stood at the end of the ledge looking after them.

For ten days thereafter Slippy wandered the heights, miserably searching for his friends along all the streets and avenues of the high goat cities. And each day two bald eagles sailed close to him expectantly, waiting for some mischance to strike him down. But Slippy, with a surprising ruggedness and craft, was doing the unbelievable—meeting and beating the winter wild in its cruelest and grimmest aspect.

A fighting spirit had awakened in him, a spirit that harked back to his hardy ancestors. His clever brain, that had formerly contrived small tricks of mischief, now worked overtime for self-protection. He had profited by all the object lessons of the deer and goats, and added numerous observations of his own. The fierce winds of the heights, he knew, could be depended upon to uncover enough herbage to keep life in his body, and at night he kept from freezing to death by huddling close to Sounder on the sheltered side of the peaks. But his civilized nature was dying the seven deaths in those mountain solitudes, and many times a day his lonesome whinny echoed among the crags.

Sounder too was doing the incredible, surpassing through necessity all normal bounds of his nature. Wolfish instincts came uppermost in him, instructing him how to consume enough snow for the water he needed, how to tell from afar when a deep snowbank held sleeping partridge, and how to dig out wood mice in their deep runways when all other food failed. He grew lean and gaunt as a specter, but somehow he survived.

A third week went by and January came, bringing with it a still cold unlike anything Slippy had yet known. He still searched the heights for his friends, and at length one afternoon he sighted a number of white specks against a far-off cliff. A valley lay between, but Slippy, undaunted, descended clear to timber line, bucked the deep drifts, and labored grimly up the other slope. Before nightfall he had come up with the goat band again, whinnying his satisfaction.

January was a terrible month up on the roof of the world. Storm after storm swept the heights. From the forested valleys below the hunger call of wolves and coyotes sounded nightly, and sometimes the whining scream of a cougar would split the breeze. Even the wild goats began to feel the pinch of hunger, for the snows were such that the highest peaks became mantled with white.

Now came the time of greatest peril, when hunting in the valleys grew lean and the mountain lions sought the peaks for meat. The broad pads of these killers held them up on the deep snow where the sharp hoofs of the goats cut through. The deadly stalking of the great cats could not wholly be guarded against, no matter what the craft of the goats. The cougars would prowl the heights until they found some point where the goats would have to pass. Lying in wait for hours until the band approached, the lion would drop like a bolt from some overhanging rock, and one of the band would pay with its life.

After each attack by a lion the goats would take refuge for days among the rim rocks. But they could not remain there indefinitely, and when hunger drove them down again the killers would again hang like a bad conscience to their trail. By the end of January five of the original fifteen goats had been killed, and still there was no break in the weather.

Slippy came through that grim month unscathed, partly because he was always struggling along at the tail end of the file of goats, and partly because the lions were suspicious of him, associating him and his scent with man, their greatest enemy. The old leader of the goats also escaped attack. That hoary patriarch would have welcomed facing a lion in fair combat. But the killers were cowards at heart, and had no stomach for tackling a four-hundred-pound fighting machine, with sinews of whalebone and a hide like a thick wool rug.

As February came and the deep snows still made hunting in the lower forests impossible for the cougars, the contest between the goats and the great cats came to an inevitable dramatic head. For weeks the goats had been growing warier and warier. They never approached a rock cliff without beating carefully up wind, eyes and nostrils alert for a sign of the enemy. For a fortnight there had been no casualties in the band, for they had lived on the leanest fare in order to avoid every possible ambush.

At last, on a still night when a dying moon bathed the white peaks in a spectral light, the lions, driven by unbearable hunger, brought the battle to the old patriarch.

Slippy and Sounder were some five hundred feet below the band this night. All were bedded near the brink of a broad, open ledge, where no enemy could possibly approach without first appearing boldly in the open. It was that hour before the dawn when night hunters that have found no kill turn desperate.

The jagged peaks roundabout leaned toward the morning stars, when an eddy of breeze carried the rank scent of lion to the sensitive nostrils of the old leading goat. He had the band on their feet in an instant. Then, after long minutes of tension, a mountain lion showed among the rocks of the distant cliff, another close behind. This was the pair that had ravaged the peaks all winter. Beyond all caution now, they advanced into the wash of moonlight, red-eyed with hunger.

The goats backed to the brink of the ledge, the old patriarch well to the fore, facing the cliff. Minutes of waiting passed. The lions flattened themselves to the snow, advancing but a few inches at a time, their eyes holding the goats with a murderous fixity. Never before had they carried the war into the open like this. Their every instinct was for waiting and indirection, but fiercer even than their blood lust was the gnaw of hunger. The big muscles of their shoulders bulged above their gaunt, crouched bodies.

Slippy, standing five hundred feet down slope, was trembling faintly, unable to make any other move. Weakened by cold and privation, he wanted only to sink down in the snow; wanted only to creep away and sleep. But the lions came on—so stealthily that they seemed not to move at all, save for their long tails that twitched like snakes. Puffs of icy wind sent sprays of snow across the ledge from the rocks above.

Even old Sounder seemed to have no battle challenge in him this night. For once he made no sound, but merely got to his feet, his hackles rising stiffly along his gaunt shoulders. As yet the lions had not seen him.

Abruptly the foremost lion launched himself forward in an attempt to pass the old leader's guard. But the bulky patriarch, agile as any kid, reared and whirled on his hind legs with a bawl of defiance, and a lightning thrust of his crinkly black horns caught the killer in mid-air. The lion was jerked to one side as if by invisible wires. Almost in the instant he alighted he returned to the attack, in a succession of short rushes and angry snarls. The *wheep-wheep* of his great mailed paws tore patches from the old goat's white coat but, wheeling and pivoting with flashing horns, the leader still managed to block the lion at every turn.

Back to the very brink of the ledge they maneuvered, till another step would have pitched them both into oblivion. Still by a miracle the cougar was unable to break through the guard to the huddled kids and nannies behind.

Then, into the breach, help came flying in a shaggy wolfish form. Old Sounder, who might have crept away unnoticed from that place of death and danger, had hesitated but a brief minute. Straight into the face of the cougar he launched his hundred and fifty pounds. What followed was a storm of tawny arms and legs and flying snow, amid a crescendo of screams and growls and the white flesh of fang and claw.

The lion's mate, meanwhile, had been circling the rocks to come in from the opposite side and make a swift kill while the old patriarch was engaged. But no opening offered. Instead, there stood Slippy in her way, a chunky, sorrel-colored horse trembling in every limb but with white teeth bared, hoofs dancing, nostrils ruckling in a frenzy of defiance. Even as Sounder attacked, the lioness sprang from haunches like coiled springs. Slippy moved in the same instant. He pivoted and powerful hind legs shot out, catching the lioness a glancing blow on the shoulder.

With a fiendish squall the big cat struck the snow, then bounded to the pony's back, her four sets of claws sinking deep into his quivering sides. Slippy staggered, pitched to his nose but struggled up again, his wild whinnies of protest blending with the battle cry of the patriarch.

The mailed paw of the lioness crooked beneath Slippy's neck and wrenched cunningly. Her custom was to kill by dislocation. Slippy bucked like a demon. His blunt teeth caught one silky ear of the attacker and ground it into a bleeding rag. The lioness screamed with rage and sprang free—unable, like all cats, to stand pain. She crouched for another spring, perilously close to the lip of the ledge, as Slippy wheeled with a desperate whinny. In that instant old Sounder was beside him. Somehow the dog had broken free of the lion and come to the aid of his friend.

Sounder sprang in with a roar; the lioness struck and sprang aside. Once more, terrible and avenging, Slippy swung around to deliver a broadside kick with his powerful hind legs. It landed squarely and soddenly against the big cat's ribs, flinging her back. She teetered a moment on the very brink, her claws rasping on the ice and snow, and Slippy kicked again. A moment the tawny body dangled over the snowy ledge, then slipped and pitched downward, writhing and screaming, into the gulf below.

The male lion, circling the old goat, turned his head at the death cry of his mate. It was only an instant, but for the patriarch, dancing on his hind legs preparing for a charge, it was enough. He drove in with a mighty thrust of lowered horns that rolled the killer over. Before he found his feet the old goat hit him again like a pile-driver, while from the opposite side old Sounder was closing in to finish the kill.

It was too much for the lion. Before either opponent could reach him again, the killer of the peaks was streaking, belly down, for the shelter of the cliffs.

At that point Slippy and Sounder might have established themselves as masters of the mountain wilderness and all its inhabitants. To them it was an empty glory, however; particularly to old Sounder, wounded far more seriously than he knew. Torn and red and hardly recognizable, he collapsed presently on his side, his blood staining the snow. He gave but a few feeble thumps of his tail when Slippy came and stood above him.

The lioness pitched downward, writhing and screaming.

It was two hours before his fevered wounds stopped bleeding. All that day Slippy stayed close to his friend. The goat band, too, hovered near in a strange concern, drawn by the bond that had been established between them in battle.

That victory over the cougars seemed a winning over famine and the winter hardships as well, for at nightfall there came an abrupt break in the weather.

Before morning the snowy slopes were melting in a thousand tiny rivulets and through the silence sounded the occasional long, sucking *chug* of sinking snow. Mountain and forest seemed to relax and breathe again. There might come other freezes, but the worst of the winter was now over.

Meanwhile Sounder was fighting with the last supreme Enemy, and barely holding his own. Somehow Slippy seemed to know. By gentle nudges of his warm, inquiring nose, he kept rousing the old dog from his coma of pain and fever, urging him to follow down the mountain to the ranch house. Again and again through that long day the dog would rally and rise on shaky legs and follow Slippy for a hundred and fifty yards, only to sink down again and rest until strength was renewed.

Night had fallen when they reached the ranch. All was deserted still, but the corrals and pastures were almost free of snow, the warm breeze was like a benison, and the air was filled with the soft chuckle of trickling water. Stretched out on the ranch porch, Sounder let the old familiar scents and sounds slide through his ears and nose. His heart took strength and the shadowy Enemy faded away, defeated.

It was about noon next day, as the goat band fed slowly along the snowline above the ranch, that something startled them into sudden flight. Slippy saw them go and flung up his head, then wheeled at another movement and the old familiar sound of human voices.

Jesse Hunnicutt, with Jake Marden and young Jesse behind him, had just rounded a bend in the valley trail, each mounted and leading a pack animal. Releasing their pack horses at sight of Slippy, all three spurred forward with incredulous whoops and yells.

And Slippy? Flinging up his head with a wild whinny, he sprang from complete rest to full speed in a single shutter-click of time. Down the length of the great pasture he thundered to meet his friends, running with all that was in him, his small mountain-hardened legs moving like pistons in perfect rhythm. To the watching men his flying hoofs seemed never to strike the ground.

The riders reined in to gape, sitting their horses as though struck in stone. On he came, until he was eight feet in front of the horsemen. In the final instant before head-on collision, Slippy jerked aside with no slightest slackening of speed, then swept round and round them in great wild circles, whinnying again and again with happiness. The men continued to watch in silent fascination.

Always slimly built and lightly muscled, Slippy was now leaned down to the point of emaciation, the tendons like slender skeins at his wrists and hocks—but skeins of steel. He looked more than ever as if he might drift before the wind.

Jesse Hunnicutt was muttering as he watched. "Look at him, just look at him!" he cried. "There's an antelope and a greyhound rolled up in him—to say nothin' of a cannon ball! And that legwork! And to think I left him for dead!"

They waited till Slippy had worked off some of his steam and joy and come to a stand. Then Jesse Hunnicutt dismounted, while young Jesse spurred toward the ranch house to look for his dog. The rancher was aware of a vague but definite shame as he approached the game little horse. He was guilty, as he saw it now, of rank desertion. Slippy's mane was a gnarled and matted mass from the winter winds; his lean sides were no longer sleek, but woolly as a range horse's—nature's desperate effort to help ward off the cold. The man's eye picked out the wounds along his back.

"Cougars, Boss!" cried Jake Marden. "The pore little cuss! I reckon he saw a thing or two besides cold and hunger up there among the peaks!"

"Well, I'll be John Brown!"

Jesse put a hand on Slippy's sturdy neck, then bent to run exploring, incredulous fingers over the solid chest and hocks and pasterns. He swore soulfully again. Never had he dreamed of seeing a two-year-old in such superb condition. In spite of cougars and cold, winter and hunger, or perhaps because of them, he was looking at a champion.

For a space man and horse stood gazing at each other across the great gulf of silence that hangs forever between the human and animal world. Had Slippy been human the gulf might never have been spanned after what had happened in the fall. But being animal, he bent his head to rub it lovingly against the man's sleeve. It was enough for him that the voices of his human friends once more fell blessedly on his ears.

Up at the ranch house old Sounder too had rubbed away that gulf as if it had never been, and young Jesse was kneeling on the porch steps, his arms full of his old dog.

FROM

Salute

C. W. ANDERSON

---

*Peter grew up on a farm near the famous race-track at Sara-
toga, thinking and reading about and loving horses. Even
as a tiny boy, tending the farm horses was always a joy instead of a chore to him. He would sit on the broad backs of
the work horses, his small legs sticking straight out, and
pretend he was racing. But of course it was not like having a
real riding horse of his own. That was Peter's dream. And
it was realized most unexpectedly one day at Saratoga as he
watched a beautiful bay horse stumble and injure his leg in
a practice race. Rather than have him destroyed, the trainer
offered him to Peter on the promise of a good home. Here
begins one of the finest passages ever written about what it
feels like to ride a fine horse.*

Learning to Ride Together

THE morning sun was shining brightly through the small-
paned window when Peter awoke. For a moment he lay wondering what it was that made him feel so light and happy. Then he
remembered and leaped out of bed. He had a horse! Even when
he was wide awake he had a horse. It might be on its way even
now. With his clothes thrown on hurriedly and his hair tangled
and on end, Peter dashed downstairs. The smell of bacon and
eggs came from the kitchen, where his mother stood over the
stove. She smiled and shook her head.

"Not yet," she said. "He won't be here until later. Call your father for breakfast."

There was much to talk about at breakfast, but it was mostly about Mohawk. Peter's father recalled many instances of horses that were thought to be hopelessly crippled but had been cured by care and rest.

When breakfast was over, Peter hurried out where he could see the road that led to Saratoga winding like a ribbon through the hills and valleys. There was nothing in sight, but it was still early. He ran down to the barn to feed Ned and Brownie and to look at the new stall. It seemed light and cheerful in the morning sun. Surely Mohawk would be comfortable and happy here.

When he hurried out again the road was still empty; so he climbed up on the top rail of the fence, where he could get a good view. As he waited, Peter tried to remember just how Mohawk looked. He was bay, a beautiful dark bay with a wonderful shine to his coat. But did he have one white foot or two? He remembered the white star on his forehead and how large and intelligent his eyes were. It was the look in the eyes that made Peter forget his shyness before all those people.

A long time passed by. There was still nothing in sight but some cows being driven across the road. Perhaps the man had changed his mind. What if Mohawk was so much better this morning that the trainer decided to keep him?

But what was this that was just coming over the farthest hill? It was much bigger than a car; it must be the horse van. Peter had never seen a horse van; but he felt that it must be something like a big truck, and certainly this was big enough for a horse. The road dipped into a valley, and he waited breathlessly. Now it was coming up the hill. . . . Peter's heart sank. It was only a milk truck.

Dark despair was upon him. Deep in his heart he had known it was too good to be true. People didn't give away beautiful horses. He would have to wait until he was big enough to earn money to buy a horse. But it was all so far away—so long to wait. His eyes smarted, and he swallowed hard as he climbed down from the fence.

As he turned slowly toward the house he saw something on the road. It was bigger than the milk truck, much bigger. If the man hadn't changed his mind it might be the horse van. Peter's heart beat fast as he waited for it to come up the hill. Then he saw the top, and on it was lettered, "Horses." The truck stopped, and the driver asked if Peter Folwell lived there.

Peter knew that his dream had come true.

Three weeks had passed since Mohawk had limped out of the van and into his new home. He now moved much more easily, and the swelling in his leg was almost gone. The trainer had sent instructions for his treatment, and Peter spent all his spare time putting cold bandages on the injured leg. Every day he took Mohawk down to the brook to stand for a long time in the cool, flowing water. This was very good to take the soreness out of a muscle or tendon. The soft yielding meadow was very pleasant to a horse whose legs had become sore from many years of racing over hard tracks, and soon he began to have a spring in his walk.

Although Peter was still very fond of Ned and Brownie his feeling about Mohawk was different. Not only because this was his own horse, but because he was so intelligent and gentle and sensitive that Peter found it hard to leave him, even for a short time. Mohawk seemed to miss Peter just as much, for he was always standing with his head over the stall door waiting for him to come back. For a shy boy who had few playmates it was an ideal companionship.

One day several weeks later Peter's father stood watching Mohawk as Peter led him back from the brook.

"I think you could start riding him a little now," he said. "He isn't limping at all, and you're very light. I'll see if I can borrow a saddle and bridle from the Washburns. They have no saddle horse now, so they don't use them."

Peter had never ridden except on Ned's or Brownie's wide

back; but he had read everything he could find about riding, and he had no fear of horses. He felt sure that Mohawk would know he was learning and try to help. For so long, now, he had been riding in his dreams that he did not feel like a beginner at all.

When Peter's father saw how Mohawk opened his mouth to take the bit, and lowered his head so that Peter could reach to put on the bridle, he said that he would never worry about Peter's safety with such a horse. Then the saddle was put on and tightened, and Peter proudly led Mohawk out of the stable. His father helped him into the saddle, and as Peter gathered up the reins he felt that the great moment of his life had come. He was riding his own horse.

They started off for the meadow, where the footing would be soft, and now Peter realized the difference between the walk of a saddle horse and a work horse. Mohawk's was so smooth and springy it was like flowing water; and when he pranced a little because he felt so gay, Peter tingled from head to foot. Certainly nothing in the world was as fine as this.

As they crossed the brook and went into the pasture beyond, Peter was surprised to find how natural it felt to be in the saddle. When they came back to the stable an hour later no one, seeing how easily he sat his horse, would think that this boy was coming back from his first ride.

The second week they were going longer distances, and there was no sign of soreness in Mohawk's leg. They were still going only at a walk, to give the leg a chance to become strong and supple before trying a faster pace. This was the best possible thing for Peter also. Each day he was feeling more at home in the saddle and in rhythm with Mohawk's every movement. Most beginners are so anxious to start galloping that they are impatient of any details, and as a result they usually do everything a little wrong afterward.

It was enough for Peter just to be with his horse; he would have been happy to ride at a walk for months if necessary. There were so many things to remember: the heels down, the knees gripping just so, the hands light and firm on the reins. To Peter, who wanted perfection in this above all else, no detail was too small or unimportant.

Coming back across the meadow one day, Mohawk began prancing very lightly, then a little faster, and in a moment he was in a trot. At first Peter sat close to the saddle; then as he felt the trot lengthen he found himself rising a little with the rhythm of it, and soon he was in perfect unison with the gait.

It had seemed wonderful before, but now Peter saw life stretched out before him in a succession of golden days. He rode up to the kitchen door and called to his mother excitedly. She came out to watch and was really surprised to see how well Peter rode. When they came back from their circle of the farm-yard Mohawk stopped expectantly. He was a great favorite with Peter's mother and knew she would always have something for

Mohawk seemed overflowing with energy and spirit.

him: an apple or a carrot or a lump of sugar; sometimes even a cooky, which he liked especially.

Needless to say, Mohawk received more care than most horses get. His coat was brushed many times a day until it shone like burnished metal in the sun. His mane and tail were dark and silky, and he carried his head in such a spirited way that he was a very handsome sight. No one in the countryside had ever owned anything like him, and the neighbors always stopped work to see him go by.

The crispness in the air acted as a tonic on Mohawk; he pranced and seemed overflowing with energy and spirit. Peter now rode at a canter as easily as at a trot, and sometimes when they came to a stretch of smooth road he would let Mohawk go at a fast gallop if he wanted to. Speed was what Mohawk had been bred for, generation after generation; so it was only natural that he should remember his racing days and sometimes like to hear his feet drumming and feel his mane flying. To Peter it was very thrilling.

All through the winter there was scarcely a day when Peter did not take Mohawk out for a ride after school. Even snow and cold did not stop them; for Mohawk had his heavy winter coat, and he always seemed pleased and surprised at the strange white world outside.

When the buds were showing on the trees again, Peter and Mohawk understood each other as horse and rider seldom do. The reins were hardly necessary; Mohawk responded to Peter's voice, even in the excitement of galloping at full speed.

As the hills and meadows grew greener and the days lengthened, Peter and Mohawk went farther and farther over the countryside. Nearly all errands were done on horseback. If Peter's mother needed something from the store in the village a few miles away, it seemed they had been gone only a few minutes before she heard Mohawk's neigh outside as he waited to be rewarded. By the time summer had come there was scarcely a road or trail within ten miles that they had not explored.

The muscles under Mohawk's shining coat stood out clear and sharp and rippled and flowed as he moved. Peter's father said he had never seen a horse in finer condition. Often on a Saturday, after he had done his chores, Peter would put a sandwich in his pocket and go out with Mohawk for all day.

He had never realized before how many wild animals were near by. Several times they came upon startled deer and were thrilled to see the long graceful bounds that carried them over the highest walls with ease. Occasionally a fat woodchuck would scurry away with his awkward, waddling gait; often they saw pheasants and partridge, and once a fox that vanished so quickly and completely that Peter was not sure whether he saw or imagined it.

There were chores to be done each day, and Peter often helped in the fields with work that was not too heavy for an eleven-year-old boy. But there was always time for riding too. Peter's father realized that his son's interest in horses was much more than a childish enthusiasm, so he encouraged him to learn as

much as possible about them. He was wise enough to realize that a person may accomplish more in the direction of his interest than in any other.

The small bookshelf in Peter's room was now almost full of books about horses, and all of them had been read many times. Whether it was the record of his hero, Man o' War, or the best way to treat a cracked hoof, it all stayed clearly in his mind.

In late July the papers were full of news of the opening of the Saratoga racing season. One day Peter noticed the name of Mr. Harley, the trainer who had given him Mohawk. He was at Saratoga with horses he was training for the races there. Peter felt that he had never thanked Mr. Harley for Mohawk, and he wished for a long time that he could show the trainer how well Mohawk was. He told his father about it and asked if he could ride over the next day. It was only ten miles away, and since the training track was in the outskirts of the city there would be

Half a dozen horses were on the track.

very little traffic early in the morning. His father gave his consent, and Peter spent all the afternoon grooming Mohawk and cleaning and polishing the saddle and bridle.

The moon was pale in the sky, and only a faint pink glow showed in the east when Peter dressed next morning. He hurried down to the stable to feed Mohawk, and then came back to eat the breakfast which his mother had set out for him the night before.

By the time he had brushed and saddled Mohawk it was quite light. They had the road to themselves, and mile after mile was quickly covered by Mohawk's long swinging trot. Before Peter realized it they were in the outskirts of Saratoga. Soon the Oklahoma Training Track loomed ahead, and they could hear the galloping of horses. Mohawk's head went up and he sniffed the air, pranced, and blew loudly through his nostrils. There was no doubt that he remembered the old scenes well and that the spirit of competition still flamed strong in him.

Peter rode through the gate and into a very colorful and exciting scene. Half a dozen horses were on the track galloping, while many others were being led around and cooled after their workouts. The rail of the track was lined with grooms who had colored blankets over their arms, exercise boys in breeches and boots, and trainers who were timing their horses. A chestnut horse and a gray came galloping by, head and head, at almost racing speed. Mohawk kept snorting and prancing; he wanted to be racing with them.

When Peter could take his fascinated eyes off the horses he began to look for Mr. Harley. Soon he saw him talking to a man, and he waited near by. As the trainer turned around he caught sight of Mohawk; then he walked over and looked more closely. Peter could see how surprised he was.

"Why, Mohawk, old-timer, I wouldn't have known you," he said as he patted his nose. "How did you do it, Sonny?" he said to Peter. "He never looked any better, not even in his younger days."

Peter told all about it, and the trainer nodded his head as he studied him.

"You like horses," he said. "You'll be a real horseman someday."

This was the greatest praise possible, and Peter flushed with pleasure.

The Potato Race

HELEN TRAIN HILLES

Bumps jumped out of bed and looked at the large round potato, thoroughly scrubbed, that lay on her bedside table. Beside it was a shining silver soup spoon. It was only six o'clock in the morning, and she giggled at the thought of how she would practice secretly for the steeplechase. She was not so good a rider as her twin cousins, Patrick and Pamela, and their young English friends, but she was determined to uphold the honor of America in the steeplechase.

She couldn't put on her riding habit this morning, for if the cousins caught her coming back from the stables in her riding habit, they might suspect what was going on. So she slipped on an old sweater and an old pair of her brother's breeches that had somehow got stuffed into her suitcase. The boots fitted so she decided to wear those, and leave them somewhere in the stables. Then she could come home barefoot, as the twins often did, over the soft, smooth lawns.

When she reached the stables she saw Dragon Fly, already saddled, his bit gleaming in clear morning sun. James, the groom, came out of the stable whistling, as Bumps' quick footsteps crunched on the gravel.

"'Ello!" he smiled at the young visitor from America. "Your 'orse is waiting," he said. "Now, up you go!"

Bumps was up in the air and on Dragon Fly's back almost before she knew what was happening.

"I think we'll shorten the stirrups a bit," James went on.

"Now, you just let your 'orse take you over the jumps. He was schooled on them jumps."

How free and easy she felt! The loose breeches and sweater didn't hamper her a bit, and no one was there to watch her. She was much better! If only she could do it as well the day of the show! One, two, three jumps, all cleared well. But when Bumps came to the last jump, she felt herself stiffen. Because she had fallen once didn't mean she was going to again, she told herself. But it was no use. Stiff as a log she sat in that saddle, and with a jerk she was off. Dragon Fly cleared the jump by himself, then stopped short and looked reproachfully at the little heap on the ground on the other side of the jump.

Bumps was not hurt, but she lay there a little dazed and quite ashamed of herself. James picked her up.

"Now!" he said quietly. "Over that jump again!"

"Do I have to?" said Bumps a little fearfully.

"Yes," said James, "until you do it right. You won't hurt yourself. You fall like a real rider."

"It's something to be told you fall well," Bumps giggled.

"It's half the battle," said James gravely.

So Bumps tried the jump again—and again she fell off. But the third time she managed by the skin of her teeth to stay on, coming down on the saddle with a terrific, shaking jerk. The fourth time she *wanted* to try it.

"That was good," said James. Bumps was glad she had stuck to it. Oh, the feeling it gave you to go over that high jump well!

"That's all for today," said James, "except to practice with the potato."

Bumps picked up the potato. She put it in the deep soup spoon. It seemed very top-heavy, and the minute she started walking the potato wobbled about and finally fell out.

"I'll never be able to do it on a horse!" she said. She mounted Dragon Fly and James handed her the spoon and potato. She sat for a moment, holding the end of the spoon in her right hand. Then she touched the horse gently with her heels.

And with a jerk she was off.

"Oh, please," she breathed, "please walk evenly—and don't look at me, or you'll spoil everything." She laughed as Dragon Fly turned his long neck and stared at her with a perplexed eye. She let him walk around in a circle as she concentrated on the potato. At first her fingers felt cramped, but soon she discovered that if she relaxed the potato did not wobble so much.

"Very good, Miss," said James. At that moment Bumps heard a distant laugh.

"Oh!" she said. "I almost forgot! What time is it? That was Pat!" She scrambled off Dragon Fly and the spoon clattered to the ground. "Will you hide my spoon and potato and—and these?" She sat down on the grass and peeled off her shining boots. "I'm sorry to leave everything in such a mess—and thanks ever so much, but I've got to dash now."

She raced off barefoot, keeping an eye out for her cousins. When she reached the house she slipped noiselessly up the back stairs. At the top, with a quick glance down the long hall, she slid into her room. She mopped her face, put on a pair of sneakers, and brushed the fresh dirt off her clothes. Then she ambled down the hall, and stifled a yawn as she met her cousins in the schoolroom.

"Sleepy-head!" teased Pat. "I knocked and knocked, and then Mother said if you were that sleepy to let you sleep yourself out!"

"I—I hope there's some breakfast left," said Bumps. She couldn't lie, and yet she didn't want them to find out where she'd been.

The next three mornings Bumps got up early and practiced hard. She learned to jump well. James said she was as good as Pat and almost as good as Pam. But she still couldn't stop herself from going stiff before that last jump.

The children were all so excited about the steeplechase they almost forgot Bumps was to leave the day after. All the boys and girls invited to the party—eleven of them—had accepted, and a number of parents were to come and swell the grandstand. Bumps' Aunt Grace went around counting things on her fingers and murmuring about sandwiches. A parcel appeared for Uncle John who ducked with it into a closet and locked the door before the children had time to feel it. He said something about shirts, but the shape hadn't looked like shirts at all.

Somehow, until today, the steeplechase had seemed quite far off, but when Bumps went to bed that night it came to her in a rush that the party was really the next day. That evening James had said for her not to think about it, and to get a good night's rest. "But I can't very well stop my heart thumping," Bumps thought, as she climbed into bed. She only had one more night in England! Then she was going home to her family—and yet England seemed almost like home now.

All the children hung around restlessly the next morning. Everywhere they went some one told them to go some place else. They couldn't ride because James and the boy were so busy grooming the horses.

"Oh, dear! Do you think afternoon will ever come?" groaned Pat.

At last it was only an hour too soon to go and dress, so the children went upstairs. Bumps, in her room, went to the wardrobe and pulled out her new habit. Then she remembered what she had forgotten on those days when she had ridden in her loose old clothes. Her habit was a tight fit! She'd never do as well in her habit! And yet it was so beautiful! Even modest Bumps had become used to the pleased murmurs when she appeared so trimly dressed. She frowned. She was going to uphold the honor of America. How she did was more important than how she looked! She stuck her habit back into the wardrobe and slipped into her brother's breeches and her own shirt. Then she put on her little brown felt riding hat with the feather, and her shining boots. She was ready. She snatched up her ivory-headed crop as she heard Pam calling.

"Hurry! We're all ready and Father says we may see the grandstand now!"

Bumps gave a last glance at the wardrobe and a doubtful one at herself in the glass and ran downstairs.

Pat and Pam were much too interested in what was going on to notice how she looked. But Bumps stared at them in amazement. They were all dressed up for the show! They had on regular, well-fitting riding habits and trim derby hats. Their necks were held a little stiff by high white stocks. For a moment Bumps felt slightly uncomfortable.

The grandstand was so shiny white that Bumps wondered if the paint were quite dry yet. It smelled very strong, and if you pressed your finger down hard on it, it gave, though the top was dry. On one side was hung a faded Union Jack, and as Bumps peered around the other, she saw a clean new American flag. She knew that was for her and it made her feel very important. Aunt Grace in a flowered dress and floppy hat was already greeting some strange people. Uncle John had on a lovely pink hunting coat, white stock, and glossy black hat.

Several new horses and two or three men that looked rather like James were about.

"Whose horses are those?" Bumps asked.

"The Hanbridges' and Sylvia Dale's horses—they had to send them over because they live too far away," explained Pam.

"The others all live near and will ride over," added Pat. "Oh, and here comes Cedric!"

So the cousins dashed off to welcome a tall boy on a beautiful small hunter. There also were two girls too small to be really interesting, and quite an array of parents and grooms. The grandstand was filling up now, and Bumps suddenly noticed a lady who was staring at her through a monocle. She felt hot as she remembered her clothes.

"And this is our young niece from America," explained Aunt Grace, as Bumps shook hands with the lady.

"Oh," said the lady, as though that had explained everything.

Everyone had come, and Uncle John was going over the list of events with James.

The first class was to be a very simple one. Everyone, even younger children who had only ponies, could join in. They were all to ride around the outer ring, paying special attention to form. Everyone was mounted, the youngest little boy so small that he had to be lifted onto his pony.

"Walk!" shouted Uncle John through his megaphone. Bumps felt very much at home. This was just like the Bar Harbor show, in which she had ridden since she was four!

"Trot!" Bumps kicked Dragon Fly gently. Toes up. Back straight. Heels down.

"The little American rides well." She heard a murmur from the grandstand as she passed.

"Canter! Turn around! Stop!" It was fun, obeying orders, making the horse do as you wanted.

When the class was dismissed, no one was sorry that Uncle John gave the prize to the small boy on the Shetland pony. He was so overcome that he ran to his mother, much to his older brother's disgust.

The parent and child class came next. Bumps could not enter it, as she did not have a parent with her, but she watched with interest. It was won by Cedric and his father, dressed exactly alike, the boy's light hunter keeping pace with his father's heavy one.

Bumps was thinking of the jumping class that was coming next. Something like stage fright was creeping up from the soles of her sleek boots, till it lodged in a lump under her shirt. She sat quite still and so cramped that, when her class was called, her right foot was prickly and felt weak.

"Oh, dear, now my foot's asleep!" thought Bumps, as she limped down to where the hunters and children were waiting their turns.

Pat went first and everyone watched as he rode all around the course, getting over every jump, but knocking down two rails. Cedric's horse was unused to the course, and not yet very well trained in jumping. It refused the first jump. "Oh," thought Bumps, heartsick for him, "how awful!" But Cedric's face was set and serious. He turned his horse towards the jump again, and there was a burst of applause as he got over at last. He cleared the next jump, but his horse refused again at the last.

Cedric doggedly tried again. As he rode out, having finally cleared every jump, there were loud cheers. Uncle John called out, "Good boy!" Bumps decided she liked Cedric.

Pam next. There was a hum of admiration from the stands as she mounted gracefully, turned her big hunter towards the first jump and cleared it easily. Round the course she went, not hurrying, taking each jump, even the last, perfectly.

"She's good," thought Bumps. Of course, it was thrilling to see anyone ride so well. But she had a little sinking feeling. She hadn't a chance.

It was Bumps' turn. She got up on Dragon Fly.

"You can do it," whispered James.

"She's only dressed for riding at the top and bottom—not in the middle," Bumps heard some child say as she started off.

"Loosen up!" she told herself. Anyway, she couldn't win. No one could beat Pam. It made it a little easier, knowing that. She must do just as well as she could. Dragon Fly cleared his first jump. Bumps forgot it was a contest, forgot her clothes, forgot everything but the joy of jumping. Why, it was easy! The sound of applause at the third jump brought her back. They were clapping her! She felt very pleased. She smiled happily at the blurred pink spot that was Uncle John. Then coming towards her she saw the fourth jump. She stiffened, then she made herself unbend. The awful feeling of stage fright came over her again. She had to jump it. She could. The jump loomed towards her and she could feel Dragon Fly gather himself beneath her. Oh! Dragon Fly sprang. Bumps jerked high from the saddle, lost a stirrup, then came down again. She clutched Dragon Fly's bristly mane and righted herself with a bump in the saddle. At least she was on—and she thought all her teeth were in.

As she rode out she was clapped, and though she was furious with herself for not doing better, she smiled as she got off her horse a little stiffly.

For the events up to this one, ribbons had been given. Bumps guessed Aunt Grace had made them. But this time, when Pam was told she was the winner, Uncle John gave her a lovely little silver cup.

"It's not quite correct for the hostess to get the prize," he said, "but you won it, so you must have it."

Everyone cheered, and Bumps ran up to her cousin.

"Oh, Pam, you were wonderful!" she said wistfully. "Do you think I could ever be as good?"

"I dare say you could, easily, in time," said Pam modestly. Uncle John patted Bumps' shoulder.

"You're a credit to America," he said. "If it hadn't been for that last jump, you would have won the prize!"

Bumps, her disappointment bravely squashed down, smiled happily at the praise Uncle John rarely gave.

"Really?" she beamed.

James came over with a great burlap bag and opened the top.

"Now!" announced Uncle John. "The last event, the potato race, will take place!" There was a chorus of surprise and giggles as Uncle John doled out the large silver spoons.

"The last person with a potato in his spoon wins! And remember, only one hand, and you may not touch the potato! Here's the bag. Everyone puts his hand in and draws a potato, and that is the one he must keep!"

The children grouped themselves about the bag and reached in all at once and drew out potatoes. There was a good deal of shuffling and pulling. Bumps, who had grabbed several strange hands instead of potatoes, felt somehow that she knew all these children much better than she had. She finally came up laughing with a great big potato that had already begun to sprout.

The children all mounted and were handed their spoons and were busy arranging their potatoes in the firmest possible way before the race started. Bumps' potato had a large hump in it, and would not lie properly in the spoon. She turned it the other way, and just as Uncle John said, "Ready!" it seemed to turn and fall into a comfortable place. It really felt quite firm.

"Walk!" called Uncle John. There was a clatter and a spoon fell to the ground. But Bumps didn't look, intent on her own potato. Three more potatoes or spoons fell amidst a shower of giggles. The riders who had lost their potatoes got off their horses. Out of eleven who had started, only seven were now left and some of the potatoes were very wobbly.

"Trot!" called Uncle John. There was a gasp from the children left in the ring. Pat's potato jolted. Though he leaned way over to try and catch it, it was gone. He laughed, and slid off his horse. Bumps suddenly looked around and saw that she and Cedric were the only ones left! But her glance shot back to her potato. This was no time to be looking around! Shrieks were beginning from the other children.

Each time he rose his potato hopped a little.

"Bumps! Bumps! Bumps!" shouted Pat and Pam.

"Cedric! Hold on!"

Bumps remembered to hold her arm loose as she trotted around the track. And she tried to keep steady. Instead of posting as she had been taught, she stuck to the saddle as you did when riding a western pony. Her potato felt almost steady.

Cedric was posting. Each time he rose his potato hopped a little into the air.

"Canter!" cried Uncle John. Cedric's potato bounced high in the air.

"Ah!"

Cedric was off his horse, almost before the potato flopped on the ground.

"Bumps wins!"

She got off her horse, still with her potato in its spoon. She was surrounded by the other children and Uncle John.

"Good for you, Bumps!" cried Pat excitedly. "It's because she rode so much out in Arizona that she has such a steady seat," he explained proudly to the others.

"She's most awfully good, even if she does look a little odd," said Cedric generously.

Bumps was laughing and quite red. Her back hurt pleasantly from the whacks everyone was giving her. She picked her potato carefully out of its spoon, to save, but as she did so she noticed that the hump had really fitted right into the spoon and made it much easier.

Uncle John came up to her with a shiny silver cup which had been in that mysterious parcel he had hidden in the closet several days before. He made a very solemn little speech about the cup going to America despite ten British contestants and handed her the cup. But Bumps was a little worried. She wanted that cup awfully—but—

She took a deep breath and burst out, "Uncle John, here's my potato. See, it had quite a hump and I think that helped and I'm not sure it's fair."

All the other children were silent as Uncle John roared with laughter. "But you all drew your potatoes—and if yours had a hump, that was your good luck. But, my dear, don't worry. You would have won anyway."

"And—and I practiced in the mornings, early, before anyone but James was awake." Bumps felt she must tell all.

"Everyone always practices before races," said Uncle John, "and everyone here had a list of the events and could have done so if he had wished."

"Of course, she deserves it," said Cedric, as though it had been settled long ago. Bumps heaved a deep sigh, then reached out eagerly for the cup. "Thank you ever so much!" she said, grabbing it close to her. "Thank you, everybody!"

Pam and Bumps were the heroines of the day, and the rest of the afternoon passed pleasantly.

When the last guest had left, the three cousins went off arm in arm to the house. Pat and Pam were to help Bumps pack, and the first thing that went into her suitcase was the gleaming cup, wrapped in a felt silver bag and a great bulge of tissue paper.

FROM

Red Horse Hill

STEPHEN W. MEADER

A few days before Cedar, a big sorrel colt, is to be entered in the New Hampshire trotting races, Uncle John has an accident which fractures his hand so that he will be unable to drive. Luckily he is able to get permission to have his nephew Bud substitute for him. The youngster has had plenty of practice with Cedar and is elated at the chance to test the big red pacer on the snow course. He hasn't the proper clothes or proper equipment for racing. But he does have guts—and a wonderful horse.

Elimination Race

Bud got up at four-thirty and dressed, in the bleak dark of that Washington's Birthday morning. The cold and the excitement made him shake all over like a leaf as he went stumbling out into the barn. But he climbed the mow and dug into the hay savagely with the fork to pull himself together. And when he came down Tug was there to give his hand a warm, reassuring lick.

Bud hustled through the work in time to give Cedar a last brushing down, then fed and watered him with care and went in to breakfast. For Aunt Sarah's sake he made a valiant effort to eat, but he was keyed too high that morning to enjoy the taste of food. Uncle John came out with him to help harness, and by eight o'clock they were ready to start. Bud waved good-by to

Aunt Sarah and drove the colt out of the dooryard to the musical jingle of bells. Tug went too, sitting erect between their feet.

All down the snowy miles to Riverdale Bud had to check Cedar's pace, soothing him constantly by voice and hand, for the colt felt like skylarking.

"This jog to town is a good thing fer him," Uncle John said. "It'll take some o' the devilment out of him, an' maybe he'll be ready fer business at race time."

At the outskirts of the town they overtook the Hunters' sleigh, in which Cal and his father were riding, and accompanied them to the speedway. There was still nearly an hour before the first heat was scheduled to begin, and Bud blanketed the colt and walked him slowly up and down while the others were getting their tickets for the grandstand. Uncle John reported his injury to the race committee and made the necessary arrangements for having a substitute drive in his place.

The holiday had brought out a far larger crowd than had been present the afternoon before. Not only had many come afoot, but there were rows of cutters ranged along the sides of the track, with an occasional automobile among them. The sky was overcast and the air sharply cold.

"Looks as if it might snow later," said Uncle John, casting a weatherwise eye aloft. He had come back for a last look at Cedar before the race.

A gong began to clang at the judges' stand. "Ten minutes," said Uncle John. "Warm him up a bit back here, then take him up over the course so it won't be strange to him. Good-by, lad."

Bud took Cedar's blanket off and let him stretch his legs a trifle on the road back of the stand. When he seemed well limbered up the boy swung his horse to the foot of the speedway and jogged him up past the grandstand. Then along the line of jingling sleighs and pungs he guided Cedar toward the starting-point. There were laughter and a few jeers as they passed—the strong young horse, with his winter coat as smooth as Bud could brush it, but looking a bit rough and uncouth about the legs; the scarred old cutter, its moth-eaten cushions well dusted and its steel runners polished till they gleamed; and sitting very straight under an ancient buffalo robe, the serious-faced boy with his eyes to the front.

Eight horses besides Cedar were moving up to the start. Most of them were local trotters. They had beautiful, clipped legs, and right at their tails—on them, in fact—sat their drivers, in sulky sleighs that were no more than light skeletons of braced steel, with ridiculous little shells of seats above.

As they swung into position Bud looked off down the mile straight-away with a pounding heart. He felt himself in a sort of daze, his arms heavy, helpless. Then almost before he knew it the starting gun had sounded. Ahead of him flew the other eight, close-bunched.

A laugh went up as the boy gritted his teeth and urged the sorrel colt after them. Hot tears of anger filled his eyes. But the swift rhythm of Cedar's haunches under the taut reins brought back his confidence and even a thrill of pride. He steeled himself for the job ahead.

And now from the crowds that lined the snow path came scattering cheers as they went by, for some of the men from the upper end of the county and some of Bud's schoolmates recognized them. Slowly, very slowly, it seemed to the boy, they were coming up—overhauling first one rival and then another, till, as the wire drew close, there were six behind them.

Cedar finished in third place. Bud swung him around to pass the grandstand on the return journey. He could not bring himself to look up. He was red with shame. But there were many good horsemen along the track who had seen the colt's fine spurt and who threw Bud a word of encouragement as he went back for the second heat.

Well, there should be no leaving at the post this time! Bud gathered the reins, and the sorrel picked up speed as he neared the start. Over the line he went like a shot, right abreast of the leaders. Halfway down the track Bud looked sidewise. The winner of the first heat, a game little chestnut gelding named Billy D., was holding even with the boy's sleigh seat, trotting with all that

was in him. The rest were trailing behind. Bud thrilled to see
the red colt then. As his grip on the reins tightened, Cedar responded, speeding faster and faster, with the wind in his mane,
over the hard-packed snow he loved. And he crossed the finish
line with a good three lengths to spare.

There was a yell from the crowd as the time went up. Bud
looked at the board and nearly choked with surprise. Two-eight,
it said. Surely there was a mistake. In a minute they would find
it out and change the "o" to a "1." But no, the crowd was still
cheering. "Cedar! Cedar!" cried the voices in the stand, hailing
a new popular favorite. And flushed this time with pride, Bud
grinned up at the throng, trying to find Uncle John and Cal and
Tug.

The colt was over his first nervousness now, and Bud let him
take plenty of time in going back for the final test. When they
reached the start the boy got out of the sleigh and stooped to
rub down Cedar's steaming legs with a dry piece of sacking. A
man spoke, so close to his shoulder that it startled him.

"Give 'im the whip, this last heat," he said in a low voice.

"Give 'im the whip, this last heat."

"They're goin' after yuh. That colt's got better time in 'im, yet, an' you'd better use it. Don't look around, but drive like the devil, all the way!" And the man was gone before Bud could open his mouth to reply. The single glimpse he got of him had shown a sallow, thin fellow with a black mustache, wearing a great coonskin coat.

Already the horses were back on the track. Bud was thinking quickly, disturbed by the uncalled-for advice of the stranger. It was true enough that he must do his best to win this last heat, but why had the man been so anxious to tell him so? Was he betting on Cedar? Uncle John's words came back to Bud as distinctly as if he were hearing them spoken: "Don't let anybody tell you how to do. Drive your own race." And the boy resolved that, green as he was in such matters, he would use his own judgment and disregard all outside counsel. Still worrying a little, he swung the big red colt into place above the start.

Down they came, all together, like a cloud before the wind, as the flag dropped.

Cedar was rocking along, smoothly as ever, almost in the center of the group. Suddenly Bud saw two horses moving up, one on each flank, and though less than a quarter of the course was finished their drivers were plying the whip savagely. As the sleighs drew even with Cedar's head both men pulled inward a barely perceptible distance. The colt's flying forefeet were very near to striking their runners.

In another instant he might have broken, for he was disconcerted and tossed back his head. But Bud pulled him far off to the left and spoke to him once or twice as Uncle John would do. The young pacer held his stride and a second later was going again like the wind, outside and nearly abreast of the others.

Beyond the half mile they had passed all but the little chestnut, Billy D. He fought them hard all the way down, but Cedar's mighty strength was too great a handicap. Bud was slacking off on the reins at the finish, and the colt drifted easily under the wire, a length to the good.

The spectators came pouring out of the stand as Bud guided Cedar off the track. A crowd of curious men and boys surrounded them, staring open-mouthed at the young stallion while Bud wiped down his legs and blanketed him. After a moment Uncle John shouldered through the onlookers, followed by Tug and the Hunters. No words were needed to express the farmer's joy. It glowed in his square, brown face.

"That was drivin', boy!" he said, and gripped Bud's hand. Then he looked around at the crowd. "Here, let's git the colt out o' this an' give him a chance to rest," he added.

In the lee of a pine thicket near the upper end of the speedway they found a sheltered place to tie the horses and eat their lunch. When Cedar was cool enough they gave him a light feed and a little drink.

"What was it happened up there near the start in the last heat?" asked Uncle John as they consumed Aunt Sarah's sandwiches and pie.

"Two of the drivers tried to box me," said Bud, and he went on to tell how Cedar had escaped from the trap. "There was another funny thing happened," the boy remarked. "Just before the last heat a man came and warned me to drive for all I was worth and lay into the colt with the whip. Do you suppose he really meant to help me? I didn't like his looks, so I didn't pay much attention to him."

"He might've wanted Cedar to win," said Uncle John, "but it sounds more to me as if he'd been tryin' to use the colt up—kill his speed fer this afternoon. Who was the feller?"

Bud described the stranger, but neither Uncle John nor Myron Hunter could remember having seen him.

The next two hours were hard for the youthful jockey. No one talked much. They all took turns at leading the blanketed pacer up and down to keep his legs from stiffening. Now that the first flush of winning the elimination race had passed, Bud had moments of bitter doubt. He thought of the crudeness of their preparations for the final and compared them mentally with what was going on in the big, steam-heated box stalls at the hotel stable, where grooms and trainers were even then putting the last fine touches on Chocorua and Saco Boy.

He thought of Cedar—a raw young colt, driven down that forenoon over ten miles of country road, raced in three hard heats in the morning, and handled clumsily by an amateur driver. What chance had he to win against those famous pets of the racing-game, fresh from a night's rest and maneuvered by wise and tricky hands?

Then he looked up at the big red horse stepping proudly along at his side, saw the courage that glowed in his eye and the strength of his arched neck—and shame filled the boy's heart. Cedar, at least, had no yellow streak.

Two o'clock came, and the young pacer was put back between the shafts of the cutter. Uncle John pulled the last buckle tight with his left hand and gave the colt's cheek a lingering pat. "I guess it's time to go down to the judges' stand," he said. "They'll likely make the three hosses parade past 'fore the first heat."

They led Cedar down the track, still in his blanket, as far as the upper end of the grandstand. There the wraps were taken off and Bud took his place once more in the sleigh while the others climbed to their seats in the pavilion.

There was a great throng gathered at the track that cold, gray afternoon. The governor had come over from Concord, and by his side in the decorated box loomed the gigantic figure of a famous New Hampshire Congressman who never missed a good harness race if he could help it.

Driving up past the crowds to the judges' stand, Bud realized with dismay that he and Cedar were a part of the spectacle that these thousands had come to watch. Luckily his stage-fright did not pass through the reins into the horse. He was as gay as ever, and even danced a little as the band played.

Close by, their blanketed forms the center of deep knots of men, were the colt's two opponents. Bud watched them as their coverings were stripped off. Saco Boy stood forth magnificent—a great black stallion with fire in his eyes and mighty muscles leaping in his neck and shoulders. He was more massive and even taller than Cedar, but, Bud felt, no better proportioned.

Then his glance shifted to Chocorua. Instantly the old hatred he had felt when he first saw her returned. It seemed as if no horse had a right to such slim, long racing shanks. She was built like a greyhound, and the similarity was made more striking by her blue roan color and the clipped smoothness of her chest and legs. Her head was long and narrow and wicked. With her ears back she was like a reptile—venomous.

As Bud looked past her his eye was caught by a coonskin coat and a thin, dark-mustached face above it. It was the stranger of the morning, standing close by the mare's head and engaged in an earnest conversation with two men. One was a hard-faced, smallish man in black furs—Andy Blake, the mare's driver. The other was Sam Felton himself. The fat-jowled magnate's eye met Bud's and flashed with recognition. Was it Cal who had said that the Feltons never forgot a grudge? There was something of vindictive triumph in that glance that the boy did not like. And the mystery that had puzzled him was cleared up at last. Instead of a friend the man who had given him the tip was an enemy—one of Chocorua's backers. No wonder he had urged Bud to drive the colt to a needless whipping finish in the morning race. Perhaps it was he who had engineered the attempt to box Cedar, as well. The boy thanked his stars he had followed Uncle John's advice.

From the judges' booth sounded the sharp, impatient banging of the gong. "Ten minutes!" came the call, and Bud gathered the reins once more for action.

Final Race

Bud took Cedar on a little warm-up spin along the track, then came back with the others to the judges' stand. There was another laugh at the rude racing turnout from Red Horse Hill, for many people in the crowd had not been present that morning. Andy Blake, mounted close behind the tall hind-quarters of his mare, grinned spitefully at Bud's reddening face. But old Billy Randall, who held the reins over Saco Boy, gave the lad a friendly nod.

"Sorry 'bout John gittin' hurt," he said, "but you drove a good race this mornin'. That's a great youngster you've got there."

From the judges' stand the horses' and drivers' names were read out and the conditions of the race announced. Three heats were to be driven and the championship decided on points if no horse won twice. As the announcer put down his megaphone a babel of sound rose from the stands—cheers and shouts of encouragement. The three drivers turned their horses' heads and jogged slowly up the track toward the start.

Bud had an entirely different feeling from the one with which he had entered the morning race. He was alert and tense now, determined to fight. They swung around at the head of the snow path and got under way. Nearing the start the big, black trotter flashed out ahead, fiercely impetuous. He left the line a good four lengths beyond the others, and Bud expected to hear the jangling of the recall bell. Instead came the report of the gun, and the starter's flag fell. In spite of an outcry from the crowd and the wild gesticulations of Andy Blake the heat was on.

A great excitement entered Bud's veins. His grip on the reins tightened, and he shouted to Cedar through the whipping wind. The colt was pacing swift and sure as in the forenoon, one pointed ear cocked back for Bud's voice, the other forward. Chocorua's evil head, close by their sleigh-seat at first, dropped back and back till Bud could see her no longer, and the colt drew up little by little on the great trotting stallion.

It was such a finish as horsemen dream of. Scarcely half a length apart down the last quarter fought the sorrel and the black. There was so little to choose that many called it a dead heat. But with the sting of Randall's whip on his shining side, Saco Boy flung himself under the wire a nose ahead.

"Two-five and a quarter!" bawled the timekeeper. And as Bud

came out of the spell of the race he realized that thousands of voices had been calling on Cedar to win.

Again the long mile back to the starting-point, and then a little breathing-spell as they got ready for the second heat. Blake, sullen and resentful, had saved his mare after the uneven start. She stood there, poised on her slim legs, hardly breathing as yet, while the black stallion puffed and pawed and flung white spume flecks back over his ebony neck. Cedar was quieter, but the exertions of the day had begun to tell on him. His deep sides rose and fell with the effort he had made. Bud soothed him with pet names and rubbed him unceasingly as they stood waiting.

It had begun to snow when the starter called them out— long, slanting darts of white hurled across the track by the keen north wind.

They brought their horses to the right about and came down to the post again. The tall roan mare leaped to the front this time, with Randall and Bud driving close at her heels. Blake was not lagging now. From the start he drove her—drove her with hard hand and hard voice, the whip ever poised above her lean back. And still, as she fled away, came Cedar after her, eager as a hawk, his swift feet thudding on the firm-packed snow. Off to the right the great black horse held the pace for a while, then burst into a thunderous gallop, and they left him and sped on.

It was a terrific gait the mare was making. And she held it to the end, for Blake began using the whip at the three-quarter post and brought her in under a flying lash. Gallantly Cedar followed, but at the finish there was still a length that his weary legs could not make up.

Bud had to shut his jaw hard, for he wanted to cry as he stood by Cedar's side after that second heat. There was a faint, constant trembling in the steel muscles under the colt's damp hide and his coat was bright no longer, but dark with sweat. Rubbing and working at those beautiful legs as if his life depended on it, the boy talked to him breathlessly, pleading with him, begging forgiveness for the one last trial that Cedar must endure. Twice he had given his best and lost. The race and the purse

The tall roan mare leaped to the front.

were gone, of course—utterly beyond their reach, but Bud knew
they must keep on and see it through.

When he looked up for a moment men were jumping in the
air in excitement, shouting and pointing toward the judges'
pavilion. On the board were figures which at first Bud read without believing. They said: "2.04."

Then at his elbow he saw Billy Randall standing. The old
trainer's voice was queer and husky as he spoke.

"I wanted to look at that colt o' yours, lad," he was saying. "I
guess we're through—Saco Boy an' I. Once he breaks in a race
he's done for the day. But you've got the greatest snow horse in
New England there under that blanket—"

"Ye're durn right!" interrupted a voice behind them, and Bud
turned quickly to see Long Bill Amos. "The finest pacer I ever
see!" continued the teamster. "An' if you don't beat that roan
she-devil—now—" He choked. "Look at her! By gosh, I didn't
come all the way from Boston to see this colt get trimmed."

Bud looked at Chocorua. There she stood, ears back and
head hung low, her eyes rolling wickedly at the grooms who
toiled over her legs. She was fresh no longer.

Randall nodded at Bill in full agreement.

"Now look here, boy," said the veteran driver to Bud. "It
would ruin some horses to give 'em the punishment that Cedar's
takin' today. But I know him. Know his blood. Know his
trainin'. He'll stand it. You beat the mare an' you've *won!*"

"Wh-what?" Bud gasped.

"Sure!" put in Amos. "It'll be decided on points. Take a look
at that board, front o' the judges' stand."

Bud's eye followed his pointing finger, and a gust of hope
swept through him. The board on the pavilion read:

	First Heat	Second Heat	Third Heat
SACO BOY	1	3	—
CHOCORUA	3	1	—
CEDAR	2	2	—

To put a figure "1" after Cedar's name in the third heat would give him a first and two seconds, while the best either of the others could make would be a first, a second, and a third.

With Long Bill helping him, Bud bent down and redoubled his efforts on the colt's legs. As he worked he whispered to the brave young horse, over and over, that this time he *must*, and he felt Cedar's soft lips fumbling playfully at his ear.

The stand was in an uproar when the red colt and the roan mare went back for the final heat. But through the shouting Bud heard a deep, familiar bark and looked up to see the white terrier between Uncle John and Cal. The farmer was bent forward, his face gray and strained, and Cal was giving vent to shrill yells of encouragement. Bud waved a stiff mitten and went on as if in a dream.

Driven whirls of snow were cutting their faces as the jockeys turned above the start once more. Men along the track were huddled close together for warmth and thrashing their arms to shake off the numbness. It was blowing hard, and Bud knew the temperature must be near zero.

There were only two of them left to race, for Saco Boy had been withdrawn. Bud looked down the track through the white storm that hid the far-off grandstand and the town. The wind had swung to the northeast now, and into it they must go. The boy gathered the reins. Cedar's red haunches quivered into action. For the last time they crossed the starting-line.

How they got down to the half-mile post Bud never knew. The air was full of white, and snow particles bit at his eyelids, half blinding him. He was calling the colt's name again and again and leaning forward, always watching the roan mare's head where she raced longside.

The smoothness was gone out of Cedar's gait. Every tired muscle of him was in revolt, and he was racked with a mighty effort at every stride. Yet on and on he held and never slackened. Into the final hundred yards they came at last, with the lean gray head still on their flank. And now the sorrel labored hard, his sides all streaked with frozen sweat, his head and neck stretched out. But he paced on with weary legs.

Cut by the whip, the mare came up desperately, inch by inch. Bud knew that no whip could better the valiant fight the red pacer was making. "Cedar—Cedar, boy!" he cried, and to the anguish of his voice some last reserve of the colt's great heart responded, for his nose was still beyond Chocorua's when they lunged under the line of the wire.

It was late afternoon of the day following Cedar's victory when Bud brought the colt home. Slant beams of frosty sunlight gleamed on a blanket of unbroken snow all up across the mountain's shoulder. The storm that had swept the speedway during the race had passed in the night.

Quietly, without effort, the good red pacer picked his way through the drifted snow of the hill road. Bud sat in the cutter and wondered if any boy had ever been quite as happy as he was at that moment.

FROM
Black Beauty

ANNA SEWELL

This story was written in the hope of influencing people to be kind to animals, and certainly this gentle and gallant black horse makes a terrific appeal to the emotions. Probably more tears have been shed over Black Beauty than over any other animal. The chapters given here show what varied and heart-breaking experiences the once beautiful horse had to undergo after his legs had been injured by a careless rider. It is now more than 80 years since Black Beauty first appeared, but it still retains an old-fashioned warmth and moving quality that makes it one of the most popular of all children's books today.

A Fair Start

THE name of the coachman was John Manly; he had a wife and one little child, and they lived in the coachman's cottage very near the stables.

In the morning he took me into the yard and gave me a good grooming, and just as I was going into my box, with my coat soft and bright, the Squire came in to look at me, and seemed pleased.

"John," he said, "I meant to have tried the new horse this morning, but I have other business. You may as well take him around after breakfast. Go by the common and the Highwood,

Black Beauty.

and back by the water mill and the river; that will show his paces."

"I will, sir," said John.

After breakfast he came and fitted me out with a bridle. He was very particular in letting out and taking in the straps, to fit my head comfortably. Then he brought a saddle, but it was not broad enough for my back; he saw it in a minute and went for another, which fitted nicely. He rode me first slowly, then a trot, then a canter, and when we were on the common he gave me a light touch with his whip, and we had a splendid gallop.

"Ho, ho! my boy," he said, as he pulled me up, "you would like to follow the hounds, I think."

We came back through the park and met the Squire and Mrs. Gordon walking; they stopped and John jumped off.

"Well, John, how does he go?"

"First-rate, sir," answered John. "He is as fleet as a deer, and has a fine spirit, too; but the lightest touch of the rein will guide him. At the end of the common we met one of those traveling carts hung all over with baskets, rugs, and such like. You know, sir, many horses won't pass those carts quietly. He just took a good look at it, and then went on as quiet and pleasant as could be. They were shooting rabbits near the Highwood, and a gun went off close by; he pulled up a little and looked, but didn't stir a step to right or left. I held the rein steady and didn't hurry him, and it's my opinion he has not been frightened or ill-used while he was young."

"That's well," said the Squire; "I will try him myself tomorrow."

The next day I was brought up for my master. I remembered my mother's counsel and my good old master's, and I tried to do exactly what he wanted me to do. I found he was a very good rider, and thoughtful for his horse, too. When he came home, the mistress was at the hall door as he rode up.

"Well, my dear," she said, "how do you like him?"

"He is exactly what John said," he replied, "a pleasanter creature I never wish to mount. What shall we call him?"

"Would you like Ebony? He is as black as ebony," she said. "No, not Ebony."

"Will you call him Blackbird, like your uncle's old horse?"

"No, he is far handsomer than old Blackbird ever was."

"Yes," she said, "he is really quite a beauty, and he has such a sweet, good-tempered face and such a fine, intelligent eye—what do you say to calling him Black Beauty?"

"Black Beauty—why, yes, I think that is a very good name. If you like, it shall be his name," and so it was.

When John went into the stable he told James that the master and mistress had chosen a good sensible name for me, that meant something; not like Marengo, or Pegasus, or Abdallah. They both laughed, and James said:

"If it was not for bringing back the past, I should have named him Rob Roy, for I never saw two horses more alike."

"That's no wonder," said John. "Didn't you know that Farmer Gray's old Duchess was the mother of them both?"

I had never heard that before; and so poor Rob Roy who was killed at that hunt was my brother! I did not wonder that my mother was so troubled. It seems that horses have no relations; at least they never know each other after they are sold.

John seemed very proud of me; he used to make my mane and tail almost as smooth as a lady's hair. And he would talk to me a great deal; of course, I did not understand all he said, but I learned more and more to know what he meant and what he wanted me to do. I grew very fond of him, he was so gentle and kind. He seemed to know just how a horse feels, and when he cleaned me he knew the tender places and the ticklish places. When he brushed my head, he went as carefully over my eyes as if they were his own, and never stirred up any ill-temper.

James Howard, the stable boy, was just as gentle and pleasant in his way, so I thought myself well off. There was another man who helped in the yard, but he had very little to do with Ginger and me.

A few days after this I had to go out with Ginger in the carriage. I wondered how we should get on together; but except laying her ears back when I was led up to her, she behaved very well. She did her work honestly, and did her full share, and I never wish to have a better partner in double harness. When we came to a hill, instead of slackening her pace she would throw her weight right into the collar, and pull away straight up.

We had both the same sort of courage at our work, and John had oftener to hold us in than to urge us forward. He never had

John had to hold us in rather than urge us forward.

to use the whip with either of us. Then our paces were much the same, and I found it very easy to keep step with her when trotting, which made it pleasant, and master always liked it when we kept step well, and so did John. After we had been out a few times together we grew friendly and sociable, which made me feel very much at home.

As for Merrylegs, he and I soon became great friends. He was such a cheerful, plucky, good-tempered little fellow, that he was a favorite with everyone, and especially with Miss Jessie and Flora, who used to ride him about in the orchard, and have fine games with him and their little dog Frisky.

Our master had two other horses that stood in another stable. One was Justice, a roan cob, used for riding, or for the luggage cart; the other was an old brown hunter, named Sir Oliver. He was past work now, but was a great favorite with the master, who gave him the run of the park. He sometimes did a little light carting on the estate, or carried one of the young ladies when they rode out with their father; for he was very gentle, and could be trusted with a child as well as Merrylegs. The cob was a strong, well-made, good-tempered horse, and we sometimes had a little chat in the paddock, but of course I could not be so intimate with him as with Ginger, who stood in the same stable.

After Black Beauty had lived in his first happy home for only three years, he and Ginger have to be sold. His new home is a fine one, but his knees are broken by a drunken groom. From then on the poor horse goes steadily down hill.

A Job Horse and His Drivers

Hitherto I had always been driven by people who at least knew how to drive; but in this place I was to get my experience of all the different kinds of bad and ignorant driving to which we horses are subjected; for I was a "job horse," and was let out to all sorts of people who wished to hire me. As I was good-tempered, I think I was oftener let out to the ignorant drivers than some of the other horses, because I could be depended upon. It would take a long time to tell of all the different styles in which I was driven, but I will mention a few of them.

First, there were the tight-rein drivers—men who seemed to think that all depended on holding the reins as hard as they could, never relaxing the pull on the horse's mouth, or giving him the least liberty of movement. They are always talking about keeping the horse well in hand, and holding a horse up, just as if a horse was not made to hold himself up.

Some poor, broken-down horses, whose mouths have been made hard and insensible by just such drivers as these, may perhaps find some support in it; but for a horse who can depend upon his own legs, and who has a tender mouth and is easily guided, it is not only tormenting, but it is stupid.

Then there are the loose-rein drivers, who let the reins lie easily on our backs, and their hands rest lazily on their knees. Of course such gentlemen have no control over a horse, if anything happens suddenly. If a horse shies, or starts, or stumbles, they are nowhere, and cannot help the horse or themselves till the mischief is done. I had no objection to it, as I was not in the habit of either starting or stumbling, and had only been used to depend on my driver for guidance and encouragement. Still, one likes to feel the rein a little in going downhill, and likes to know that one's driver has not gone to sleep.

Besides, a slovenly way of driving gets a horse into bad and often lazy habits; and when he changes hands he has to be whipped out of them with more or less pain and trouble. Squire Gordon always kept us to our best paces and our best manners. He said that spoiling a horse and letting him get into bad habits was just as cruel as spoiling a child, and both had to suffer for it afterwards.

Besides, these drivers are often careless altogether, and will attend to anything else more than their horses. I went out in the phaëton one day with one of them; he had a lady and two children behind. He flopped the reins about as we started, and gave me several unmeaning cuts with the whip, though I was fairly off.

There had been a good deal of road mending going on, and even where the stones were not freshly laid down there were a great many loose ones about. My driver was laughing and joking with the lady and the children, and talking about the country to the right and to the left; but he never thought it worth while to keep an eye on his horse, or to drive on the smoothest parts of the road; and so it happened that I got a stone in one of my forefeet.

Now, if Mr. Gordon, or John, or in fact any good driver, had been there, he would have seen that something was wrong before I had gone three paces. Or even if it had been dark, a practiced hand would have felt by the rein that there was something wrong in the step, and they would have got down and picked out the stone. But this man went on laughing and talking, while at every step the stone became more firmly wedged between my shoe and the frog of my foot. The stone was sharp on the inside and round on the outside, which, as everyone knows is the most dangerous kind that a horse can pick up, at the same time cutting his foot, and making him most liable to stumble and fall.

Whether the man was partly blind, or only very careless, I can't say; but he drove me with that stone in my foot for a good half mile before he saw anything. By that time I was going so lame with the pain that at last he saw it, and called out, "Well, here's a go! Why, they have sent us out with a lame horse! What a shame!"

He then chucked the reins and flipped about with the whip, saying, "Now, then, it's no use playing the old soldier with me; there's the journey to go, and it's no use turning lame and lazy."

Just at this time a farmer came riding up on a brown cob; he lifted his hat and pulled up.

"I beg your pardon, sir," he said, "but I think there is something the matter with your horse; he goes very much as if he had a stone in his shoe. If you will allow me, I will look at his feet; these loose scattered stones are confounded dangerous things for the horses."

"He's a hired horse," said my driver. "I don't know what's the matter with him, but it is a great shame to send out a lame beast like this."

The farmer dismounted, and took up my near foot. "Bless me, there's a stone! Lame! I should think so!"

"Bless me, there's a stone!"

At first he tried to dislodge it with his hand; but as it was now very tightly wedged, he drew a stone pick out of his pocket, and very carefully, and with some trouble, got it out. Then holding it up, he said, "There, that's the stone your horse had picked up; it is a wonder he did not fall down and break his knees into the bargain!"

"Well, to be sure!" said my driver, "that is a queer thing! I never knew that horses picked up stones before."

"Didn't you?" said the farmer rather contemptuously, "but they do, though, and the best of them will do it, and can't help it sometimes on such roads as these. And if you don't want to lame your horse you must look sharp and get them out quickly. This foot is very much bruised," he said, setting it gently down and patting me. "You had better drive him gently for a while; the foot is a good deal hurt, and the lameness will not go off directly." Then mounting his cob and raising his hat to the lady, he trotted off. Needless to say, I was very grateful to him.

When he was gone my driver began to flop the reins about and whip the harness, by which I understood that I was to go on, which of course I did, glad that the stone was gone, but still in a good deal of pain. This was the sort of experience that we job horses often came in for.

Poor Ginger

One day, while our cab and many others were waiting outside one of the parks where music was playing, a shabby old cab drove up beside ours. The horse was an old, worn-out chestnut, with an ill-kept coat, and bones that showed plainly through it; the knees knuckled over, and the forelegs were very unsteady.

I had been eating some hay, and the wind rolled a little of it that way. The poor creature put out her long, thin neck and picked it up, and then turned round and looked about for more. There was a hopeless look in the dull eye that I could not help noticing, and then, as I was thinking where I had seen that horse before, she looked full at me and said, "Black Beauty, is that you?"

It was Ginger! but how changed! The beautifully arched and glossy neck was now straight and lank and fallen in; the clean, straight legs and delicate fetlocks were swelled; the joints were grown out of shape with hard work; the face, that once was so full of spirit and life was now full of suffering, and I could tell by the heaving of her sides, and her frequent cough, how bad her breath was.

Our drivers were standing together a little way off, so I sidled up to her a step or two, that we might have a little quiet talk. It was a sad tale that she had to tell.

After a twelve-months' run off at Earlshall she was considered to be fit for work again, and was sold to a gentleman. For a while she got on well, but after a longer gallop than usual the old strain returned, and after being rested and doctored she was again sold. In this way she changed hands several times, but always getting lower down.

"And so at last," said she, "I was bought by a man who keeps a number of cabs and horses, and lets them out. You look well off, and I am glad of it, but I could not tell you what my life has been. When they found out my weakness, they said I was not worth what they gave for me, and that I must go into one of the low cabs, and just be used up. That is what they are doing, whipping and working me with never one thought of what I suffer—they paid for me and must get it out of me, they say. The man who hires me now pays a deal of money to the owner every day, and so he has to get it out of me, too; and so it's all the week round and round, with never a Sunday rest."

I said, "You used to stand up for yourself if you were ill-used."

"Ah!" she said, "I did once, but it's no use. Men are strongest, and if they are cruel and have no feeling, there is nothing we can do but just bear it—bear it on and on to the end. I wish the end was come; I wish I was dead. I have seen dead horses, and I am sure they do not suffer pain. I wish I may drop down dead at my work, and not be sent off to the knacker's."

I was very much troubled and I put my nose up to hers, but I could say nothing to comfort her. I think she was pleased to see me, for she said, "You are the only friend I ever had."

Just then her driver came up, and with a tug at her mouth backed her out of the line and drove off, leaving me very sad indeed.

A short time after this, a cart with a dead horse on it passed our cab stand. The head hung out of the cart tail, the lifeless tongue was slowly dropping with blood, and the sunken eyes! but I can't speak of them; the sight was dreadful. It was a chestnut horse with a long, thin neck. I saw a white streak down the forehead. I believe it was Ginger; I hoped it was, for then her troubles would be over.

Hard Times

I shall never forget my new master. He had black eyes and a hooked nose, his mouth was as full of teeth as a bulldog's, and his voice was as harsh as the grinding of cart wheels over gravel stones. His name was Nicholas Skinner, and I believe he was the same man that poor Seedy Sam drove for.

I have heard men say that seeing is believing, but I should say that feeling is believing; for much as I had seen before, I never knew until now the utter misery of a cab-horse's life. Skinner had a low set of cabs and a low set of drivers; he was hard on the men, and the men were hard on the horses. In this place we had no Sunday rest, and it was in the heat of summer.

Sometimes on a Sunday morning a party of fast men would hire the cab for the day, four of them inside and another with the driver, and I had to take them ten or fifteen miles out into the country and back again. Never would any of them get down to walk up a hill, let it be ever so steep, or the day ever so hot—unless, indeed, when the driver was afraid I should not manage it; and sometimes I was so fevered and worn that I could hardly touch my food. How I used to long for the nice bran mash with niter in it that Jerry used to give us on Saturday nights in hot weather, that used to cool us down and make us so comfortable. Then we had two nights and a whole day for unbroken rest, and on Monday morning we were as fresh as young horses again; but here there was no rest, and my driver was just as hard as his master.

He had a cruel whip with something so sharp at the end that it sometimes drew blood, and he would even whip me under the belly, and flip the lash out at my head. Indignities like these took the heart out of me terribly, but still I did my best and never hung back, for, as poor Ginger said, it was no use; men are the stronger.

My life was now so wretched that I wished I might, like Ginger, drop down dead at my work, and be out of my misery, and one day my wish very nearly came to pass.

I went on the stand at eight in the morning, and had done a good share of work, when we had to take a fare to the railway. A long train was expected in, so my driver pulled up at the back of some of the outside cabs, to take the chance of a return fare. It was a very heavy train, and as all the cabs were soon engaged, ours was called for. There was a party of four; a noisy, blustering man with a lady, a little boy, and a young girl, and a great deal of luggage. The lady and the boy got into the cab, and while the man ordered about the luggage, the young girl came and looked at me.

"Papa," she said, "I am sure this poor horse cannot take us and all our luggage so far, he is so very weak and worn out; do look at him."

"Oh! he's all right, miss," said my driver, "he's strong enough."

The porter, who was pulling about some heavy boxes, suggested to the gentleman, as there was so much luggage, that he had better take a second cab.

"Can your horse do it, or can't he?" said the blustering man.

"Oh! he can do it all right, sir; send up the boxes, porter; he could take more than that," and he helped to haul up a box so heavy that I could feel the springs go down.

"Papa, papa, do take a second cab," said the young girl beseechingly. "I am sure it is cruel."

"Nonsense, Grace; don't make all this fuss. A pretty thing it would be if a man of business had to examine every cab horse before he hired it—the man knows his own business. There, get in and hold your tongue!"

My gentle friend had to obey; and box after box was lodged on the top of the cab, or settled by the side of the driver. At last all was ready, and with his usual jerk at the rein, and slash of the whip, he drove out of the station.

The load was very heavy, and I had had neither food nor rest since morning; but I did my best, as I always had done, in spite of cruelty and injustice.

I got along fairly till we came to Ludgate Hill, but there the load and my own exhaustion were too much. I was struggling to keep on, goaded by constant chucks of the rein and use of the whip, when, in a single moment—I cannot tell how—my feet slipped from under me; and I fell heavily to the ground on my side.

The suddenness and the force with which I fell seemed to beat all the breath out of my body. I lay perfectly still; indeed, I had no power to move, and I thought now I was going to die. I heard a sort of confusion round me, loud angry voices, and the getting down of the luggage, but it was all like a dream. I thought I heard that sweet, pitiful voice saying, "Oh! that poor horse! it is all our fault."

Someone came and loosened the throat strap of my bridle, and undid the traces which kept the collar so tight upon me. Someone said, "He's dead, he'll never get up again." Then I could hear a policeman giving orders, but I did not even open my eyes; I could only draw a gasping breath now and then. Some cold water was thrown over my head, and some cordial was poured into my mouth and something was covered over me.

I cannot tell how long I lay there, but I found my life coming back, and a kind-voiced man was patting me and encouraging

My feet slipped and I fell heavily.

me to rise. After some more cordial had been given me and after one or two attempts, I staggered to my feet, and was gently led to some stables which were close by. Here I was put into a well-littered stall, and some warm gruel was brought to me, which I drank thankfully.

In the evening I was sufficiently recovered to be led back to Skinner's stables, where I think they did the best for me they could. In the morning Skinner came with a farrier to look at me. He examined me very closely and said:

"This is a case of overwork more than disease, and if you could give him a run off for six months, he would be able to work again; but now there is not an ounce of strength in him."

"Then he must just go to the dogs," said Skinner. "I have no meadows to nurse sick horses in—he might get well or he might not. That sort of thing don't suit my business. My plan is to work 'em as long as they'll go, and then sell 'em for what they'll fetch at the knacker's or elsewhere."

"If he was broken-winded," said the farrier, "you had better have him killed out of hand, but he is not. There is a sale of horses coming off in about ten days; if you rest him and feed him up, he may pick up, and you may get more than his skin is worth, at any rate."

Upon this advice, Skinner, rather unwillingly, I think, gave orders that I should be well fed and cared for, and the stableman, happily for me, carried out the orders with a much better will than his master had in giving them.

Ten days of perfect rest, plenty of good oats, hay, bran mashes, with boiled linseed mixed in them, did more to get up my condition than anything else could have done. Those linseed mashes were delicious, and I began to think, after all, it might be better to live than to go to the dogs. When the twelfth day after the accident came, I was taken to the sale, a few miles out of London. I felt that any change from my present place must be an improvement, so I held up my head, and hoped for the best.

Black Beauty is now sold to Farmer Thoroughgood who takes good care of him and restores much of his vanished good looks. His last home turns out to be almost as good as his first, and to house a pleasant surprise in the new groom.

My Last Home

One day, during this summer, the groom cleaned and dressed me with such extraordinary care that I thought some new change must be at hand. He trimmed my fetlocks and legs, passed the tar brush over my hoofs, and even parted my forelock. I think the harness had an extra polish. Willie seemed anxious, half merry, as he got into the chaise with his grandfather.

"If the ladies take to him," said the old gentleman, "they'll be suited and he'll be suited; we can but try."

At the distance of a mile or two from the village we came to a pretty, low house, with a lawn and shrubbery at the front and a drive up to the door. Willie rang the bell and asked if Miss Blomefield or Miss Ellen was at home. Yes, they were. So, while Willie stayed with me, Mr. Thoroughgood went into the house.

In about ten minutes he returned, followed by three ladies; one tall, pale lady, wrapped in a white shawl, leaned on a younger lady, with dark eyes and a merry face; the other, a very stately looking person, was Miss Blomefield. They all came and looked at me and asked questions. The young lady—that was Miss Ellen—took to me very much; she said she was sure she would like me, as I had such a good face. The tall, pale lady said she should always be nervous—riding behind a horse that had once been down, as I might come down again, and if I did she should never get over the fright.

"You see, ladies," said Mr. Thoroughgood, "many first-rate horses have had their knees broken through the carelessness of their drivers, without any fault of their own, and from what I see of this horse I should say that is his case; but, of course, I do not wish to influence you. If you desire, you can have him on trial, and then your coachman will see what he thinks of him."

"You have always been such a good adviser to us about our horses," said the stately lady, "that your recommendation would go a long way with me. If my sister Lavinia sees no objection, we will accept your offer of a trial, with thanks."

It was then arranged that I should be sent for the next day. In the morning a smart-looking young man came for me; at first he looked pleased; but when he saw my knees he said, "I don't think, sir, you should have recommended my ladies a blemished horse like that."

" 'Handsome is that handsome does,' " said my master. "You are only taking him on trial, and I am sure you will do fairly by him, young man. If he is not as safe as any horse you ever drove, send him back."

I was led to my new home, placed in a comfortable stable, fed, and left to myself. The next day, when my groom was cleaning my face, he said, "That is just like the star that 'Black Beauty' had; he is much the same height, too; I wonder where he is now?"

A little farther on he came to the place in my neck where I was bled, and where a little knot was left in the skin. He almost started, and began to look me over carefully, talking to himself.

"White star in the forehead, one white foot on the off side, this little knot just in that place." Then looking at the middle of my back—"and as I am alive, there is that little patch of white hair that John used to call 'Beauty's three-penny bit.' It must be 'Black Beauty!' Why, Beauty! Beauty! do you know me? Little Joe Green that almost killed you?" And he began patting and patting me as if he was quite overjoyed.

I could not say that I remembered him, for now he was a fine, grown fellow, with black whiskers and a man's voice, but I was sure he knew me, and that he was Joe Green. I was very glad. I put my nose up to him and tried to say that we were friends. I never saw a man so pleased.

"As I am alive, it must be Black Beauty!"

"Give you a fair trial! I should think so indeed! I wonder who the rascal was that broke your knees, my old Beauty! You must have been badly served out somewhere. Well, well, it won't be my fault if you haven't good times of it now. I wish John Manly was here to see you."

In the afternoon I was put into a low Park chair and brought to the door. Miss Ellen was going to try me, and Green went with her. I soon found that she was a good driver, and she seemed pleased with my paces. I heard Joe telling her about me, and that he was sure I was Squire Gordon's old "Black Beauty."

When we returned the other sisters came out to hear how I had behaved myself. She told them what she had just heard, and said, "I shall certainly write to Mrs. Gordon and tell her that her favorite horse has come to us. How pleased she will be."

After this I was driven every day for a week or so, and as I seemed quite safe, Miss Lavinia at last ventured out in a small close carriage. After this it was quite decided to keep me and call me by my old name of "Black Beauty."

I have now lived in this happy place a whole year. Joe is the best and kindest of grooms. My work is easy and pleasant, and I feel my strength and spirits all coming back again. Mr. Thoroughgood said to Joe the other day:

"In your place he will last till he is twenty years old—perhaps more."

Willie always speaks to me when he can, and treats me as his special friend. My ladies have promised that I shall never be sold, and so I have nothing to fear; and here my story ends. My troubles are all over, and I am at home; and often before I am quite awake, I fancy I am still in the orchard at Birtwick, standing with my old friends under the apple trees.

Ellen Rides Again

BEVERLY CLEARY

THE arrival of spring meant different things to different people. To Mrs. Tebbits it meant spring cleaning. To Mrs. Allen it meant planting seeds and setting out new flowers. To Ellen and Austine spring meant something much more important. It meant no more winter underwear.

The two girls were walking home from the library one warm spring afternoon. They felt light and carefree in their summer underwear. It was a wonderful feeling. It made them want to do something exciting.

At the library Austine had been lucky enough to find two horse books. "I wish I could ride a horse sometime," she said.

"Haven't you ever ridden a horse?" asked Ellen.

"No. Have you?" Austine sounded impressed.

"Oh, yes," said Ellen casually. "Several times."

It was true. She had ridden several times. If she had ridden twice she would have said a couple of times. Three was several times, so she had told the truth.

"Where? What was it like? Tell me about it," begged Austine.

"Oh, different places." That was also true. She had ridden at the beach. Her father had rented a horse for an hour and had let Ellen ride behind him with her arms around his waist. The horse's back had been slippery and she had bounced harder than was comfortable, but she had managed to hang on.

And she had ridden at Uncle Fred's farm. Uncle Fred had lifted her up onto the back of his old plow horse, Lady, and led her twice around the barnyard. Lady didn't bounce her at all.

And then there was that other time when her father had paid a dime so she could ride a pony around in a circle inside a fence. It hadn't been very exciting. The pony seemed tired, but Ellen had pretended it was galloping madly. Yes, it all added up to several times.

"Why haven't you told me you could ride?" Austine demanded. "What kind of saddle do you use?" Austine knew all about different kinds of saddles, because she read so many horse books.

"Oh, any kind," said Ellen, who did not know one saddle from another. "Once I rode bareback." That was true, because Lady had no saddle.

"Golly," said Austine. "Bareback!"

Ellen was beginning to feel uncomfortable. She had not meant to mislead Austine. She really did not know how it all started.

"Oh, Ellen, you have all the luck," exclaimed Austine. "Imagine being able to ride horseback. And even bareback, too."

"Oh, it's nothing," said Ellen, wishing Austine would forget the whole thing.

But the next day at school Austine did not forget about Ellen's horseback riding. She told Linda and Amelia about it. They told Barbara and George. Barbara and George told other boys and girls. Each time the story was told, it grew.

Even Otis was impressed and he was a difficult boy to impress. When the girls started home after school, he was waiting on the edge of the school grounds. He had a piece of chalk and was busy changing a sign from "Bicycle riding forbidden at all times" to "Bicycle riding bidden at all times." Otis crossed out "for" every time he had a chance, but the rain always washed away the chalk marks.

"Hello, Ellen," he said, walking along beside her in his cowboy boots. Since Christmas Otis had worn boots instead of Oxfords. He was not wearing spurs today. Miss Joyce had asked him not to wear them to school.

Ellen and Austine ignored him.

Otis kicked at the grass along the edge of the sidewalk. "Say, Ellen, is it true you ride a lot? Even bareback?"

"Of course it's true," said Austine.

"I wish people would stop talking about it," said Ellen crossly. "What's so wonderful about riding a horse, for goodness' sake?"

"Gee whiz," said Otis enviously. "Some people have all the luck."

The girls continued to ignore him. He followed them for a while, kicking at the grass, and then turned down another street.

When the girls came to Austine's house, they found Mrs. Allen on her knees beside a flat box of pansy plants. She was taking them out of the box and setting them into a border along the driveway.

"Hello there," she said. "Since tomorrow is Memorial Day and there isn't any school, how would you like to go on a picnic?"

Ellen did not say anything. She thought Mrs. Allen meant her, too, but she was not sure. She hoped so. That was the trouble with the word *you*. Sometimes it meant one person and sometimes it meant a lot of people. Maybe Mrs. Allen was talking to Austine and not to both of them.

Mrs. Allen said, "Ellen, I have already asked your mother and she says you may go."

"Thank you. I'd love to go." Maybe a picnic would make Austine forget about horses. And if they went on a picnic, Austine couldn't come to Ellen's house to play and perhaps say something about horseback riding in front of Mrs. Tebbits. Ellen was worried about what her mother would say if she found out how Ellen had exaggerated.

"Where are we going?" asked Austine.

"We're going to drive out toward Mount Hood. The rhododendrons are beginning to bloom, and I thought it would be nice to see them blooming in the woods."

The next morning at ten o'clock Ellen ran down Tillamook Street and around the corner to Austine's house. For her share of the picnic she carried eight deviled eggs carefully packed in a cardboard box. Mr. Allen was backing out the car. Mrs. Allen sat in the front seat and Austine in the back.

"Hop in," said Mr. Allen. "Bruce isn't going with us. The Boy Scouts are marching in a parade."

Ellen was glad she and Austine could each sit by a window. That made it easier to look for white horses and to play the alphabet game. The first one to see a white horse got to make a wish. Ellen was going to wish Austine would forget about her horseback riding.

The girls always played the alphabet game when they rode in a car. Each watched the signs on her own side of the road for the letters of the alphabet. Each letter had to be found in order or it did not count. The *k* in a Sky Chief gasoline sign could not be used unless a *j* had already been seen. The girl who had a Burma Shave sign on her side of the road at the right time was lucky because it contained in the right order both *u* and *v*, two hard letters to find. The game went quickly at first, because there were lots of signs, but as they neared the mountains the signs became more scarce.

Ellen was looking for a Texaco filling station for an *x* when Austine shouted, "Look, a white horse! I've got dibs on it." She shut her eyes to wish.

Ellen was sorry she had not seen the horse first. She needed a wish. Finally both girls were down to *z*. By then the car was winding along the mountain roads.

"Z!" shouted Ellen. "I win. There was a sign by that bridge that said 'Zigzag River.' "

"That's all right," said Austine generously. "I'm going to get my wish."

It was a few more miles along the highway that Austine saw the horses. "Look, Daddy! Horses for rent, fifty cents an hour! Please stop," she begged.

Mr. Allen drew over to the side of the road near some horses in a makeshift corral. Austine scrambled out of the car and ran to the horses, while the others followed.

"Daddy, please let us go horseback riding. All my life I've wanted to ride a horse. Please, Daddy. You and Mother could go on and look at the rhododendrons and come back for us."

"Would it be safe for the girls to ride alone?" Mrs. Allen asked the man with the horses.

"Please, Mother," begged Austine. "Make my wish come true."

"Sure. Kids do it all the time," answered the man. "They ride up that dirt road as far as the old sawmill and turn around and come back. The horses know the way. Takes about half an hour. Road runs right along the highway."

"They won't be thrown from the horses?" asked Mrs. Allen.

"From these horses?" said the man. "No, lady. These horses worked at a riding academy for years."

"You're sure they're gentle?"

"Yes, ma'am. Gentle as kittens."

"The girls could hang onto the saddle horns," suggested Mr. Allen.

"Oh, Daddy, you aren't supposed to hang onto the saddle horn. Only tenderfoots, I mean tenderfeet, do that. We'll be safe, because Ellen has ridden a lot and I know all about riding from books."

Ellen wished Austine would keep still. She was not at all sure she wanted to ride, especially without a grownup along.

"I suppose it would be safe to let the girls ride for half an hour," said Mrs. Allen. "We could walk along the dirt road and look at the rhododendrons while they rode. That way they would be within shouting distance."

"All right, girls, which horses do you want to ride?" asked Mr. Allen, taking a handful of change out of his pocket.

Ellen thought she had better act brave even if she didn't feel that way. "The spotted horse is nice, but I think I'd rather have the brown one over in the corner of the pen." She thought the brown horse looked gentle.

"I'll take the pinto on this side of the corral," said Austine, glancing at Ellen.

Oh dear, thought Ellen. I've said the wrong thing. I wish I'd read some horse books.

Austine watched eagerly and Ellen watched uneasily while the man saddled and bridled the two horses. "O.K., kids," he said.

Ellen walked over to the brown horse and patted him gingerly. He seemed awfully big when she stood beside him. But he looked down at her with large gentle eyes, and Ellen felt braver.

The man held out his hand, palm up.

Oh, I wonder if he wants me to give him some money, thought Ellen. It must be that, but I'm sure Austine's father paid him. Or maybe he wants to shake hands. A sort of farewell.

"Come on, girlie. Step up," said the man. "Don't be scared. Brownie isn't going to hurt you."

My goodness, thought Ellen. I guess he expects me to step in his hand. I suppose it's all right. His hand is dirty anyway.

She put her foot into his hand and he boosted her onto the horse. The ground seemed a long way below her. And Ellen had forgotten how wide a horse was. The man shortened her stirrups and then helped Austine onto the pinto. Ellen patted Brownie on the neck. She was anxious to have him like her. If only she had a lump of sugar in her pocket.

"Look," cried Austine. "I'm really on a horse."

Ellen knew she was expected to take the lead. "Giddap," she said uncertainly. Brownie did not move.

The man gave each horse a light slap on the rump. They walked out of the corral and ambled down the dirt road as if they were used to going that way. Austine's mother and father followed on foot.

Ellen carefully held one rein in each hand. As she looked at the ground so far below, she hoped Brownie wouldn't decide to run.

"I'm going to call my horse Old Paint like in the song," said Austine, who never missed the Montana Wranglers on the radio and knew all about cowboy songs. "I wish I'd worn my cowboy neckerchief."

"Yes," said Ellen briefly. She didn't feel like making conversation.

When Austine's horse moved in front, Ellen took hold of the saddle horn. It wasn't so much that she was scared, she told herself. She just didn't want to take unnecessary chances.

"I wish we'd worn our pedal pushers," said Austine. "It's sort of hard to feel like a cowgirl in a dress."

"I wish we had, too."

Maybe this wasn't going to be so bad after all. The horses seemed to know the way, and Ellen found the rocking motion and the squeak of the saddle rather pleasant. She was even able to look around at the trees and enjoy the woodsy smell.

Then when they had gone around a bend in the road, Brownie decided it was time to go back to the corral. He turned around and started walking in the direction from which they had come.

"Hey," said Ellen anxiously. She pulled on the right rein, but Brownie kept on going. "Stop!" she ordered, more loudly this time.

"What are you going that way for?" asked Austine, turning in her saddle.

"Because the horse wants to," said Ellen crossly.

"Well, turn him around."

"I can't," said Ellen. "He won't steer."

Austine turned Old Paint and drew up beside Ellen. "Don't you know you're supposed to hold both reins in one hand?" Austine was scornful.

Ellen didn't know. "I just held them this way to try to turn him," she said. She took them in her left hand. They were so long she wound them around her hand.

Austine leaned over and took hold of Brownie's bridle with one hand. "Come on, Old Paint," she said, and turned her horse forward again. Brownie followed.

"Thanks," said Ellen. "My, you're brave."

"Oh, that's nothing," said Austine modestly. "You don't steer a horse," she added gently. "You guide him."

"Oh . . . I forgot." Ellen wondered how she would ever explain her ignorance to Austine. What would her best friend think when she found out how Ellen had misled her?

The horses plodded on down the woodsy road. Through the trees the girls could see the highway and hear cars passing. Austine's mother and father appeared around the bend, and Ellen began to feel brave again.

"Let's gallop," suggested Austine.

Ellen's legs were beginning to ache. "How do you make them gallop?"

"Dig your heels in," said Austine.

"Oh, I wouldn't want to hurt the horse," said Ellen.

"You won't hurt him, silly. Cowboys wear spurs, don't they?"

Ellen timidly prodded Brownie with her heels. Brownie ambled on.

Austine dug in her heels. Old Paint began to trot. At first Austine bounced, but soon she rode smoothly. Then her horse began to gallop.

When Old Paint galloped, Brownie began to trot. Ellen began to bounce. She hung onto the saddle horn as hard as she could. Still she bounced. Slap-slap-slap. Her bare legs began to hurt from rubbing against the leather of the saddle flap. Slap-slap-slap. Goodness, I sound awful, she thought. I hope Austine doesn't hear me slapping this way.

Austine's horse, after galloping a few yards, slowed down to a walk. "Whoa, Old Paint," cried Austine anyway, and pulled on the reins. Old Paint stopped and Austine panted a minute.

"I did it, Ellen!" she called. "It was just a few steps, but I really, truly galloped. I hung on with my knees and galloped just like in the movies."

"Wh-wh-oa-oa!" Ellen's voice was jarred out between bounces. Brownie trotted on. Slap-slap-slap.

Austine began to laugh. "I can see trees between you and the saddle every time you go up. Oh, Ellen, you look so funny!"

Slap-slap-slap. Ellen didn't think she could stand much more bouncing. It was worse than being spanked.

"I can see trees between you and the saddle."

"Ellen Tebbits! I don't think you know a thing about horse-back riding."

"Wh-wh-oa-oa!" When Brownie reached Old Paint he stopped. After Ellen got her breath, she gasped, "I do, too. It's just that the other horses I rode were tamer."

The horses walked on until the road curved down to the edge of a stream.

"Oh, look. There's a bridge," exclaimed Ellen, looking up.

"I guess the highway crosses to the other side of the stream," said Austine. "I wonder if the poor horses are thirsty."

There was no doubt about Brownie's wanting a drink. He left the road and picked his way down the rocky bank to the water.

"Poor horsie, you were thirsty," said Ellen, patting his neck.

But Brownie did not stop at the edge of the stream. He waded out into it.

"Whoa," yelled Ellen, above the rush of the water. "Austine, help!"

Brownie waded on.

"Austine! What'll I do? He's going swimming!"

"Here, Brownie! Here, Brownie!" called Austine from the bank. Her voice sounded faint across the surging water.

When Brownie had picked his way around the boulders to the middle of the stream, he stopped and looked around.

"Look, he's in over his knees!" Ellen looked down at the swirling water. "Giddap, Brownie!"

"Kick him in the ribs," yelled Austine from across the stream.

"I don't want to hurt him," called Ellen, but she did kick him gently. Brownie did not appear to notice.

"Slap him on the behind with the ends of the reins," directed Austine from the bank.

Ellen slapped. Brownie turned his head and looked at her reproachfully.

By this time some hikers had stopped on the bridge. Looking down at Ellen, they laughed and pointed. Ellen wished they would go away.

Brownie lowered his head to drink. Because Ellen had the reins wound around her hand, she could not let go. As she was pulled forward, the saddle horn poked her in the stomach.

"Oof," she said. Hanging over the horse's neck, she clung to his mane with one hand while she unwound her other hand.

Brownie looked at her with water dripping from his chin. Ellen thought it was his chin. Maybe on a horse it was called something else.

Austine broke a branch from a huckleberry bush that grew out of an old log at the edge of the stream. She waved it toward Brownie. "Here, horsie. Nice horsie."

Brownie glanced at her with mild interest.

"Oh, go on, Brownie," said Ellen in disgust. She kicked him hard this time. Brownie looked at her sadly and swished his tail.

A couple of cars stopped on the bridge and the occupants

looked down at Ellen and laughed. "Yippee!" yelled one of the hikers and everyone laughed. "Ride 'em, cowboy!"

"Do something, Austine," Ellen called across the water. "Our half hour must be nearly up."

"Maybe I could ride back and get the man who owns the horses," Austine yelled back.

"No, Austine. Don't leave me here alone," begged Ellen. "Maybe I could get off and wade. I don't think the water would come up to my shoulders."

"The current's too strong," called Austine. "And anyway, we're supposed to bring the horses back. You can't go off and leave Brownie."

Austine was right. Ellen knew that she couldn't leave Brownie. She might lose him, and the man would probably make her pay for him. At least, she thought he would. She had never heard of anyone losing a horse, so she wasn't sure. "I can't stay here forever," she called.

"Mother and Daddy should catch up with us in a minute," Austine called. "They'll know what to do."

That was just what was worrying Ellen. She didn't want the Allens to see her in such a predicament. What would they think after Austine had told them she had ridden before? Maybe they had wandered off to look at rhododendrons and were lost in the woods by now.

Still Brownie did not move. Ellen wondered what it would be like to try to sleep on a horse. Again she wished she had brought some lumps of sugar. She could have eaten them herself when she became hungry.

One of the hikers climbed down the bank to the edge of the water. "Need some help, little girl?" he called.

"Oh yes, please," answered Ellen gratefully.

Jumping from boulder to boulder, the man drew near her, but he could not get close enough to reach Brownie's bridle. "Throw me the reins, little girl," he directed.

Ellen threw them as hard as she could. They fell into the

Jumping from boulder to boulder, the man drew near.

water, but the man grabbed them as the current carried them toward him.

"Come on, old fellow," he said, pulling at the reins. Meekly Brownie began to pick his way around the boulders toward the bank.

"Oh, thank you," said Ellen, when they reached dry ground. "I guess I would have had to stay out there all day if you hadn't come for me."

"That's all right," said the man. "The trouble is, you let the horse know you were afraid of him. Let the old nag know you're boss and you won't have any trouble."

"Thank you, I'll try," said Ellen, taking a firm grip on the reins. "Good-by."

Just then Austine's mother and father appeared around the bend in the road. "Enjoying your ride, girls?" asked Mr. Allen.

"Oh yes," said Austine. "We just stopped to give the horses a drink."

"It's time to turn back now," said Mrs. Allen.

"All right, Mother," said Austine.

The girls headed their horses toward the corral. Ellen was so embarrassed she didn't know quite what to say to Austine. What would Austine think of her after this? What would she tell the kids at school?

Finally, when Austine's mother and father were a safe distance behind, Ellen said in a low voice, "I guess I didn't know quite as much about horseback riding as I thought I did."

"Your horse was just hard to manage, that's all," said Austine generously.

"Austine?" said Ellen timidly.

"What?"

"You won't tell anybody, will you? You won't tell that Otis Spofford what happened, will you?"

Austine smiled at her. "Of course I won't tell. We're best friends, aren't we? It'll be a secret like our winter underwear. Giddap, Old Paint."

"Thank you, Austine," said Ellen gratefully. "You're a wonderful friend. And you know what? I'm going to look for some horse books the next time we go to the library."

The horses, knowing they were headed toward hay, showed more spirit. Ellen held the reins firmly. That Brownie was going to know who was boss. She began to enjoy herself. She pretended she was returning to a ranch after a hard day riding the range.

"I didn't know horses had such long hair," she remarked.

"It's their winter coat," explained Austine. "They'll shed it this summer."

Ellen laughed. "Just like winter underwear," she said.

The Black Stallion
and the Red Mare

GLADYS F. LEWIS

AT FIRST Donald lay still. Scarcely a muscle moved. The boulders and the low shrubs screened him from view. Excitement held him motionless. His hands gripped the short grass and his toes dug into the dry earth. Cautiously he raised himself on his elbows and gazed at the scene below him.

There, in his father's unfenced hay flats, was the outlaw band of wild horses. They were grazing quietly on the rich grass. Some drank from the small hillside stream. Donald tried to count them, but they suddenly began moving about and he could not get beyond twenty. He thought there might be two hundred.

Donald knew a good deal about that band of horses, but he had never had the good luck to see them. They were known over many hundreds of square miles. They had roamed at will over the grain fields and they had led away many a domestic horse to the wild life. Once in that band, a horse was lost to the farm.

There in the flats was the great black stallion, the hero or the villain of a hundred tales. Over the far-flung prairie and grass lands there was scarcely a boy who had not dreamed of wild rides, with the great body of the stallion beneath him, bearing him clean through the air with the sharp speed of lightning.

There was the stallion now, moving among the horses with the sureness and ease of a master. As he moved about, teasingly kicking here and nipping there, a restlessness, as of a danger sensed, stirred through the band. The stallion cut to the outside of the group. At a full gallop he snaked around the wide circle, roughly bunching the mares and colts into the smaller circle of an invisible corral.

He was a magnificent creature, huge and proudly built. Donald saw the gloss of the black coat and the great curving muscles of the strong legs, the massive hoofs, the powerful arch of the neck, the proud crest of the head. Donald imagined he could see the flash of black, intelligent eyes. Surely a nobler creature never roamed the plains!

Off-wind from the herd, a red mare came out from the fold of the low hills opposite. She stood motionless a moment, her graceful head held high. Then she nickered. The black stallion drew up short in his herding, nickered eagerly, then bolted off in the direction of the mare. She stood waiting until he had almost reached her; then they galloped back to the herd together.

The shadows crept across the hay flats and the evening stillness settled down. A bird sang sleepily on one note. Donald suddenly became aware of the monotonous song, and stirred from his intent watching. He must tell his father and help send news around the countryside. He was still intensely excited as he crept back from the brow of the hill and hurried home. All the time his mind was busy and his heart was bursting.

Donald knew that three hundred years ago the Spaniards had brought horses to Mexico. Descendants of these horses had wandered into the Great Plains. These horses he now was watching were of that Spanish strain. Thousands of them roamed the cattle lands north to the American boundary. This band now grazed wild over these park lands here in Canada—four hundred and fifty miles north of the boundary.

His father and the farmers for many miles around had determined to round up the horses and make an end of the roving band. As a farmer's son, Donald knew that this was necessary and right. But a certain respect for the band and the fierce loyalty that he felt toward all wild, free creatures made him wish in his heart that they might never be caught, never be broken and tamed. He, who was so full of sympathy for the horses, must be traitor to them!

There had been conflicts in his heart before, but never had there been such a warring of two strong loyalties. He saw himself for the first time as a person of importance because he, Donald Turner, had the power to affect the lives of others. This power, because it could help or harm others, he knew he must use wisely.

When he stood before his father half an hour later, he did not blurt out his news. It was too important for that. But his voice and his eyes were tense with excitement. "That band of wild horses is in the hay hollow west of the homestead quarter," he said. "There must be close to two hundred."

His father was aware of the boy's deep excitement. At Donald's first words he stopped his milking, his hands resting on the rim of the pail as he looked up.

"Good lad, Donald!" he said, quietly enough. "Get your supper and we'll ride to Smith's and Duncan's to start the word around. Tell Mother to pack lunches for tomorrow. We'll start at sunup." He turned to his milking again.

The other men were in the yard shortly after daylight.

Donald afterward wondered how long it would have taken ranch hands to round up the band of horses. These farmers knew horses, but not how to round up large numbers of them as the men of the ranch country knew so well. The farmers learned a good deal in the next two weeks.

Twenty men started out after the band as it thundered out of the hay flats, through the hills and over the country. The dust rose in clouds as their pounding hoofs dug the dry earth. The herd sped before the pursuers with the effortless speed of the wind. The black stallion led or drove his band, and kept them well together. That first day only the young colts were taken.

At sunset the riders unsaddled and staked their horses by a poplar thicket, ate their stale lunches and lay down to sleep under the stars. Their horses cropped the short grass and drank from the stream. Some slept standing, others lay down.

At dawn the herd was spied moving westward. With the coming of night, they, too, had rested. For a mile or more they now sped along the rim of a knoll, swift as bronchos pulled in off the range after a winter out. The black stallion was a hundred feet ahead, running with a tireless, easy swing, his mane and tail streaming and his body stretched level as it cut through the morning mists. Close at his side, but half a length behind him, ran the red mare. The band streamed after.

After the first day's chase and the night under the stars, Donald had ridden back home. Not that he had wanted to go back. He would have given everything that he owned to have gone on with the men. But there were horses and cattle and chores to attend to at home, and there was school.

The roundup continued. Each day saw the capture of more and more horses. As the men doubled back on their course, they began to see that the wild horses traveled in a great circle, coming back again and again over the same ground, stopping at the same watering holes and feeding in the same rich grass flats. Once this course became clear, fresh riders and mounts in relays were posted along the way, while others drove on from behind. The wild band had still to press on with little chance for rest and feeding. The strain of the pursuit took away their desire for food, but they had a burning thirst and the black stallion would never let them drink their fill before he drove them on. Fatigue grew on them.

As the roundup continued, the whole countryside stirred with excitement. At every town where there was a grain elevator along the railroad, people repeated the latest news of the chase. On the farms the hay went unmown or unraked, and the plows rested still in the last furrow of the summer fallow. At school the children played roundup at recess. Donald, at his desk, saw the printed pages of his books, but his mind was miles away running with the now almost exhausted wild horses.

Near the end of the second week of the chase, Donald's father rode into the yard. Donald dropped the wood he was carrying to the house and ran to meet his father.

"Dad, they haven't got the black stallion and the red mare, have they?" Donald could scarcely wait for his father's slow reply.

"No, Donald, lad," he said. "Though those two are the only horses still free. They're back in the flats. We'll get them to-morrow."

Donald felt both relief and fear.

In the yellow lamplight of the supper table his father told of the long days of riding, of the farms where he had eaten and rested, and of the adventures of each day.

"That was a gallant band, lad!" he said. "Never shall we see their equal! Those two that are left are a pair of great horses. Most wild horses show a weakening in the strain and grow up with little wind or muscle. But these two are sound of wind and their muscles are like steel. Besides that, they have intelligence. They would have been taken long ago but for that."

No one spoke. Donald felt that his father was on his side, the side of the horses. After a long pause, Mr. Turner continued.

"With his brains and his strength, that stallion could have got away in the very beginning. He could have got away a dozen times and would now be free south of the border. But that was his band. He stayed by them, and he tried to get them to safety. This week, when his band had been rounded up, he stuck by that red mare. She is swift but she can't match his speed. It's curious the way they keep together! He stops and nickers. She nickers in reply and comes close to him, her nose touching his flank. They stand a moment. Then they are away again, she running beside him but not quite neck to neck. Day after day it is the same. They are no ordinary horseflesh, those two, lad!"

There was a lump in Donald's throat. He knew what his father meant. Those horses seemed to stand for something bigger and greater than himself. There were other things that made him feel the same—the first full-throated song of the meadow lark in the spring; ripe golden fields of wheat with the breeze rippling it in waves; the sun setting over the rim of the world in a blaze of rose and gold; the sun rising again in the quiet east; the smile in the blue depths of his mother's eyes; the still whiteness of the snow-bound plains; the story of Columbus dauntlessly sailing off into unknown seas.

These things were part of a hidden, exciting world. The boy belonged to these things in some strange way. He caught only glimpses of that hidden world, but those glimpses were tantalizing. Something deep within him leaped up in joy.

That night Donald dreamed of horses nickering to him but, when he tried to find them, they were no longer there. Then he dreamed that he was riding the great, black stallion, riding over a far-flung range, riding along a hilltop road with the world spread below him on every side. He felt the powerful body of the horse beneath him. He felt the smooth curves of the mighty muscles. Horse and rider seemed as one.

A cold dawn shattered his glorious dream ride. With his father he joined the other horsemen. From the crest of the slope from which Donald had first seen them, the pair of horses was sighted. They were dark moving shadows in the gray mists of the morning.

They had just finished drinking deep from the stream. Not for two weeks had the men seen the horses drink like that. Thirsty as they were, they had taken but one drink at each water hole. This last morning they were jaded and spent; they had thrown caution to the winds.

At the first suspicion of close danger, they stood still, heads and tails erect. Then they dashed toward the protecting hills. There the way forked.

It was then Donald saw happen the strange thing his father had described. At the fork the stallion halted and nickered. The mare answered and came close. She touched his flank with her head. Then they bounded off and disappeared in the path that led northwest to the rougher country where the chase had not led before.

Then they bounded off and disappeared.

Along the way the horses had been expected to take, grain-fed horses had been stationed. These had now to move over northwest. But the men were in no hurry today. They were sure of the take before nightfall. The sun was low in the west when two riders spurred their mounts for the close in. The stallion and the mare were not a hundred yards ahead. They were dead spent. Their glossy coats were flecked with dark foam. Fatigue showed in every line of their bodies. Their gallant spirits no longer could drive their spent bodies. The stallion called to the mare. He heard her answer behind him. He slowed down, turning wildly in every direction. She came up to him, her head drooped on his flank and rested there. In a last wild defiance, the stallion tossed his magnificent head and drew strength for a last mighty effort. Too late!

The smooth coils of a rope tightened around his feet. He was down, down and helpless. He saw the mare fall as the rope slipped over her body and drew tight around her legs. It maddened him. He struggled wildly to be free. The taut rope held. The stallion was conquered. In that last struggle something went out of him. Broken was his body and broken was his spirit. Never again would he roam the plains, proud and free, the monarch of his herd.

Donald saw it all. He felt it all. His hands gripped the pommel of the saddle and his knees pressed hard against his pony's sides. Tears blinded his eyes and from his throat came the sound of a single sob. It was as if he himself were being broken and tied.

The sun dipped below the rim of the plains. The day was gone; the chase was ended. The men stood about smoking and talking in groups of two's and three's, examining the two roped horses. Donald's father knelt close to the mare, watching her intently. Donald watched him. His father remained quiet for a moment, one knee still resting on the ground, in his hand his unsmoked pipe. Donald waited for his father to speak. At last the words came.

"Boys," he said, without looking up, and with measured words, "do you know, this mare is blind—stone blind!"

A week later, Donald and his father stood watching those two horses in the Turner corral. They were not the same spirited creatures, but they were still magnificent horses.

"I figured," his father said, turning to the boy, "that they had won the right to stay together. I've brought them home for you, Donald. They are yours, lad. I know you will be good to them."

"Instead of saying 'Good day,' I muttered 'Kick, gal,' spurred her lightly, and—the whole centaur bowed and was covered with glory and conceit."   *—Boy on Horseback*

Boy on Horseback

LINCOLN STEFFENS

---

*These chapters are from the first part of the famous writer's
complete* Autobiography. *Lincoln Steffens' early days in
San Francisco of the 70's were centered mainly in his love
for and adventures with horses. So much so that when the
story of his boyhood appeared as a separate book, it was
called* Boy on Horseback.

A Miserable Merry Christmas

WHAT interested me in our new neighborhood was not the
school, nor the room I was to have in the house all to myself,
but the stable which was built back of the house. My father let
me direct the making of a stall, a little smaller than the other
stalls, for my pony, and I prayed and hoped and my sister Lou
believed that that meant that I would get the pony, perhaps for
Christmas. I pointed out to her that there were three other stalls
and no horses at all. This I said in order that she should answer
it. She could not. My father, sounded, said that some day we
might have horses and a cow; meanwhile the stable added to the
value of a house.

"Some day" is a pain to a boy who lives in and knows only
"now." My good little sisters, to comfort me, remarked that
Christmas was coming, but Christmas was always coming and
grownups were always talking about it, asking what you wanted
and then giving you what they wanted you to have. Though

everybody knew what I wanted, I told them all again. My mother knew that I told God, too, every night. I wanted a pony, and to make sure that they understood, I declared that I wanted nothing else.

"Nothing but a pony?" my father asked.

"Nothing," I said.

"Not even a pair of high boots?"

That was hard. I did want boots, but I stuck to the pony. "No, not even boots."

"Nor candy? There ought to be something to fill your stocking with, and Santa Claus can't put a pony into a stocking."

That was true, and he couldn't lead a pony down the chimney, either. But no. "All I want is a pony," I said. "If I can't have a pony, give me nothing, nothing."

Now I had been looking myself for the pony I wanted, going to sales stables, inquiring of horsemen, and I had seen several that would do. My father let me "try" them. I tried so many ponies that I was learning fast to sit on a horse. I chose several, but my father always found some fault with each one. I was in despair. When Christmas was at hand I had given up all hope of a pony, and on Christmas Eve I hung up my stocking along with my sisters, of whom, by the way, I now had three. I haven't mentioned them, or their coming, because, you understand, they were girls, and girls, young girls, counted for nothing in my manly life. They did not mind me, either; they were so happy that Christmas Eve that I caught some of their merriment. I speculated on what I'd get; I hung up the biggest stocking I had, and we all went reluctantly to bed to wait till morning. Not to sleep; not right away. We were told that we must not only sleep promptly, we must not wake up till seven-thirty the next morning—or if we did, we must not go to the fireplace for our Christmas. Impossible.

We did sleep that night, but we woke up at six A.M. We lay in our beds and debated through the open doors whether to obey till, say, half past six. Then we bolted. I don't know who started it, but there was a rush. We all disobeyed; we raced to get first to the fireplace in the front room downstairs. And there they were, the gifts, all sorts of wonderful things, mixed-up piles of presents; only as I disentangled the mess, I saw that my stocking was empty; it hung limp; not a thing in it; and under and around it —nothing. My sisters had knelt down each by her pile of gifts. They were squealing with delight, till they looked up and saw me standing there in my nightgown with nothing. They left their piles to come to me and look at my empty place. Nothing. They felt my stocking: nothing.

I don't remember whether I cried at that moment, but my sisters did. They ran with me back to my bed, and there we all cried till I became indignant. That helped some. I got up, dressed, and driving my sisters away, I went alone out into the yard, down to the stable, and there, all by myself, I wept. My mother came out to me by and by. She found me in my pony stall, sobbing on the floor, and she tried to comfort me. But I heard my father outside; he had come part way with her, and she was having some sort of angry words with him. She tried to comfort me; besought me to come to breakfast. I could not; I wanted no comfort and no breakfast. She left me and went on into the house with more sharp words for my father.

I don't know what kind of breakfast the family had. My sisters said it was "awful." They were ashamed to enjoy their own toys. They came to me, and I was rude. I ran away from them. I went around to the front of the house, sat down on the steps, and, the crying over, I ached. I was wronged, I was hurt—I can feel now what I felt then. I am sure that if one could see the wounds upon our hearts, there would be found still upon mine a scar from that terrible Christmas morning. And my father, the practical joker, he must have been hurt, too, a little. I saw him looking out of the window. He was watching me or something for an hour or two, drawing back the curtain ever so little lest I catch him. But I saw his face, and I think I can see now the anxiety upon it, the worried impatience.

I saw a man riding a pony down the street—a pony and a brand new saddle.

After—I don't know how long—surely an hour or two—I was brought to the climax of my agony by the sight of a man riding a pony down the street, a pony and a brand new saddle; the most beautiful saddle I ever saw, and it was a boy's saddle. The man's feet were not in the stirrups; his legs were too long. The outfit was perfect; it was the realization of all my dreams, the answer to all my prayers. A fine new bridle, with a light curb bit. And the pony! As he drew near, I saw that the pony was really a small horse, what we called an Indian pony, a bay, with black mane and tail, and one white foot and a white star on his forehead. For such a horse as that I would have given, I could have forgiven, anything.

But the man, a disheveled fellow with a blackened eye and a fresh-cut face, came along, reading the numbers on the houses. As my hopes—my impossible hopes—rose, he looked at our door and passed by, he and the pony, and the saddle and the bridle.

Too much. I fell upon the steps, and having wept before, I broke now into such a flood of tears that I was a floating wreck when I heard a voice.

"Say, kid," it said, "do you know a boy named Lennie Steffens?"

I looked up. It was the man on the pony, back again, at our horse block.

"Yes," I spluttered through my tears. "That's me."

"Well," he said, "then this is your horse. I've been looking all over for you and your house. Why don't you put your number where it can be seen?"

"Get down," I said, running out to him.

The man went on saying something about "ought to have got here at seven o'clock; he told me to bring the nag here and tie him to your post and leave him for you . . ."

"Get down," I said.

He got down, and he boosted me up to the saddle. He offered to fit the stirrups to me, but I didn't want him to. I wanted to ride.

"What's the matter with you?" he said, angrily. "What are you crying for? Don't you like the horse? He's a dandy, this horse; I know him of old. He's fine at cattle; he'll drive 'em alone."

I hardly heard, I could scarcely wait, but he persisted. He adjusted the stirrups, and then, finally, off I rode, slowly, at a walk, so happy, so thrilled, that I did not know what I was doing. I did not look back at the house or the man. I rode off up the street, taking note of everything—of the reins, of the pony's long mane, of the carved leather saddle. I had never seen anything so beautiful. And mine! I was going to ride up past Miss Kay's house. But I noticed on the horn of the saddle some stains like raindrops, so I turned and trotted home, not to the house but to the stable. There was the family—father, mother, sisters—all waiting for me, all happy now. They had been putting in place the tools of my new business: blankets, currycomb, brush, pitchfork—everything, and there was hay in the loft.

"What did you come back so soon for?" somebody asked. "Why didn't you go on riding?"

I pointed to the stains. "I wasn't going to get my new saddle rained on," I said. And my father laughed. "It isn't raining," he said. "Those are not raindrops."

"They are tears," my mother gasped, and she gave my father a look which sent him off to the house. Worse still, my mother offered to wipe away the tears still running out of my eyes. I gave her such a look as she had given him, and she went off after my father, drying her own tears.

My sisters remained and we all unsaddled the pony, put on his halter, led him to his stall, tied and fed him. It began really to rain; so all the rest of that memorable day we curried and combed that pony. The girls plaited his mane, forelock, and tail, while I pitchforked hay to him and curried and brushed, curried and brushed. For a change we brought him out to drink. We led him up and down, blanketed like a race horse; we took turns at that. But the best, most inexhaustible fun, was to clean him.

When we went reluctantly to our midday Christmas dinner, we smelt of horse, and my sisters had to wash their faces and hands. I was asked to, but I wouldn't, till my mother bade me look in the mirror. Then I washed up—quick. My face was caked with muddy lines of tears that had coursed over my cheeks to my mouth. Having washed away that shame, I ate my dinner, and as I ate I grew hungrier. It was my first meal that day, and as I filled up on the turkey and the stuffing, the cranberries and the pies, the fruit and the nuts—as I swelled, I could laugh. My mother said I still choked and sobbed now and then, but I laughed, too. I saw and enjoyed my sisters' presents till—I had to go out and attend to my pony, who was there, really and truly there, the promise, the beginning, of a happy double life. And—I went and looked to make sure—there was the saddle, too, and the bridle.

But that Christmas, which my father had planned so carefully, was it the best or the worst I ever knew? He often asked me that; I never could answer as a boy. I think now that it was both. It covered the whole distance from broken-hearted misery to bursting happiness—too fast. A grownup could hardly have stood it.

I Get a Colt to Break In

Colonel Carter gave me a colt. I had my pony, and my father meanwhile had bought a pair of black carriage horses and a cow, all of which I had to attend to when we had no "man." And servants were hard to get and keep in those days; the women married, and the men soon quit service to seize opportunities always opening. My hands were pretty full, and so was the stable. But Colonel Carter seemed to think that he had promised me a horse. He had not; I would have known it if he had. No matter. He thought he had, and maybe he did promise himself to give me one. That was enough. The kind of man that led immigrant trains across the continent and delivered them safe, sound, and together where he promised would keep his word. One day he drove over from Stockton, leading a two-year-old which he brought to our front door and turned over to me as mine. Such a horse!

She was a cream-colored mare with a black forelock, mane, and tail and a black stripe along the middle of her back. Tall, slender, high-spirited, I thought then—I think now that she was the most beautiful of horses. Colonel Carter had bred and reared her with me and my uses in mind. She was a careful cross of a mustang mare and a thoroughbred stallion, with the stamina of the wild horse and the speed and grace of the racer. And she had a sense of fun. As Colonel Carter got down out of his buggy and went up to her, she snorted, reared, flung her head high in the air, and, coming down beside him, tucked her nose affectionately under his arm.

"I have handled her a lot," he said. "She is kind as a kitten, but she is as sensitive as a lady. You can spoil her by one mistake. If you ever lose your temper, if you ever abuse her, she will be ruined for ever. And she is unbroken. I might have had her broken to ride for you, but I didn't want to. I want you to do it. I have taught her to lead, as you see; had to, to get her over here. But here she is, an unbroken colt; yours. You take and you break her. You're only a boy, but if you break this colt right, you'll be a man—a young man, but a man. And I'll tell you how."

Now, out west, as everybody knows, they break in a horse by riding out to him in his wild state, lassoing, throwing, and saddling him; then they let him up, frightened and shocked, with a yelling broncho-buster astride of him. The wild beast bucks, the cowboy drives his spurs into him, and off they go, jumping, kicking, rearing, falling, till by the weight of the man, the lash, and the rowels, the horse is broken—in body and spirit. This was not the way I was to break my colt.

"You must break her to ride without her ever knowing it," Colonel Carter said. "You feed and you clean her—you; not the stable man. You lead her out to water and to walk. You put her on a long rope and let her play, calling her to you and gently pulling on the rope. Then you turn her loose in the grass lot there and, when she has romped till tired, call her. If she won't come, leave her. When she wants water or food, she will run to your call, and you will pet and feed and care for her." He went on for half an hour, advising me in great detail how to proceed. I wanted to begin right away. He laughed. He let me lead her around to the stable, water her, and put her in the stable and feed her.

There I saw my pony. My father, sisters, and Colonel Carter saw me stop and look at my pony.

"What'll you do with him?" one of my sisters asked. I was bewildered for a moment. What should I do with the little red horse? I decided at once.

"You can have him," I said to my sisters.

"No," said Colonel Carter, "not yet. You can give your sisters the pony by and by, but you'll need him till you have taught the colt to carry you and a saddle—months; and you must not hurry. You must learn patience, and you will if you give the colt time to learn it, too. Patience and control. You can't control a young

horse unless you can control yourself. Can you shoot?" he asked
suddenly.

I couldn't. I had a gun and I had used it some, but it was a
rifle, and I could not bring down with it such game as there was
around Sacramento—birds and hares. Colonel Carter looked at
my father, and I caught the look. So did my father. I soon had a
shotgun. But at the time Colonel Carter turned to me and said:

"Can't shoot straight, eh? Do you know what that means?
That means that you can't control a gun, and that means that
you can't control yourself, your eye, your hands, your nerves.
You are wriggling now. I tell you that a good shot is always a
good man. He may be a 'bad man' too, but he is quiet, strong,
steady in speech, gait, and mind. No matter, though. If you break
in this colt right, if you teach her her paces, she will teach you to
shoot and be quiet."

He went off downtown with my father, and I started away
with my colt. I fed, I led, I cleaned her, gently, as if she were
made of glass; she was playful and willing, a delight. When Colonel Carter came home with my father for supper, he questioned
me.

"You should not have worked her today," he said. "She has
come all the way from Stockton and must be tired. Yes, yes, she
would not show fatigue; too fine for that, and too young to be
wise. You have got to think for her, consider her as you would
your sisters."

Sisters! I thought; I had never considered my sisters. I did not
say that, but Colonel Carter laughed and nodded to my sisters.
It was just as if he had read my thought. But he went on to draw
on my imagination a centaur; the colt as a horse's body—me, a
boy, as the head and brains of one united creature. I liked that. I
would be that. I and the colt: a centaur.

After Colonel Carter was gone home I went to work on my
new horse. The old one, the pony, I used only for business: to
go to fires, to see my friends, run errands, and go hunting with
my new shotgun. But the game that had all my attention was
the breaking in of the colt, the beautiful cream-colored mare,

who soon knew me—and my pockets. I carried sugar to reward her when she did right, and she discovered where I carried it; so did the pony, and when I was busy they would push their noses into my pockets, both of which were torn down a good deal of the time. But the colt learned. I taught her to run around a circle, turn and go the other way at a signal. My sisters helped me. I held the long rope and the whip (for signaling), while one of the girls led the colt; it was hard work for them, but they took it in turns. One would lead the colt round and round till I snapped the whip; then she would turn, turning the colt, till the colt did it all by herself. And she was very quick. She shook hands with each of her forefeet. She let us run under her, back and forth. She was slow only to carry me. Following Colonel Carter's instructions, I began by laying my arm or a surcingle over her back. If she trembled, I drew it slowly off. When she could abide it, I tried buckling it, tighter and tighter. I laid over her, too, a blanket, folded at first, then open, and, at last, I slipped up on her myself, sat there a second, and as she trembled, slid off. My sisters held her for me, and when I could get up and sit there a moment or two, I tied her at a block, and we, my sisters and I, made a procession of mounting and dismounting. She soon got used to this and would let us slide off over her rump, but it was a long, long time before she would carry me.

That we practiced by leading her along a high curb where I could get on as she walked, ride a few steps, and then, as she felt me and crouched, slip off. She never did learn to carry a girl on her back; my sisters had to lead her while I rode. This was not purposeful. I don't know just how it happened, but I do remember the first time I rode on my colt all the way around the lot and how, when I put one of the girls up, she refused to repeat. She shuddered, shook and frightened them off.

While we were breaking in the colt a circus came to town. The ring was across the street from our house. Wonderful! I lived in that circus for a week. I saw the show but once, but I marked the horse-trainers, and in the mornings when they were not too busy I told them about my colt, showed her to them, and asked them

how to train her to do circus tricks. With their hints I taught the
colt to stand up on her hind legs, kneel, lie down, and balance on
a small box. This last was easier than it looked. I put her first on a
low big box and taught her to turn on it; then got a little smaller
box upon which she repeated what she did on the big one. By and
by we had her so that she would step up on a high box so small
that her four feet were almost touching, and there also she would
turn.

The circus man gave me one hint that was worth all the other
tricks put together. "You catch her doing something of herself
that looks good," he said, "and then you keep her at it." It was
thus that I taught her to bow to people. The first day I rode her
out on to the streets was a proud one for me and for the colt,
too, apparently. She did not walk, she danced; perhaps she was
excited, nervous; anyhow I liked the way she threw up her head,
champed at the bit, and went dancing, prancing down the street.
Everybody stopped to watch us, and so, when she began to sober
down, I picked her up again with heel and rein, saying, "Here's
people, Lady," and she would show off to my delight. By constant repetition I had her so trained that she would single-foot,
head down, along a country road till we came to a house or a
group of people. Then I'd say, "People, Lady," and up would go
her head, and her feet would dance.

But the trick that set the town talking was her bowing to any
one I spoke to. "Lennie Steffens' horse bows to you," people
said, and she did. I never told how it was done; by accident.
Dogs used to run out at us, and the colt enjoyed it; she kicked
at them sometimes with both hind hoofs. I joined her in the
game, and being able to look behind more conveniently than she
could, I watched the dogs until they were in range, then gave the
colt a signal to kick. "Kick, gal," I'd say, and tap her ribs with
my heel. We used to get dogs together that way; the colt would
kick them over and over and leave them yelping in the road. Well,
one day when I met a girl I knew I lifted my hat, probably muttered a "Good day," and I must have touched the colt with my
heel. Anyway, she dropped her head and kicked—not much; there

The trick that set the town talking was her bowing.

was no dog near, so she had responded to my unexpected signal by what looked like a bow. I caught the idea and kept her at it. Whenever I want to bow to a girl or anybody else, instead of saying "Good day," I muttered "Kick, gal," spurred her lightly, and—the whole centaur bowed and was covered with glory and conceit.

Yes, conceit. I was full of it, and the colt was quite as bad. One day my chum Hjalmar came into town on his Black Bess, blanketed. She had had a great fistule cut out of her shoulder and had to be kept warm. I expected to see her weak and dull, but no, the good old mare was champing and dancing, like my colt.

"What is it makes her so?" I asked, and Hjalmar said he didn't know, but he thought she was proud of the blanket. A great idea. I had a gaudy horse blanket. I put it on the colt and I could hardly hold her. We rode down the main street together, both horses and both boys, so full of vanity that everybody stopped to smile. We thought they admired, and maybe they did. But some boys on the street gave us another angle. They, too, stopped and looked, and as we passed, one of them said, "Think you're hell, don't you?"

Spoilsport!

We did, as a matter of fact; we thought we were hell. The recognition of it dashed us for a moment; not for long, and the horses paid no heed. We pranced, the black and the yellow, all the way down J Street, up K Street, and agreed that we'd do it again, often. Only, I said, we wouldn't use blankets. If the horses were proud of a blanket, they'd be proud of anything un-usually conspicuous. We tried a flower next time. I fixed a big rose on my colt's bridle just under her ear and it was great—she pranced downtown with her head turned, literally, to show off her flower. We had to change the decoration from time to time, put on a ribbon, or a bell, or a feather, but, really, it was not necessary for my horse. Old Black Bess needed an incentive to act up, but all I had to do to my horse was to pick up the reins, touch her with my heel, and say, "People"; she would dance from one side of the street to the other, asking to be admired. As she was. As we were.

I would ride down to my father's store, jump off my prancing colt in the middle of the street, and run up into the shop. The colt, free, would stop short, turn, and follow me right up on the sidewalk, unless I bade her wait. If any one approached her while I was gone, she would snort, rear, and strike. No stranger could get near her. She became a frightened, frightening animal, and yet when I came into sight she would run to me, put her head down, and as I straddled her neck, she would throw up her head and pitch me into my seat, facing backward, of course. I whirled around right, and off we'd go, the vainest boy and the proudest horse in the State.

"Hey, give me a ride, will you?" some boy would ask.

"Sure," I'd say, and jump down and watch that boy try to catch and mount my colt. He couldn't. Once a cowboy wanted to try her, and he caught her; he dodged her forefeet, grabbed the reins, and in one spring was on her back. I never did that again. My colt reared, then bucked, and, as the cowboy kept his seat, she shuddered, sank to the ground, and rolled over. He slipped aside and would have risen with her, but I was alarmed and begged him not to. She got up at my touch and followed me so close that she stepped on my heel and hurt me. The cowboy saw the point.

"If I were you, kid," he said, "I'd never let anybody mount that colt. She's too good."

That, I think, was the only mistake I made in the rearing of Colonel Carter's gift-horse. My father differed from me. He discovered another error or sin, and thrashed me for it. My practice was to work hard on a trick, privately, and when it was perfect, let him see it. I would have the horse out in our vacant lot doing it as he came home to supper. One evening, as he approached the house, I was standing, whip in hand, while the colt, quite free, was stepping carefully over the bodies of a lot of girls, all my sisters and all their girl friends. My father did not express the admiration I expected; he was frightened and furious. "Stop

"Stop that," he called, and came running into the lot.

that," he called, and he came running around into the lot, took the whip, and lashed me with it. I tried to explain; the girls tried to help me explain.

I had seen in the circus a horse that stepped thus over a row of prostrate clowns. It looked dangerous for the clowns, but the trainer had told me how to do it. You begin with logs, laid out a certain distance apart; the horse walks over them under your lead, and whenever he touches one you rebuke him. By and by he will learn to step with such care that he never trips. Then you substitute clowns. I had no clowns, but I did get logs, and with the girls helping, we taught the colt to step over the obstacles even at a trot. Walking, she touched nothing. All ready thus with the logs, I had my sisters lie down in the grass, and again and again the colt stepped over and among them. None was ever touched. My father would not listen to any of this; he just walloped me, and when he was tired or satisfied and I was in tears, I blubbered a short excuse: "They were only girls." And he whipped me some more.

My father was not given to whipping; he did it very seldom, but he did it hard when he did it at all. My mother was just the opposite. She did not whip me, but she often smacked me, and she had a most annoying habit of thumping me on the head with her thimbled finger. This I resented more than my father's thoroughgoing thrashings, and I can tell why now. I would be playing Napoleon and as I was reviewing my Old Guard, she would crack my skull with that thimble. No doubt I was in the way; it took a lot of furniture and sisters to represent properly a victorious army; and you might think as my mother did that a thimble is a small weapon. But imagine Napoleon at the height of his power, the ruler of the world on parade, getting a sharp rap on his crown from a woman's thimble. No. My father's way was more appropriate. It was hard. "I'll attend to you in the morning," he would say, and I lay awake wondering which of my crimes he had discovered. I know what it is to be sentenced to be shot at sunrise. And it hurt, in the morning, when he was not angry but very fresh and strong. But you see, he walloped me in my own person; he never humiliated Napoleon or my knight-hood, as my mother did. And I learned something from his dis-cipline, something useful.

I learned what tyranny is and the pain of being misunderstood and wronged, or, if you please, understood and set right; they are pretty much the same. He and most parents and teachers do not break in their boys as carefully as I broke in my colt. They haven't the time that I had, and they have not some other incentives I had. I saw this that day when I rubbed my sore legs. He had to explain to my indignant mother what had happened. When he had told it his way, I gave my version: how long and cautiously I had been teaching my horse to walk over logs and girls. And having shown how sure I was of myself and the colt, while my mother was boring into his silence with one of her reproachful looks, I said something that hit my father hard.

"I taught the colt that trick, I have taught her all that you see she knows, without whipping her. I have never struck her; not once. Colonel Carter said I mustn't, and I haven't."

And my mother, backing me up, gave him a rap: "There," she said, "I told you so." He walked off, looking like a thimble-rapped Napoleon.

If Wishes Were Horses

ADELE DE LEEUW

WEDGED between Uncle Joe and Aunt Emma and pressed hard against the rail, Stacy watched the sulkies wheeling swiftly around the bend and down the track. The two-wheeled spidery carts seemed to fly over the ground, the horses' hooves thundered in swift rhythm, and Stacy, leaning far out, clutched her bag of popcorn so hard that it broke and spilled.

"It's Mr. McGregor's mare," she cried, turning a radiant face to Aunt Emma. "It's Lady! She's winning! Isn't she wonderful? Isn't she beautiful?"

"Now, for goodness' sake—" In her excitement Stacy had dropped her purse, too. "Pick it up, Stacy, quick."

"Oh, Aunt Emma, not till Lady's won. . . . There. . . . There! She's past the stand. I knew she would! Oh, I wish—"

"If wishes were horses you'd have two dozen by now," Uncle Joe said tolerantly, but Aunt Emma pressed her lips together. "I never did see such a one for horses. I don't know why Clara and Dan didn't bring you up like other girls."

Tears stung at Stacy's lids, and her face felt hot. The cheering of the County Fair crowd drummed in her ears, but Stacy, for a nostalgic moment, wasn't there. She was back home—on the ranch that had been a kind of heaven to her all her life until tragedy had fallen like a black cloud, obliterating everything. Mother and Daddy gone . . . the ranch taken over by the bank, the horses sold. Midget and Pete and Saracen and Feather and Lucky Girl and her own sweet Janey . . .

Aunt Emma and Uncle Joe had taken her in, been good to her, given her a room newly furnished just for her, tried to make her happy. But sometimes a wave of homesickness broke over her with such force that she didn't know how she could stand it. That was when she *had* to talk about horses . . . the horses she had known and loved, the ones she was going to have when she was old enough to work and have a ranch of her own again. She could never be truly happy until she did have them. Horses were "in her blood," as Uncle Joe said. But he said it laughingly.

He didn't really understand, he or Aunt Emma. They had never known anything but this small town, the old house with its neat garden, the well-ordered, intimate life of the village. Sometimes Stacy felt that she must stifle if she stayed here much longer in this tame, hedged-about atmosphere. She would take long walks into the country, imagining herself on a horse, riding over the prairie.

It was on one of those walks that she had discovered Mr. McGregor's place. The Mansion, it was called. She had heard the townspeople refer to it. It had been a gloomy stone house, with porches falling into disrepair, and high grass blotting out the curving drive under the ancient elms. Then Mr. McGregor had bought it, had brought in carpenters and masons and landscape artists, turned the big barn into a marvelous stable, imported a trainer and two stable-boys, and filled the place with horses.

The trainer's name was Mike O'Neill, the people said. He was a terror. But nothing compared to old man McGregor himself. Rich as Croesus, with a shell like a walnut, and just as bitter. Why was he so bitter with all that money, and all those horses? The townspeople shook their heads. And what was Mrs. McGregor like? Some said she was little and faded; some said she was tall and sad-faced; but nobody had ever had a good look at her. Kept to herself. There was some kind of mystery at The Mansion, of that everyone was sure.

Stacy was remembering all that as she stooped to retrieve her purse. Suddenly she made up her mind. "Be back in a minute," she said breathlessly.

She darted through the leisurely throngs to the long open shed where the race-entrants were stabled. A little wizened man with leather leggings and a bright blue shirt was leading Lady up and down, cooling her before the rub-down. He was the same bow-legged little man who had driven Lady in the sulky like one inspired. His face was weather-brown and he clamped a cold pipe between his teeth. His cap was pulled low over his shrewd blue eyes and Stacy could see a close thatch of reddish hair. He looked a little forbidding, but she did not stop.

"You're—you're Mike O'Neill, aren't you?" she asked him.

"You're—you're Mike O'Neill, aren't you?"

He did not stop walking. "Sure, and who else? And who may you be?"

"I'm Stacy Landis . . . I live with the Holdens. I—I saw you win the race, and it was thrilling! But I knew you'd win—because you were driving Lady. She's the most beautiful mare I've ever seen. She has everything!"

His narrowed eyes studied her. "Ye think ye know a good horse when ye see one, do ye?"

"I do know. I know horses. And I know Lady's a thoroughbred. She—she makes me think of my Janey. Only she's better. I loved Janey, but of course I know Lady's a finer mare."

He was still studying her, as if trying to make up his mind. "You're a quare one, Miss," he said.

"Would Mr. McGregor mind if I stroked her nose?"

He bridled a little at that. "Sure, and how would I know what's in that one's mind? But he's not here, and I am, and *I'm* the one that handles the horses. So stroke her nose and be quick about it."

He watched her, under his low-pulled cap; watched Lady's ears and the way she stood under Stacy's hand. "You know your horses, I'll say that, Miss. You've a way with you not many has. Now where in the wide world—"

They got no further than that. Uncle Joe, red-faced and perspiring, his face creased with worry, spied her then and shouted, "Stacy! Stacy, we've been hunting the grounds over for you!"

"I'm coming to see you and Lady," Stacy managed, over her shoulder, tearing herself away. Mike said doubtfully, "I don't know about that, Miss—" but she could not be *sure* that was what he said. Uncle Joe had her by the arm, propelling her toward an even more worried Aunt Emma.

"I declare, what got into you, Stacy?"

"Oh, Aunt Emma, I'm sorry, but I had to see Lady . . ."

"Lady?"

"Mr. McGregor's mare. She won the race, don't you remember?"

"Maybe she did. They all look alike to me."

"Uncle Joe, don't you think I could have a horse—not a wonderful thoroughbred, just a nice horse I could ride—"

Uncle Joe mumbled, "You know we haven't the room."

"We could build—"

Aunt Emma said crossly, "And what about the feed? It's hard enough making ends meet nowadays, with the added expense and all, without your talking about getting a horse. I never heard such nonsense. Come along now; my feet hurt and we still have the shopping to do."

They didn't understand what it would mean to her. If she had a horse that she could take care of, that she could ride and talk to, it would bring the ranch close again . . . the ranch and the corral and Mother and Daddy—everything that spelled home.

In spite of her determination to visit The Mansion stables soon, it wasn't until Spring that Stacy managed it. Then her Uncle Joe gave her a bicycle. It wasn't a horse, of course . . . but it was motion—wind in her hair—trees whizzing by—cloud-racing—all the things she loved.

She left her bicycle by the side of the road near the McGregor meadows. Lady was in the field, and a dozen others, and three wobbly-legged colts keeping close to their mothers. At sight of them, she vaulted the fence—what was a fence to a Western girl? —and walked across the meadow toward the stable, stopping only to stroke Lady and to make friends with the fuzzy colts.

"Here I am," she told Mike. He looked around a bit nervously; the stable-boys stared at her in wonder.

"How—how'd you get in?" Mike asked.

She told him, and a slow, incredulous grin swept over his lean face. "Hmm, nothin' can keep *you* out, I see."

"D'you mind?" she asked anxiously.

"Not *me*," he answered, rather cryptically. She didn't want to ask him what he meant. "Now that you're here, look your fill," he said.

She wandered over the stable for an ecstatic hour. There were stalls of shining, varnished wood, with iron grill work between. A freshly scrubbed stone floor. High windows through which the spring sunlight filtered. A tack room with silver-mounted harness, glittering in the light, and cases of cups and ribbons—blue and red. Mike would stand near the door for a while, then come and tell her some interesting bit about one of the horses; how some of the prizes had been won.

"Begorry, it's a pleasure to talk to a knowin' lass! The dolts around here don't know a bit of good horseflesh when they see it, and care less. You're not from around here, I take it?"

"No," she said. "That is, I am now . . . but I was raised on a ranch." And under his sympathetic prodding she told him about the golden days when she had had Mother and Dad . . . and her own Janey.

Stacy and Mike got to be fast friends. "It's good to have somebody to talk to," he told her one day, clamping his unlit pipe between his teeth. "Them boys are no good at all, at all—their minds on nothin' but how to get out of workin'—and Himself no satisfaction eyether. As for Herself—" he gave a shrug. "She's a lady I feel sorry for, I do that."

"Why, Mike?"

He said briskly, "Sure, and I've said too much already." He let Stacy help him curry the horses; let her lead them around the turf ring. She pored over their histories with him, and helped Mike doctor them. It was always hard to tear herself away. Other duties seemed so prosaic after that. "When may I come again?" she'd ask, and Mike would scratch his head. After long thought he would say, "Come Wednesday . . . yes. Wednesday. And mind ye be a good gurrul in the meantime."

The days varied. Sometimes he'd ask her twice in a week; sometimes ten days would go by before he'd issue an invitation. One time there was a dreadful span of fourteen endless days. She couldn't stand it. Lady was going to foal, and she had had no news.

She rode slowly past The Mansion, back and forth, back and forth. Finally, she spurted up the drive. Someone raised a window, and called to her. She had a glimpse of a sad white face. Then the window was banged down with a crash that rattled the glass, and the shade was pulled. It puzzled her, but as soon as she got to the stable she forgot about it.

Mike was in a bad humor. One of the stable-boys was sick—or so he said—and the other was a good-for-nothing. "I'd fire the both of them," he grumbled, "but boys is hard to get these days, and I'm too old to do all the work meself."

Stacy said comfortingly, "I'll help all I can, Mike. Tell me what to do."

She worked busily beside him, going from stall to stall and renewing friendships.

"Damon's restless," Mike said. "Needs a workout. Want to take him around a bit?"

"Oh, Mike!" Stacy breathed, afraid she had only dreamt it. "Oh, Mike, may I, really?"

He held his hand out to give her a leg up, but she leaped neatly onto Damon's bare back. Mike whistled appreciatively. He watched her gentling Damon, and then out into the sunshine. "You can ride, all right," he shouted to her. She laughed with joy. It was wonderful—the feel of a horse under her again, the wind in her face, the soft thud of Damon's hooves, the sense of freedom and motion.

She circled the field a dozen times; then suddenly she saw a tall, stout man bearing down upon her, cane upraised. His face was purple with rage. She drew to a halt, and he surged forward shaking the cane in her face.

"You—you—where did you come from? What are you doing on one of my horses? What does this mean? Get off at once, get off and explain yourself."

She slid to the ground. "I'm sorry, Mr. McGregor—"

"Not a word out of you!"

Mike came running up. "Mr. McGregor, sorr—"

"Nor out of you, either. Get off this place and don't you ever come here again! The brass, the nerve of you! Get off my place, I say! I've a good mind to take this cane to you!"

"Mr. McGregor, sorr—"

"And to you, too, O'Neill! Rank carelessness! So that's what goes on behind my back, when I'm away! I saw this young scalawag coming up the drive. I couldn't believe my eyes!" His face was apoplectic. "Well, what are you waiting for? Get out!"

Stacy pedaled home furiously, the blood beating angrily in her ears. The hateful old man—hateful, hateful! Aunt Emma was horrified when she heard of the incident. "Nobody can talk like that to a Holden or a Landis! Don't you ever set foot on their place again—or near it, do you hear? That's what comes of meddling in other folks' business! You and your horses!"

But Stacy couldn't forget that ride. It had brought everything back to her, stronger, more poignantly, than ever. Her days were one long homesickness now, and she didn't see how she could live through the summer. It had been such a lovely thing while it lasted.

She lay out under the apple tree, imagining it was the hayloft; she rode her bike with closed eyes, imagining she was galloping over the field on Damon or Lady. She stared up at the stars at night, saying fervently, "Star bright, star light, first star I see tonight, I wish I may—I wish I might—" And then a long sigh. It was silly to wish. Wishes like that never came true. Never. Not here, anyway.

After that the summer dragged by in an endless succession of monotonous days. The air was hot and sultry, and even swimming did not make her feel right. She rode listlessly down the long road, one day after her swim, her thoughts ranging back to the past. Almost without her volition she found herself turning off toward the McGregor place. It wouldn't hurt just to look over the fence, would it, just to look——?

Fellow was standing under a distant tree; and she could make out Hero and Ballyhoo. But the others must be in the stable. How was Lady, she wondered? And her foal? She must have foaled by this time. Stacy's eyes turned toward the stable, and her heart stopped, then thudded fearfully. There was smoke curling from the roof, and a curl of gray wafted out of one of the windows . . . smoke on an August day.

Stacy grabbed her wet bathing suit from the bicycle basket and tied it over her nose and mouth, vaulted the fence, and sprinted across the field. The high, whinnying neighs of the frightened horses struck at her ears as she tore through the wide doors. The air was hazy with smoke and the acrid smell of it penetrated even the wet fold around her face. Where was Mike? Where were the boys? She knew what must have happened—someone had dropped a cigarette or a match in the hayloft.

Which horse first? Oh, Lady, of course, Lady and her foal. In the special box stall she found them, Lady's eyes rolling, her nostrils showing red. Stacy flung a blanket over the horse's head, spoke to her soothingly. "Come, Lady, come, Lady . . ." with one hand guiding her, with the other leading the stumbling little colt. She pleaded and coaxed and pushed. Lady reared and balked and whinnied, but Stacy's calm, urging voice forced her forward, into the blessed air.

She tied them to the stake at the far end of the ring; otherwise, she knew, they would blindly have followed her back. Damon next . . . a Damon wild-eyed with fear. The smoke was thicker now, her eyes smarted and she felt choked and breathless. The noise of their frightened cries made the stable clamorous. If only someone would help! She could never get them all out in time! What if some refused to come? She mustn't think of that.

One after the other, methodically. . . . "Come, Griselda . . . nice girl. . . ." "Sultan, quiet, Sultan!" One more now . . . King, in the last stall. He reared as she entered, and tried to throw the blanket off his head. He pawed frantically and neighed in shrill hysteria. The smoke was so thick she could scarcely see him. She strained upward to reach his halter. There were voices outside. "Good glory . . . who took them out? . . . Who's in there? Stacy, Stacy, gurrul, are ye all right?"

But she could not answer. King's rearing head jerked her arm upward and she lost her balance. She fell face forward in the stall, and everything turned black.

"It's that Mike O'Neill to see you," Aunt Emma said, her back stiff with disapproval. "I said he couldn't come in, but you could talk to him out the window."

She pushed Stacy's chair close, and laid a scarf around her shoulders. Stacy laid her bandaged hands on the sill and leaned out.

Mike was holding his cap, his red thatch gleamed in the light.

Lady reared and balked and whinnied.

"It's a wonderful gurrul ye are, Miss Stacy, a wonderful gurrul! Mr. McGregor is after wantin' to come and see you as soon as ever he can, and Herself, too."

"I'll be glad to have them," Stacy said. "Is everything all right?"

"It is that . . . in more ways than one. And I was to tell you why he was such a curmudgeon that day and chased you off. It's like his own daughter you are, and ye gave him a start. She died these twelve years ago, a fine lass about your age. He never got over it, nor Herself eyether."

So that was the mystery of The Mansion, Stacy thought. Her heart welled with pity for the McGregors.

"He was gone that day and I to fetch him with the carriage," Mike said. "So the boys went gallivantin'. If you hadn't come along, I don't like to think— Aye, it was Providence, that's what it was. And now wait a minute; I've a present from Himself."

He disappeared around the house, and Stacy could hardly contain herself. What could it possibly be? When Mike appeared again, she cried out, "Oh, Mike, not for me! Not that darling colt for *me!*"

"And who else?" he demanded. "It's Lady's own. Look at them legs, will ye, and that muzzle, and this fine back. It's many a ribbon this one will be winning!"

A colt of her own! To love and care for and talk to! It couldn't be . . . And suddenly her face fell. No, it couldn't be. "There isn't room," she said in a whisper. "And the feed—"

"And who said anything about room and feed?" Mike asked belligerently. "You'll keep it at the stables, of course, and Himself will pay for its keep. Then when you want to ride, there'll be the stable-full to choose from . . . and this one for your very own. You're to name her. Now, what will ye be after callin' her?"

Stacy cried, "Why, Janey, of course!" And the ranch and Mother and Daddy were close again, and she was happy as she hadn't been since she had lost them.

FROM
Mountain Pony

HENRY V. LAROM

---

*After Andy makes friends with his sorrel bronco, he still has
plenty of trouble and excitement ahead before Garland is
brought to justice. This is a splendid story about fine horses
and bad game rustlers in the Wyoming Rockies. The author
knows his territory intimately. And the local color is not
vaguely western, but clearly and crisply Wyoming.*

The Sorrel that Turned on a Dime

ANDY MARVIN slung the mailbag across the pommel of his
saddle, mounted his little mare, and trotted down the road from
the post office toward his uncle's ranch. It was a hot summer day
with the sun beating down on the mountain peaks, making the
snow glaciers sparkle. The little mare, called Snippy, shied deli-
cately at some wandering ranch pigs and kept her ears busy pointing here and there in search of excitement.

As she left a grove of cottonwoods, her ears jumped forward,
and Snippy stopped so suddenly that Andy almost slid over her
neck. In front of them, a heavy-set man had just opened a
wooden gate and was trying to lead a bright sorrel horse through
it. Andy watched with interest. An Eastern boy spending his
first summer in the Rockies, he wanted to learn all he could
about handling horses, and this one looked like a bronco.

The man yanked hard on the reins, and the sorrel pulled back.
He jerked again, growling names at the horse. When the horse

reared, Andy noticed that there was blood on the animal's lips. His eye showed white with fear. He was afraid of the gate and the cattle guard next to it, and he was terrified of the man.

"You loco, jug-headed fool!" the man shouted, and he struck the horse a vicious crack on the side of the jaw with the butt end of a heavy quirt. The horse grunted with pain and reared again, gasping as the man jammed down on the bit.

"Hey, don't do that!" Andy was off his mare before he realized it and running toward the sorrel horse.

The man turned to him slowly. He had a heavy, unshaven face; great muscles rippled under his dirty, blue-denim shirt, and his battered hat showed sweat along the band. "What's it to you?" he asked.

Andy stopped in his tracks. He had no right to tell this grown man, this Westerner, what to do with his horse. "Well, nothing," he said. "Only the pony's scared, and—and his mouth is bleeding."

"Uh-huh." The man looked at Andy coldly. "An' it's my horse, ain't it?"

"Sure," said Andy. "But—but, darn it! That doesn't give you the right to hit him!"

"Why not?" The man hitched his pants and looked down on Andy in disgust. "Look, sonny," he said, "maybe you better get out of the way before you get hurt." He turned and yanked the sorrel's reins again. As the horse reared, terrified of the quirt, his mouth opened, and Andy could see the spade on the bit, a long piece of metal that made the horse gasp and gag, while the side of the bit tore the flesh from the corners of his mouth. Once again the man struck the side of the horse's jaw.

Andy made a jump for his arm. It was like trying to stop a steel piston, but he hung on long enough to break the next blow. Then the man turned, grabbed him by the shirt front, and sent him spinning across the road into the ditch. For a moment he lay there, stunned. Then he felt himself lifted up and pushed backward until he was pinned against a gatepost.

He shook his head to clear it and looked up into the face close

The horse grunted with pain and reared again.

to his. He could see the sweat running through the unshaven beard. The eyes, a cold, watery blue, stared into his. "What's your name, sonny?" the man asked, softly.

"Andy Marvin," Andy said, trying to get his breath. He could feel the great fist against his chest, pushing him against the post, grinding it into his back. "Let me go!"

"Wes Marvin's nephew, huh?" the man went on. "I shoulda knowed. You look like him."

Andy began to get his breath back. "You let go of me," he said, "or I'll tell my uncle. He'll pin your ears back."

He felt the fist push him harder into the gatepost. "Let me tell *you* somethin', sonny," the man growled, and his eyes narrowed. "If Wes Marvin starts anythin', I'll tear him apart, see? An' you can tell him Randy Garland said so. An' you! You're a big boy now, sonny. You got somethin' to learn. Out here a horse is a man's property. If I wanna hit him, I'm agoin' to hit him. Unless you wanna buy him, you got nothin' to say, see? Now git!"

Once again he grabbed Andy's shirt front and, after first drawing him close, pushed him staggering across the road into a pile of rocks.

Andy felt sick at his stomach. He closed his eyes a moment to try and stop the dizziness, and when he opened them again Garland had turned to the horse and was yanking on the bit.

Andy looked at the horse's bright sorrel coat, the silver mane, the broad forehead with the crooked blaze running down the nose. Then he saw the blood on the mouth, the swelling on the side of the jaw. He couldn't stand it any longer.

"All right, I'll buy him," he said.

Garland stopped pulling on the reins and turned in astonishment. "You'll what?"

"I said I'll buy him."

Garland tied the sorrel's reins to the gatepost. His whole attitude seemed to change when he saw the chance to make money. He walked to where Andy was sitting and looked down at him. "How much money you got?" he asked.

Andy was so relieved to see the horse-beating stop that it took him a moment to gather his wits. "I've got some," he ended lamely. Why tell him he had only forty dollars?

Garland scratched his head and made a sucking noise with his teeth. "That horse'll cost you sixty dollars," he said.

Andy's heart sank. He didn't have sixty dollars, and he shouldn't buy a horse anyway. His dad had told him, "Now this money is to make sure you pay your own expenses. Don't waste it!"

And here he was trying to spend it all on a horse, a pony he knew nothing about. A bronc! Maybe a killer!

"Sixty dollars is too much," Andy said.

Garland looked at him shrewdly, a smirk on his lips. "You don't know a good horse from a bad un," he said. "This horse is worth a hundred if I wait an' sell it to the Army feller. I think I'll do that." He turned from Andy and started toward the horse, swinging his quirt.

Andy waited. He remembered stories about how people bargain for horses. Maybe this was a bluff. Garland reached the horse, who immediately began to pull back on the reins. Garland spoke over his shoulder. "You want to make me an offer?"

"Thirty dollars," Andy said.

Garland laughed. "The Army man'll do better."

"The Army won't touch that horse," Andy said bitterly. "You've ruined his mouth. Anyway, I bet he's too small."

Garland turned and studied Andy for a long time. Andy stared back. He began to feel better. The man was uncertain. He wanted that money. And, by golly, the horse *was* too small for the Army. That was a lucky guess.

"I'll tell you what I'll do," Garland said, slowly. "I ain't got time to gentle this bronc. I'll give you him for fifty. An' that's my last offer."

"I'll give you forty," said Andy suddenly. "And that's *my* last offer."

"It ain't enough."

"It's all I've got," said Andy honestly. He got up and walked over to where Snippy was cropping the grass. He was doing the bluffing now. He felt Garland's gaze on his back. What if nothing happened? What if Garland just went back to beating the sorrel?

Andy stalled, tightened the girth on his saddle, and reknotted the latigo strap. Trying not to let Garland see the worry on his face, he put his foot in the stirrup and was about to swing into the saddle, when Garland spoke.

"How do I know you even got that much money?"

"Because it's right here in my hip pocket in traveler's checks," said Andy quickly. "I can turn them into cash at the post office any time I want."

Garland sucked on his tooth and scratched himself. "All right," he said finally. "It's a deal. Meet me at the post office in ten minutes." He unhitched the reins and swung into the saddle. The little horse, wild-eyed, its ears back, feeling a cuff on the side of its head, turned on a dime and broke into a dead run, the man slapping its flanks with the quirt.

Andy gazed after them in awe. "Gee," he thought. "That's my horse. *And can he run!*" Then he looked at little Snippy munching grass. "Holy cow, Snip," he said. "What'll Uncle Wes say when he finds out I bought a bronc?"

Returning to the post office, Andy cashed his checks, paid the money into Garland's hands, and in return received a dirty slip of paper stating that he had paid in full for "One sorrel gelding branded R Quarter Box on the right shoulder."

"There's your bronc," said Garland, pointing through a window. "I used your rope and tied him to the hitchin' rack." He folded the money into his pocket and disappeared through the doorway.

To Andy it seemed a simple matter to lead the little sorrel home, but the horse was still frightened. The moment Andy approached, he began to weave and spin at the end of the rope like a trout on a fishline.

Andy unhitched the lead rope from the rail and untied Snippy. Keeping the rope in his right hand, he started to mount the mare. His body, looming suddenly over the mare's back, scared the sorrel, who started backing off. Andy swung into the saddle as quickly as he could, paying out the lead rope as he did so. This seemed to excite Snippy, who began to prance and pivot on her tiny feet. The sorrel, running behind the mare's rump, twisted the rope around Andy's body. Desperately Andy hung on, afraid that, once he let go, the sorrel would get away for good. With both horses twisting and turning, Andy was soon so badly tangled in the lead rope, that there was danger he might suddenly be pulled from the saddle and dragged. He tried his best to unwind himself by turning Snippy, but the rope cut across his chest and hindered his hands.

In the middle of the excitement, a voice said, "Leave go, cowboy. I'll hold your bronc."

Andy let go the lead rope, turned—and blushed to the roots of his sandy hair. Standing behind him, holding the lead rope in his hand, was Uncle Wes's best friend, Tex Blackwell, the county sheriff.

Wes was the head game warden, and, whenever he and the sheriff met, there were long discussions concerning the condition of elk, bear, deer, and Big Horn sheep. No man in all Wyoming understood animals, wild or tame, better than Tex Blackwell, and there was no one Andy would rather have for a friend.

And now Tex had found Andy all balled up in rope, like a kitten with a ball of yarn. "Gosh, thanks!" Andy murmured, hoping the old man wouldn't laugh at him.

But Tex wasn't looking at Andy, he was watching the sorrel. He shook his head slowly. "You couldn'ta done that, Andy," he said. "Look at that mouth and jaw!"

"Gee, no!" Andy said, hastily. "I didn't do it, sir. I stopped somebody else from doing it."

Tex turned. He had what Andy thought was the most beautiful and luxuriant mustache in all the world, drooping around his mouth, and on his hip he carried a pearl-handled forty-five, the only one Andy had ever seen outside the movies.

"How, Andy?" asked the sheriff. "How'd you stop it?"

"I—I—" Andy felt sillier than ever. "I bought the horse," he blurted.

Tex gazed at him solemnly, with just the faintest twinkle in his eyes. "You got a bronc here," he said. "He's been spoiled. May never be no good. What'd you pay for him?"

"Forty dollars."

"Better give him back, Andy." The old man was trying to be kind. "He's too tough for you, boy. You've only been out here a month or two. Wes'll never let you ride him."

Andy felt a kind of lump in his throat. If Tex said so, it *was* so. He looked at the little horse, his sturdy legs spread wide, his ears cocked forward as if listening to them decide his fate. Give him back to that killer!

"Don't you think I could gentle him, Tex? I mean if I took lots of time?"

Tex smiled. "You sure love horses, don't you, Andy? But you ain't up to handling a bronc yet. You might get hurt bad. You

The sorrel twisted the rope around Andy's body.

better give him back. I'll fix it for you, an' you won't get in trouble with Wes. Who'd you buy him off?"

"A man named Garland."

The sheriff looked up quickly. "Randy Garland!" He started biting his lip and chewing on his mustache. Andy was surprised. He had never seen Tex show excitement about anything before.

"What's the matter, Tex?" he asked. "Have I done something terribly wrong?"

"You better tell me the story, Andy." The sheriff was deadly serious.

Andy's face fell. What had he done? He told the whole story carefully, leaving out nothing.

When he had finished, Tex spoke quietly. "Look, Andy," he said. "When you tell Wes about this, just forget Garland's name, if you can. An' whatever you do, don't tell how you got pushed around. Meantime, I'll see Garland and arrange for him to take the horse back."

"But, Tex—" Andy felt the lump swelling in his throat again.

"I don't like to spoil anybody's fun," Tex said, kindly. "But

I'm only savin' you trouble. A Garland horse ain't worth a plug of tobacco in this country, Andy. He spoils 'em. Most of 'em get sold for bear bait. Now here's your lead rope. Take the horse home. I'll see you in the morning."

Once they got started, the sorrel followed Snippy quietly, and for the first time Andy had a chance to think. He felt cornered, desperate. He couldn't bear to give the sorrel back. He had just naturally fallen in love with him. And he was in a worse jam than ever with his Uncle Wes!

He had made enough mistakes with Uncle Wes already, he thought. He had done foolish "dude tricks," like walking his horse through an irrigation dam and flooding the wrong field, and leaving the corral gate unhooked and letting the work horses wander out onto the front lawn.

Now he had spent all his money without permission to bring home a spoiled bronc. He wouldn't be allowed to ride it, and he didn't even have enough cash left to pay for its feed.

And what was all this about Randy Garland? Buying from him was evidently the worst mistake of all.

Andy rode along wondering whether he hadn't better wire his father that he was coming East immediately. "I bet Uncle Wes would be glad to get rid of me," he thought. "He works hard all the time and has enough troubles without me." Well, there was nothing to do but face it. Andy tried to screw up his courage.

But when he got to the ranch all he had to face was a big letdown. Unce Wes had taken his adopted daughter, Sally, and gone to a game wardens' meeting and would not be back until the following morning. Andy felt tired and discouraged. He ate his supper quickly and said nothing to his Aunt Ida concerning the new horse. She would find out soon enough!

After supper he went down to the corral. The sorrel was tied to the hayrack, eating contentedly. Andy got some salve from the saddle house. Speaking softly, he walked up to the horse and began rubbing his neck. The sorrel tossed his head, but he was over his fright, and Andy finally managed to smear some salve on the sides of the horse's mouth and on the bruised jaw. Then he turned the horse loose in the corral with little Snippy for company.

Andy climbed dejectedly to the top of the fence and sat watching the horses. Snippy munched hay steadily, her head completely out of sight in the rack, but every now and then the sorrel would stop eating and raise his head. His jaws would stop grinding and his ears point forward as though listening to some faint sound far away. Andy wondered if it was the mustang in him, the wild horse listening for a possible enemy.

Once, when he raised his head, a shaft of evening sunlight seemed to pick out the little horse on purpose, and his sorrel coat blazed as bright as a new penny.

"Gee," Andy thought. "If he was really mine! If I could only keep him! I'd call him Sunny."

Dusk rose from the valley like a curtain, crawling up the cliffs. Andy still sat on the fence dreaming, watching the horse, and thinking, "I'll never get to ride him."

Suddenly he sat up quickly, as though stuck with a pin. "Hey!" he said aloud. "Nobody's told me I couldn't ride him—not yet, anyway." Excitement filled him. "Suppose—suppose I *proved* I could handle him! Suppose I got up early before Uncle Wes got home—"

Andy let out a cowboy yip that echoed up the valley. Sunny pulled his head out of the rack and spun around inquiringly. "You wait!" Andy shook his finger at the horse. "We've got a date at sunrise."

Just before dawn on the next morning, a cold breath of wind blew off the snow glaciers and drifted down the valley of the South Fork. It sent shivers down Andy Marvin's spine as he closed the kitchen door softly and started for the saddle house. He dragged his saddle to the corral, turned Snippy into the cow corral, and closed the gate behind him. A sorrel head with a crooked little blaze peered at him from around the corner of the hayrack. Andy started speaking to him quietly. "Nobody's ever going to hit you again, old boy," he said.

As Andy approached, the sorrel snorted frosty vapor, then spun swiftly around the corral as close as he could get to the fence. He trotted high, as though on springs. He waggled his ears, shook his head, made ruffling noises with his nose. He felt just fine.

But Andy finally cornered him. He worked slowly. The horse was head-shy and tried to avoid the hackamore Andy was attempting to put over his ears so that no bit would be necessary. It took quite a while but finally it was on. Then came the blanket and the saddle. He dropped them on the pony's back gently, talking to him all the time. It seemed to Andy that the saddle didn't fit very well. It humped up on the back. But finally it was tightly cinched and the latigo tied securely.

The time had come! Andy felt a tautness in his stomach. His heart was pounding; his hands felt clammy. This was the moment—the one chance to prove he was man enough to ride his own horse. Sunny seemed to sense the excitement, too. He didn't move as Andy mounted. He just stood hunched a little, his front feet spread wide, his hind legs tucked under him. Andy got well seated, took a grip on the reins, and kicked gently with his heels.

Sunny's head dove between his legs. The legs themselves slammed straight and hard into the ground. Andy felt the horse explode. He thought he had been shot from a cannon. He grasped frantically for the saddle horn, but it was too late. Up, up he sailed. Then he hit the ground with a thudding, stunning bump. Pretty sparklers sputtered before his eyes and from a distance he heard a voice say, "Ride him, cowboy! Ride him!"

When his head cleared, he saw the pony in front of him, snorting with excitement. Leaning on the fence were two laughing men, Sheriff Blackwell and Uncle Wes. Behind them, her feet hanging from a wagon box, sat Sally Marvin.

"Doggone it," Andy grunted, spitting dust and climbing to his feet. He was angry—mad clear through. They were laughing at him and maybe at the horse, too. He reached the sorrel, climbed on him as fast as possible, and kicked with his heels again.

Up, up he sailed.

As the pony bucked, Andy gripped with his knees. Each jolt shook him, but he hung on grimly, sitting well back in the saddle and keeping his neck stiff. Gradually the jolting ceased, until finally the little horse lined out into a springy trot as easy to ride as a four-door sedan. Andy stayed with it until he was sure that he was in complete control. Then he pulled up in front of the two men.

"I guess Tex told you," he said, looking straight at Uncle Wes. "I—I bought him."

Much to his surprise he saw that Wes was smiling, a bigger, friendlier smile than he had ever seen on his uncle's face before. "Yes," he said, "and—and, by golly, you rode him!"

"You mean," Andy said, "you mean it's all right? I can ride him, and have him and gentle him?"

"You can try," said Uncle Wes.

"And it wouldn't surprise me none if you succeeded," added the sheriff with a grin.

FROM

Windy Foot at the County Fair

FRANCES FROST

When Toby Clark is given a pretty dapple-gray Shetland
pony on his twelfth birthday, he immediately starts dreaming about entering the pony race at the County Fair. All
summer, every day, he has been carefully training Windy
Foot. The pony is hardened and swift and sure. But on the
day before the race, Lem, an older boy and a bully, picks a
fight with Toby and leaves him with a terrific black shiner.
He is afraid that he may be disqualified. The eye does open,
however, and race day finds Toby's younger brother Johnny,
his sister Betsy, and even Tish Burnham who will be com-
peting with him on her own pony, all rooting for Toby to
win his first race.

The Pony Race

A PONY with a black mane was sitting on Toby's stomach.
He blinked at it and it was Johnny. "Wake up!" said Johnny, his
curly dark hair looking as if mice had slept in it. He bounced.

"Ouch!" said Toby. "Stop jouncing on where I'm hungry."

Johnny patted him. "Today's the day you've got to ride a
sword and buckle at your side. Wake up!"

"Oh, barnacles," said Toby. "This cot isn't big enough to tus-
sle on. Get off." He stood Johnny on the floor and sat up at the

same moment. He stretched and yawned and was suddenly wide awake. "It *is* Friday, isn't it?" He jumped out of bed, knocked Johnny over, picked him up and hugged him. "Did I hurt you? Didn't mean to."

"No," said Johnny. "But you didn't have to wake up that fast." He rubbed his impish face against Toby's. "When's the race?"

"This afternoon. Two-thirty. But I've got to get up to the stable. Thanks for sitting on me."

"Oh, that's all right," said Johnny, his arms around Toby's neck. "I'll do it again sometime."

"I don't doubt it," muttered Toby, putting him down. Betsy was still asleep with Matilda in her arms. "Don't wake her up," he told Johnny. "Get dressed yourself and come on up and talk to Windy."

Billy Blue let him exercise Appleseed with Johnny sitting on the blanket. When he took Windy Foot out, Billy said, "Take it easy this morning, Toby. Hold Windy in. Make him want to run, but don't let him. Then he'll run better this afternoon. Johnny, you want to help me?"

Johnny looked up. "Yes, sir. Can I learn how to ride horses in races?"

"Not right this minute," answered Billy Blue. "But you can learn how to take care of horses."

Johnny beamed. "I wish I could smoke a pipe like you," he said happily.

Billy Blue took his pipe out of his mouth and stared at it. "You've got to grow up first," he said. "Come on. I need help."

After breakfast, Toby went from one stable to another and made sketches of the horses. This was the last day of the Fair; he wouldn't see so many different kinds of horses again until next year. He tried to take his mind off the race by concentrating on the various characteristics of the horses, but somewhere inside him there was a hot ball of excitement. At noon he couldn't eat much and Dad advised him to lie down for half an hour.

At half-past one, Toby hurried up the road toward Burnham's

stable. He was wearing his light-blue slacks and shirt that he had been saving for the race, and his old sneakers that he had ridden Windy Foot in, all summer. The wind was warm, but he shivered.

He began to run. At the stable, Billy Blue was standing in the yard, his old pipe puffing like a stub chimney in his mouth and his safety pins gleaming on his pants leg.

"Kittens!" said Billy Blue, giving him an over-all survey. "I guessed right on my color scheme. Come on in, Toby."

Windy Foot was as clean as a whistle. His hoofs were polished. His dappled hide was spotless. And his heavy black mane and his heavy black tail were braided with narrow blue-and-white ribbons so that he looked like a pony out of a fairy tale. His forelock was tied up in a splash of ribbons and his tail was a wonder of blue and white fancy braiding. The black saddle and the black bridle had been rubbed until they held the deep gleam of excellent leather.

Toby couldn't believe his eyes. "Barnacles!" he said in a whisper.

"Barnacles, nothing," said Billy Blue. "Now you and Windy match by way of decoration, and the saddle matches those shiners you're wearing. You'd better get down to the gate and check in. The race starts at two-thirty."

"Yes, sir," answered Toby, still gazing at Windy Foot. "Mr. Blue, did you wind up Windy like this yourself?"

Billy Blue choked on his pipe smoke. "Got to do something to waste my time. Back him out! How do you think he's going to run a race standing in a stall?"

"Thanks, Mr. Blue!"

"Pshaw," said Billy Blue, looking out of the stable door.

Toby put his cheek against Windy's. "All right, boy, here we go!"

He backed the pony out of the stall, into the yard, and mounted him. "Thanks again, Mr. Blue." His voice croaked. Windy looked so beautiful that it made his throat ache.

"Oh, cats!" said Billy Blue loudly. "Stop talking and ride!"

At the checking place in the trampled field outside the track gate, Toby dismounted and held Windy's bridle, waiting his turn. His heart was acting like a hoptoad in his chest.

Ahead of him was the tow-headed boy he had seen exercising a brown pony. The boy wore tan shorts and a tan sport shirt; his hair gleamed almost white in the sunlight; and his pony wore a big yellow ribbon on her mane and another on her tail. The checker was gazing sternly at the boy's entry ticket. He nodded, filed it in a tin box, stood up and took an arm band from a pile on his table.

"All right, Jones. Stand still." With a safety pin, the man fastened the top of the white canvas band to Jones' left shoulder, then tied the bottom of the band around his arm with tapes. The large, black numeral on the band read 2. "That means you're in number two position from the inside rail," he explained. "You wait up the field there, where the Burnham girl is."

"Thank you," said Jones faintly and led his pony off.

Toby had a bad moment when he thought he had lost his entry ticket. The man watched while he dug in his pockets. He found it in his back pocket finally, tucked among the pages of his sketch pad.

"Whew!" he breathed thankfully and handed it to the checker.

"O.K., Clark," the man said and started to fasten an arm band on him. Then his hands dropped from Toby's shoulder. "Looks as if you've been in a little scrap. Can you see all right?" The man peered at him.

"Yes, sir," Toby gulped. "I can see!"

"How about that left eye?" asked the man severely.

"It's all right today." What if the man wouldn't let him ride? Toby's stomach hit his sneakers. "I can see first rate," he told the checker earnestly. "It just looks black."

"Black? Purple, you mean." The man hesitated for a moment. "Well, all right. I'll take your word for it." He finished fastening the arm band. "That must have been some fight." He smiled slightly. "Number three position from the inside rail."

"Oh, thanks!" Toby sighed with relief. He led Windy down the field as Lem Strout rode up to the checking point. Toby's heart did a back flip. Lem would be fourth, right next to him. He told himself fiercely that he wasn't afraid of Lem any more, and walked up to Tish and Jones.

"Hello, Toby." Tish wore white duck pants and a white linen shirt and had a white ribbon in her dark hair. Her arm band said 1. "How do you feel?"

She looked wonderful, he thought. He still wished he could do a portrait sketch of her. "Funny," he answered. "How do you?"

"Oh, fine," she said, smiling at him. "You won't feel funny when you get started."

He was skeptical. He patted Jigs. The heavy-footed black pony had green and gold ribbons wound in her mane and tail. "Did Billy Blue decorate Jigs, too?"

Tish looked at Windy. "He loves doing it. He's decorated my ponies every year. He had a boy of his own once who died when he was ten, and I guess Billy's thinking of him when he buys the ribbons and does all the braiding. Toby, do you know Dicky Jones? Dicky, this is Toby Clark."

Dicky's jutting jaw seemed more prominent than ever, but his blue eyes were frightened. "Hello," he murmured.

"Hello, Jones," said Toby and held out his hand. "This your first race?" He felt as scared as Jones looked, but he was older and couldn't show it. Well, maybe it would help Jones if he knew somebody else was scared, as well as he.

Jones nodded.

"Mine, too. I'm scared."

Jones' eyes lost some of their fright. "Are you? So am I."

Tish patted Jigs' side, not looking at the boys. "What are you scared about? All you have to do is ride."

Toby and Jones laughed nervously.

"Here comes Lem," said Tish.

Lem wore overalls, and his sorrel pony had pink and black ribbons twisted in his mane like the pink and black strips wound on the handles of the ten-cent whips in the whip-and-balloon stand. He gave Toby a baleful glare and led the sorrel away from the group.

"Oh, I forgot to tell you," said Tish, "your father invited Jerry and me down to your farm for Christmas, and Jerry said Yes."

"He did? Hooray!" Toby began to plan all the things they would do at Christmas—coasting and skiing and skating on Crooked River and popping corn and—

"Look at Jimmy!" said Tish.

Deep in thought, Jimmy came toward them with his head down. Tucked into his washed dungarees was a red-and-white plaid flannel shirt open at the throat. The pinto, Whistle Stop, wore simply a red-and-white saddle blanket.

"My gosh!" exclaimed Toby. "Where's his saddle?"

"He never uses one in a race. Didn't I tell you? Jimmy, wake up!" Tish was laughing.

Jimmy lifted his head in surprise. "Oh, hello." He nodded vaguely. "Isn't it nearly time to start?"

"Nearly," answered Tish. She didn't smile. "Jimmy. What are you worrying about?"

"Tractor," he answered briefly. "Oh, Toby. Hi."

"Hi," said Toby.

Here was Jimmy worrying about winning the race so he could put ten dollars toward his father's tractor, here was Tish wanting to put ten dollars toward medical college, here was Jones, wanting to win so he could—what? Toby didn't know what Jones wanted. And there was Lem Strout, wanting to win the race so he could help *his* father, probably. Well, but Dad and Windy Foot—

Jimmy interrupted his thinking. "Toby, your father spoke to my father this morning about Christmas. We'd like to, but we can't get down. We always have a lot of work planned to do during Christmas vacation—mending harness and carpenter work around the place. Thanks for asking us, though."

"I wish you could come, Jimmy."

"Here's the roan!" said Tish. "It's time!"

Toby quivered. He stroked Windy Foot's nose. "Here we go, boy," he murmured. Windy looked at him and shook his blue-

and-white plaited mane. Toby mounted him and laid an unsteady hand on the dappled neck. Windy whinnied. He wanted to start running. Toby held him in. "Easy, Windy, easy," he said and tried to stop trembling.

The young woman in the scarlet coat and the black derby hat rode up to the ponies. "All ready?" she asked with a smile.

"I guess we're all ready," Tish said, glancing around.

"I'll lead you up to the quarter-mile post," explained the young woman. "Get into position according to your numbers, starting with number one at the inside rail. When you have passed the finish post, all ponies return and line up in front of the judges' stand."

She turned the roan and Tish followed her. Dicky Jones rode after Tish. Toby walked Windy behind Jones, acutely conscious of Lem behind him on the sorrel. Jimmy and the pinto tagged the procession. The band was playing a loud, gay march and the trumpets flashed in the sun.

Toby bit his lips. He guessed he was more scared than Jones. His heart was thumping like a bass drum. He wanted to look at the grandstand and see if he could locate the family, but he knew it would be useless. Instead, he watched the young woman on the Kentucky roan and took his place at the starting post beside Jones. Jones was very pale. The poor kid, Toby thought.

He couldn't resist glancing at Lem. Lem was jerking at the sorrel's bit and muttering under his breath. Toby caught Jimmy's eye. Jimmy winked, then settled himself on Whistle Stop's red-and-white blanket. Toby tried to wink back and his shiners shut up. He opened them quickly again.

The roan pranced off around the track and out of the gate. The starter held a watch and a whistle. He was a stout red-faced man and he kept mopping his forehead with a blue bandanna. The band stopped playing with a flourish of drums. Toby's blood was roaring in his ears. The starter's whistle shrilled sharply. Toby gulped. Windy Foot shot forward.

The ponies ran together for a breath. Toby leaned forward on Windy's neck. "Excuse my dust!" he shouted.

For some crazy reason he wasn't scared now. He felt Windy gather speed and he gathered all of himself together and rode. A vast joy surged through him. He and Windy Foot had one heart and one mind.

He left Jones behind. The brown pony was slow. Then he was a neck ahead of Tish. Jimmy, crouched like an Indian on the pinto, was a shoulder's length ahead of Windy. But Lem was yelling beside him, coming closer to Windy, crowding him.

"Sissy!" screamed Lem.

Toby thought fast. If Lem pushed him over, he'd have to run into Tish and they'd both tangle with the fence, and Tish would be hurt. Clean rage swept him. They were nearing the turn.

"Tish!" he shouted at the top of his lungs. "Get ahead!" He pulled on Windy's reins, holding him up, falling behind, and Tish pounded past, rounding the turn. Then just as Lem was about to shove him into the fence, Toby yelled in Windy's ear, "Dust, Windy!" and pulled to the right.

Windy spurted forward, his hind quarters barely missing the nose of Lem's pony, and there was a crash behind him. A cry went up from the grandstand, but he couldn't look back. They were around the turn. Jigs began to lag, but Jimmy and Whistle Stop were streaking for the finish post.

Toby begged, "Dust, Windy!"

Windy dusted, and as they neared the finish post, Windy and Whistle Stop were nose and nose.

"Oh, dust!" Toby sobbed.

Windy flew past the post half a neck ahead of Whistle Stop.

Toby was panting and drenched with sweat. As he pulled his heaving pony up, he discovered that he was crying. He sniffled, heard Jimmy whistle to the pinto, and saw Whistle Stop come to a halt. He turned Windy, rubbed his arm across his wet face, and rode back, side by side with Jimmy, too breathless to speak. Tish and Jones followed. The grandstand was ominously silent.

Then Jimmy said, his voice hoarse with anger, "I saw what Lem tried to do. Look, Toby! He hit the fence himself."

Toby yelled, "Dust, Windy!" and the pinto spurted forward.

Toby looked. Lem's sorrel lay kicking at the fence. Lem was limping down the track toward the outside fence.

Toby put his hand on Windy's sweaty neck. Jimmy gently twisted Whistle Stop's mane. Tish leaned over Jigs' black neck and said something quietly to her. Jones patted the rump of his brown pony. Toby guessed they were all thinking the same thing: it might have been Windy Foot or Jigs or Whistle or the brown pony that was hurt.

Jimmy said quietly, "That'll disqualify Lem for next year."

"I guess he won't bother anyone in a race again," added Tish.

When the track was clear, one of the judges came down from the stand. Another, with a megaphone, announced loudly, "Ladies and gentlemen, we regret that this accident has delayed the awarding of the prize for the annual Webster County Fair Pony Race for ponies three years old or under. Will the owners of the ponies please dismount?" He waited until they were standing on the ground. "The prize of ten dollars for first place in the race goes this year to entry Number 3—Windy Foot, three-year-old Shetland, ridden by Tobias Clark, the young man with the shiners!"

Toby felt his face grow hot and his stomach did handsprings. He thought of Jimmy's tractor and of Tish's medical college. Then he thought of Dad's corn-cutter blade and the leaky milkhouse. The grandstand shouted and clapped.

The judge not in the stand walked up to Toby, said, "Good riding, Clark," and handed him an envelope. He shook hands, patted Windy, and returned to the stand.

Toby stared at the envelope.

Jimmy grinned at him. "What're you looking so glum about? It was a swell race!"

Tish smiled and her eyes were glowing. "Hooray for Windy!"

Toby began to feel better. "Come on, let's go," she said. "We're holding up the Fair."

Jones said timidly, "Congratulations!"

"Thanks, Jones," said Toby.

They led the ponies to the gate while the band played a lilting tune. Toby's heart lilted, too.

The judge handed him an envelope.

Well, he thought, the race was over, the Fair was over for him, and it had been wonderful. He had learned a great deal about people, and he had made four good friends—Tish and Jimmy and Mr. Burnham and Billy Blue. And he could even feel sorry for Lem. He put a finger on his left eye shiner. It was still pretty sore, but anyway he was glad he'd have some decorations to show Cliff when he got home. He could look forward to Christmas when Tish and her father would be visiting them. And next year he would enter some drawings of horses at the Fair's art exhibition.

He remembered the Roman candle feeling he'd had in his chest at the beginning of the Fair. But now, thinking of home, he felt as if he had a good warm sun glowing steadily where his heart should be.

Bucephalus, A King's Horse

ALICE C. GALL *and* FLEMING CREW

Say no more, Orestes. My mind is made up. The horse Bucephalus shall be sold."

It was on a summer day, more than two thousand years ago, that these words were spoken by Philonicus, a wealthy man of Thessaly in Greece. The two men, Philonicus the master and Orestes his slave, stood under a plane tree at one end of a green field in which a number of horses were pasturing. Around this field stretched on all sides the wide flat plains of Thessaly. And far to the north rose the lofty peaks of Mount Olympus, believed in those days to be the home of mighty gods who ruled the world.

Both master and slave were dressed in the long flowing robes of their time. But the master's robe was richly embroidered in silver, as were the sandals on his feet. About his thick brown hair he wore a band of purple. Philonicus was a man accustomed to being obeyed, and when he had spoken these words to Orestes he turned away.

But the slave put out a hand as though to detain him. "Master," he said earnestly, "there is not in all Greece another horse like Bucephalus."

"Well do I know that, Orestes," Philonicus answered. "And his new master shall pay a princely sum for him. I mean to sell him to King Philip of Macedon."

"King Philip of Macedon!" the slave repeated in amazement.

"None other," replied Philonicus. "King Philip knows horses.

His army rides into battle mounted on splendid chargers fit for the war-god Mars himself. And it is said that Philip of Macedon would rather lose six generals than one good horse of war. He will find use for Bucephalus."

"Master," Orestes pleaded, "you would not send Bucephalus into the cruel wars of Macedon? You know well how gentle has been his training. Never has he felt the sting of the lash. Surely, my master, you will not sell Bucephalus to King Philip."

"Such is my plan," Philonicus answered shortly, and a look of greed came into his eyes as he added, "King Philip's wars have brought him much wealth. His treasury is full. I mean to make him pay handsomely for Bucephalus." And without another word, Philonicus walked away.

After his master had gone, Orestes stood looking sadly off toward Olympus. If only some god would help him save Bucephalus, he thought. But the great mountain seemed very far away and he, Orestes, was a slave. He could expect little help from the gods.

Presently he whistled softly, a long clear note, and in a moment or two Bucephalus appeared at the edge of a grove of oak trees far across the field. Trotting over to where Orestes stood, the beautiful dark bay horse lowered his head so that the slave might stroke his nose and pull his silky ears. For a little while he stood so, scarcely moving at all, and then suddenly he thrust his muzzle forward, gave Orestes a playful shove, and was off down the field like the wind, his head high, his tail straight out behind him.

This was a favorite trick of his, and Orestes always expected it. But today the slave could not laugh; his heart was too heavy. From the time Bucephalus was a tiny colt Orestes had looked after him, feeding him and caring for him each day, and brushing his coat to keep it sleek and shining. It was Orestes who had put a bridle on him for the first time and taught him to carry a man on his back.

Bucephalus had not liked this. The bit hurt his tender mouth, and having a man on his back seemed a strange thing. But Orestes had been so kind and patient that soon the strangeness wore off, and Bucephalus no longer rebelled but gladly carried the slave, mile after mile, across the broad flat plains.

Thessaly is a fair land, and for Bucephalus life was pleasant. There was the wide green pasture with its soft grass and its grove of oak trees where the shade was welcome on hot afternoons. And there was a stream of cool water where he drank when he was thirsty and in whose quiet pools he stood, knee-deep, when the flies and insects annoyed him.

What would the life of Bucephalus be after this, Orestes wondered, as he watched the young horse galloping over the field. King Philip of Macedon was a powerful king, he knew, for the tales of wars and conquests had spread over all that part of the world. It was said that even now he was planning greater wars, that he longed to rule over a mighty empire, and dreamed of a day when all Greece should be his.

And now because Philonicus was greedy for gold, and King Philip of Macedon was greedy for power, Bucephalus was to have a new master!

On a morning late that summer King Philip of Macedon and his son Alexander, a lad of sixteen years, were walking through the palace gardens. They were on their way to the parade grounds to inspect the soldiers at their morning drill. But they had gone only a little way when they were met by a guardsman who saluted and stood at attention.

"Have you a message?" King Philip asked.

"Yes, Sire," the guardsman answered. "A stranger from Thessaly would see you."

"What is his errand?"

"Sire, he would sell you a horse," the guardsman said.

"A horse!" King Philip thundered. "And you come to me with such a thing! Do you take me for a stableboy? This is an affair for some petty groom. If the horse is sound, let him be bought."

"This horse is a good one, Sire," the guardsman replied, "but the price is very high and the officers who are charged with such matters feared your displeasure."

"We have gold to purchase what we need," the King told him sharply. "Go, tell my men to use their wits."

"The price the stranger asks is thirteen talents, Sire."

King Philip looked at the guardsman in amazement. "Thirteen talents!" he exclaimed. "Why, such a price would scarce be paid for twenty horses! Dismiss the man at once. Tell him King Philip is no fool."

The guardsman saluted again and turned to go, but the boy Alexander called to him. "Wait, Simonides," he said. "The stranger comes from Thessaly, did you say?"

"From Thessaly," replied the guardsman.

"It is a land of splendid horses," Alexander said. "Let us have a look at him, Father. Who knows? He may excel all horses in your stables even as you excel all other men in Macedon."

King Philip looked down at his son and laughed. "Yours is a sound head, my son," he said, laying his hand on the boy's shoulder. "Your words are well spoken. We shall see this stranger and his horse."

"Have this man of Thessaly bring his horse to the west riding field," the King told the guardsman. "And have the trainers from my stables there, to put the animal through its paces."

When King Philip and young Alexander reached the riding field, they found a number of the King's trainers already awaiting them.

"Where is this stranger from Thessaly and his horse?" the King asked impatiently.

"The Thessalonian comes yonder, Sire," said one of the men, pointing toward the stables, "but the horse is being fed a measure of oats by the Thessalonian's slave."

King Philip laughed aloud. "What say you to that, Alexander?" he exclaimed. "A king must stand waiting while a slave feeds a horse!"

The boy Alexander made no answer, for just then the Thessalonian, accompanied by a guardsman, came and knelt before the King.

"Rise, man of Thessaly," King Philip bade him. "Your land of Greece, beyond Olympus, is not unknown to me. I have seen its beautiful cities, its splendid temples, and its wide, fertile plains. A fine land it is. But tell me," he broke off, "what of this horse which now eats his measure of oats in my stables? I would know about him, for if he be worth but half the price you ask he must still be a wondrous horse."

"You shall see for yourself, O King," Philonicus replied. "He is a mount the gods might envy you. I am asking thirteen talents for him, but were he yours you would not part with him for many times that sum."

"Do you hear that, Alexander?" the King asked, turning to his son. "What think you of the Thessalonian's words?"

"Why think of them at all, Father?" the boy replied. "The horse himself will speak a truer tale than many words. See! Here he comes!"

From the stables across the riding field came the horse, with the slave Orestes on his back. Alexander grasped his father's arm excitedly and the two of them stood looking in admiration. "He is indeed a splendid creature," exclaimed the King at last.

Bucephalus was quivering with nervousness. These were strange surroundings to him. Strange voices were all about him and he had eaten his oats in a strange stable, with men he did not know staring at him. He would have been badly frightened now if Orestes had not spoken to him encouragingly and patted his back.

"Look, Father," said Alexander. "Do you note the fine, slender legs, the long body, and the narrow, well-shaped head?"

"Aye," his father answered, and then turning to Philonicus he said, "You shall have your thirteen talents, unless my trainers find some hidden flaw in him."

Two of the trainers stepped forward and grasped the bridle, one on each side, while Orestes dismounted. He stood for a moment with his hand on the horse's neck. "A good friend you have been, Bucephalus," he muttered. "May the gods send just punishment on any man who dares mistreat you!" Then with a quick look at the two trainers, the slave went over and stood quietly at his master's side.

"Get on his back and put him through his paces," the King ordered one of his trainers.

But this was easier said than done. For when the trainer made ready to mount, Bucephalus jerked his head angrily and strained at his bit. The strength of the two trainers was barely enough to hold him. Suddenly he reared straight up on his hind legs, almost pulling the two men off their feet.

"Easy, Bucephalus! Easy, good horse!" called Orestes, and leaving his master's side the slave hurried forward. "I will quiet him," he said to the trainers.

"Stay where you are, slave!" King Philip ordered, sharply. "I must learn this horse's temper before I send him to my stables." Addressing his trainers, he commanded that Bucephalus be mounted without further delay.

But King Philip's trainers, expert horsemen though they were, were not equal to this task. Bucephalus lunged and reared, kicking and biting at them if they so much as spoke to him. At last the King waved his hand in a gesture of disgust. "Take him away!" he cried angrily. "This horse is mad and altogether worthless. Turn him back to the slave. I would not give stable room to such a beast!"

The boy Alexander, who had watched these proceedings with flushed face and flashing eye, now stepped quickly forward. "Wait!" he called, and with a scornful look at the two trainers he said in a loud, clear voice so that all might hear, "What an excellent horse they lose for want of address and boldness to manage him! Shame upon them! Shame!"

King Philip turned sharply on his son. "Do you reproach those who are older than yourself," he said, "as if you knew more and were better able to manage the horse than they?"

Alexander answered boldly, "I could manage him better than the others do."

"And if you do not," said his father, "what will you forfeit for your rashness?"

Suddenly he reared straight up on his hind legs.

Alexander did not hesitate. "I will pay," he answered, "the whole price of the horse."

In spite of his annoyance the King could not help laughing at the boy's bravado. And the company joined in the laugh.

But Alexander went swiftly to the horse's head, and motioning the trainers away he took the reins in his own hands. At once he turned Bucephalus about so that he was facing the sun, for he had noticed that the horse was shying nervously at his shadow on the ground. Then, stroking the sleek neck, Alexander talked to Bucephalus gently.

Little by little the horse grew quiet. There was something in the touch of the boy's hand, something in the sound of his voice, that gave Bucephalus confidence. He knew that here was someone he could trust.

With a quick leap Alexander was on the horse's back. Bucephalus threw his head up sharply and quivered with surprise. But his fear was gone. He pawed the ground, eager to be running free over the plain with this boy on his back.

And now Alexander spoke a word of command. Instantly Bucephalus bounded away and the boy did not try to stop him. Giving him his head he urged him to even greater speed. The King and his company looked on aghast, fearing that at any moment Alexander might be thrown to his death. But Orestes the slave smiled. "The lad has fine judgment with horses," he said. "Bucephalus is in good hands."

At last the horse slackened his pace and Alexander, turning him about, came back to the riding field, his face beaming with triumph. King Philip of Macedon was more proud at this moment than he had ever been before. This boy of sixteen was destined to conquer. The gods were with him!

Scarcely waiting for Alexander to dismount, he threw his arms about the boy's neck and kissed him. "My son," he cried, "look you out a kingdom equal to and worthy of yourself! Macedon is too small for you!"

Alexander spoke and Bucephalus bounded away.

Little did King Philip think at the time how soon these words would come true.

As the days went by Bucephalus grew to love the boy Alexander more and more. Eagerly he looked forward to those times when he could run wild and free across the soft turf, the boy upon his back. This was what Bucephalus liked and it was what the boy liked. They understood each other, these two. They were friends.

But when four short years were gone, Alexander was no longer a carefree boy. He was a king. For King Philip was dead, leaving his dream of empire unfinished. His son Alexander must finish it for him. The young King's boyhood days were now over; he must turn to war and conquest. It was a hard task but he was ready.

One day there gathered on the parade ground a company of horsemen. They were no ordinary horsemen, for they had shields and long sharp spears that glistened in the sunshine. These were fighting men.

A mighty cheer was lifted as young King Alexander approached, mounted on his splendid horse Bucephalus. The fighting men lifted their spears in salute, and a moment later King Alexander and his army were on their way. Off they rode—to conquer a world.

Into far lands these Macedonians went. And always there was fighting and still more fighting. War! It was like a black cloud hiding the face of the sun. The world was turned into a world of hate, and men forgot to be kind. There were years of hardship, suffering, and bloodshed, but still Alexander's army marched on, conquering all before it.

King Philip's dream had come true, for Alexander was indeed the mightiest ruler in the world. His fame had reached into every land, and wherever men talked of heroic deeds the names of the young King and his splendid horse were heard together. Alexander the Great and Bucephalus!

At first the horse had been frightened by the din of battle. The clang of weapons, the shouting of the soldiers, and the roaring and plunging of other horses around him had filled him with

He grew accustomed to the tumult of war.

terror. But there was always the touch of his master's hand to
quiet him, the sound of his master's voice to urge him on, and
at last he grew accustomed to the tumult of war.

Through years of bitter fighting Bucephalus served his master
well, carrying him triumphantly through battle after battle. And
with each victory the ambition of King Alexander increased. With
each new conquest that he made there came to him dreams of
still greater conquest. He must go on and on, he told his men,
until the whole world belonged to him.

But it takes a long time to conquer a world, and the life of a
war horse is hard. There came a day when Bucephalus could no
longer go into battle. He was growing old.

Alexander was forced to leave him in camp far behind the
fighting lines. Here the faithful horse was well cared for. Each
day the King came and talked to him, and Bucephalus would
lower his head so that his master might stroke his nose and pull
his silky ears. And sometimes he would thrust his muzzle for-

ward and give King Alexander a playful shove, as he had done long ago with Orestes the slave in Thessaly.

Back in Thessaly the horse Bucephalus was not forgotten. Tales were told of the days when he was a colt and carried Orestes over the wide Thessalonian plains. The same flat plains still stretched away, and majestic Olympus, to the north, still raised its cloud-veiled summit. The years that had come and gone had brought little change to Thessaly.

"Orestes," said Philonicus one spring day, as again master and slave stood at the end of the green pasture, "do you remember the horse I sold for thirteen talents to King Philip of Macedon?"

"Yes, master," answered Orestes. "I shall not forget Bucephalus."

"Who would have dreamed," went on Philonicus, "that one day he would become the most famous horse in all the world? He is now almost as famous as the great Alexander himself."

"Bucephalus was always a good horse, master," Orestes said simply.

"Aye, a good horse," Philonicus repeated, turning away. "And thirteen talents was a good price, too. A handsome price, Orestes."

For a time the slave stood silent, and then walking slowly he went through the green pasture toward the little grove of trees. Midway of the field he paused and looked off at Mount Olympus. "A handsome price indeed," he said softly. "But if you had been mine, Bucephalus, not all the gold in Macedon could have bought you."

FROM
Kentucky Derby Winner

ISABEL McLENNAN McMEEKIN

*Big Jack Spratt and his grandson little Jack Spratt are as alike
as the same sandy hair, blue eyes, identical straw hats and
their talk and love of horses can make them. Except that
Gramper has a full beard while Jackie is eleven years old.
Jackie's special passion is for Risty (Aristides), a gallant
little red horse, and he is cast into despair when the colt cuts
his foot in the trial race. It heals in a few days, however,
and then there isn't a happier boy anywhere. For Risty is
slated to run in the first Kentucky Derby. The author tells
us that this is a true story. If you go to Churchill Downs,
you will find painted over the entrance the name "Aristides"
—the first winner of the great Kentucky Derby.*

Fortune Frowns

THERE was a great big calendar in the barn office and each
Saturday morning the children crossed off seven more days with
a stump of red chalk.

They put a circle around May 17th, which was the day the
Derby was to be run, and another circle, a smaller one, around
May 12th, when Risty was entered in a race on the Lexington
track. They'd get to see this one too, they knew, and were looking forward to it eagerly, bein' as how it was the first time they'd
ever get to see him stretch his legs.

At last the squares were filled up with red crosses and it was the morning of May twelfth, the calendar said.

Seemed like every last body on the home-place aimed to go to that race in Lexington. Farm wagons that hadn't been used for years on end were all gathered up and filled with straw bedding to comfortable them. Every laborer and tenant on the farm was there, dressed in his go-to-meetin' clothes. Only those who had chosen double pay as watchkeepers were left behind.

Such a like of scrubbed babies and combed-up runabouts and calicoed housewives and blue-jeaned men hadn't been seen together since the big barbecue, Jackie thought . . .

And thinking about that barbecue made him call to mind Whispery Joe and wonder where he was these days—wonder if word had got to him by the grapevine about Risty's good luck in winning those races last fall when he was a two-year-old.

Jackie, as he sat in the carryall now, waiting for Ma to bonnet herself, tried to put from his mind the remembering he had that Joe had said in that fortune Risty wasn't always going to have such good luck, that some small evil was to befall him. Surely that evil was the time he'd been stolen by Tom and Joe's own father. Surely the fortune had meant that, hadn't it? It *must* have, he decided cheerfully as Ma came down the steps in her poplin dress and bonnet with the yellow daisies on it that spoke so pretty to her red hair.

On the drive into Lexington the countryside was at its loveliest. The season had been a late one and the redbud and dogwood were still in bloom while lilacs nodded and bowed in the spring breeze from every passing farmyard.

The town itself was all a-bustle with the usual excitement of a racing day. "More crowded even than on Court Day," Gramper remarked with satisfaction, as they threaded their way through the tangle of buggies and wagons and took the road to the track.

Jackie scarce had room for a bite of the good picnic lunch of fried chicken and dressed eggs which Ma had packed up in a bushel basket for them to share with the Andersons in the free infield which centered the track. Even the chocolate cake and raspberry tart which Mrs. Anderson contributed failed to spark his eyes as they had always done before.

He was in an agony of impatience till he could get through dinner and traipse back to the barns to join Gramper and Pa and Mister Andy and see the set-up for the afternoon's events.

Risty was to be in the third race and seemed like time for it would never come, Jackie thought, as he hung around the paddock pestering the men in charge with his questions and his offers of help.

He wished mighty much as he stood there watching Bill give Risty his final rub-down under Andy's critical eye, that Mister Welch had already given Risty that namesake-blanket he had promised him so long ago. But Mister Mack said Mister Welch had written he'd bring the blanket down with him when he came this week—he had a special wish for Risty to wear it first at next Saturday's bigger and more important occasion, he'd said.

The first race was already over and the second being run now, but Jackie didn't even know that till he heard the shouts of the crowd, cheering the winner.

All he could see and think about this minute was that Mister Andy was giving final riding instructions to Oliver Lewis, while Blue Jay stood there at his brother's side, grinning peacock-proud.

Mrs. Andy hadn't let Polly come over here to the paddock with the boys, saying, no call for a girl getting on toward her teens to hear all the rough man-talk that went on around the barns. Therefore, Polly was sulking as she stayed with the other petticoats in the infield where Jackie and others would join her in a moment to get first and closest view of what Jackie knew was going to be Risty's victory.

And Risty most certainly *looked* like a victor, Jackie thought for the hundredth-and-some-odd time as he ran his hand over the shining chestnut coat, squinted admiringly at the nervous, keen-pricked ears, and said, "Good luck, feller!" to Oliver who was now being given a leg up by Mister Andy.

The thrill of the bugle call came. "Boots and Saddles!" The clarion notes seemed to sound a challenge to the half-dozen thoroughbreds who, led by their stableboys, followed the lead pony onto the track.

Jackie and Blue Jay had managed to cross the track before the first shrill of the bugle came, and they took their places beside Polly as they had promised. Her sulks were forgotten now and she was all a-tip-toe with delight, tossing her golden curls back over her shoulders and clutching the white-washed rail as tightly as the boys.

"They're off!" The cry followed the roll of the drum.

Jackie saw Risty's first gallant leap.

And then, with unbelieving eyes, he saw him falter and *stumble*. Oliver was pulling him in as the field swept on ahead!

Oliver was pulling him in!

In that awful moment of stillness, Jackie heard only Gramper's voice. "He's struck hisself. Hind foot cut the front fetlock . . . Steady, Jackie, steady, Boy. That ain't so bad. Wait, now, an' see!" . . .

Gramper was right, they all told Jackie, when the race was over and they were in the barn again and the horse-doctor had examined the cut.

It wasn't much to worry about, he said cheerfully. They were lucky. They were very lucky an artery hadn't been cut. Then they would have had to use a tourniquet. It didn't look like this would be apt to swell or heat up much. It was a small clean wound, he said. They were to keep it wet with cold pads and then apply his special Opedelso Salve he'd leave with them. He'd made a neat fortune on that stuff, he said, as he bustled out to see to another horse which had bowed a tendon in the fourth race.

Gramper tried to comfort Jackie. He said that other horse might never again be able to set foot to track but that, like as not, Risty would be fine as brass buttons this time next week.

Jackie brushed the tears out of his eyes and flung an arm against Risty's flank. Chief thing *he* cared about was that Risty was in pain now! The grownups' main concern, seemed like, was whether or not he'd be able to run in the big race next Saturday. Why, how they could so much as even *talk* about that, he didn't rightly know, when Risty's fetlock was still bleeding, the bright fresh blood staining the golden straw.

Jackie leaned down to sop it with his handkerchief and Mister Andy spoke to him sharply, "*We're* taking care of this, young man. *You* tend to your own affairs!"

Jackie said, "Yes, sir," hurt and a little scared by that unaccustomed tone.

Gramper put his hand on Jackie's shoulder, saying, "Son, Risty's goin' to be all right now. You let the men doctor him as knows how. You run on back to Ma. She'll be a-waitin' for you to go home with her. The afternoon's about over now."

"I'm not goin' home, Gramper," Jackie said quietly. "I'm goin' to spend the night here."

Gramper said, "Why, Jackie!"

And Pa said, "Son, get goin'!" in an I-mean-it tone.

Jackie said, "Please, Pa!" and his voice would have touched a heart of stone—which John Spratt's most certainly was not.

"Well," he conceded, "if Gramper'll stay here with you, I'll try to fix it up with your Ma. I've got to get on home. There's a heap of things crying to be done this very night."

Jackie, big boy that he was, caught his father about the waist and gave him a bear-hug. Pa looked right flustered and said, "Get busy choring here in the barn, or they won't let you stay. Have to earn your keep." He pointed to a line of water-pails and Jackie, with a last look to see that Risty seemed comfortable enough now, trotted off to the water trough.

That evening, after they'd supped with the hands out of the big iron kettle down in the corner of the barn lot, far enough away from the stables for there to be no threat of fire, Jackie and Gramper bedded themselves down just outside Risty's stall. Mister Andy and Bill and all the others had gone on back to the home-place knowing that Risty was in safe-keeping while Gramper was on the job.

Mister Mack himself had looked the horse over and seemed satisfied with the care he was getting. He was mighty disappointed about the accident, he said, but would be more so if he didn't have another string to his bow, in Chesapeake, for the Derby next week. He'd planned for the two to be running-mates but was bound, one way or another, for his colors to be shown on that new track.

Gramper agreed that the bay would do him proud, like as not, but still thought there was a chance of Risty making a comeback in time to be in the running, too.

Mister Mack said he'd make a wish for it on that new moon and told them good-night.

Jackie and Gramper curled up again near Risty's stall where they could hear his every movement. For a long time the two lay there talking in the darkness. That good smell of timothy and sweet clover tickled their nostrils and the other and more earthy stable smells too were not unpleasant to them.

There were a dozen horses in the big race-barn and their soft breathing and gentle snuffling made a peaceful lullaby. Jackie drifted off to sleep presently.

Seemed to him like he hadn't been asleep hardly a minute when he wakened to find Gramper gone from beside him. In an instant he was up and calling out softly.

"Here, Son, in Risty's stall," Gramper answered.

Jackie knew from the worry-tone in Gramper's voice that things weren't like they ought to be. He went, quiet as he could, into the stall and squatted up close against Gramper. There was a shaft of moonlight in the stall and he could see that Gramper was running a gentle hand over Risty's swollen fetlock.

"It's a mite filled up," Gramper said, "an' it feels right throbby to me. I'm goin' to do what I think best." He was turning Risty's head now, leading him out of the stall and down along the alleyway past the sleeping horses.

Jackie followed him with a hand on Risty's flank.

Risty was limping some but not so very much.

Gramper paused to have a word with the watchman at the barn door. "His leg's puffy, an' runnin' water's the best thing that ever was for that."

The man nodded and said, "Moon's bright. You can see your way all right, I guess."

"Sure. Us three's got cat-eyes." Gramper picked their steps carefully now, the straw-covered ground giving no sound to their feet.

In a moment or two they reached the brook. Gramper pulled off his boots and rolled up his pants legs to his knees, motioning Jackie to do the same.

He and Risty were standing in the water now, with the cooling swirl of the streamlet circling their legs. They stayed there for what seemed to Jackie like an awful long time. He leaned up against Risty's flank and most dropped off to sleep again.

Then Gramper said, "That's enough, Young Spratt. We'll take him back now, an' this time I aim to use some of my 'brocation on his leg. That hoss-doctor can have *his* long-soundin' salve. We'll jest see what *mine* does, afore now an' mornin'!"

"You think it'll help, don't you, Gramper? Honest Injun, you think Risty's leg'll be better by mornin'? If it worsened—if he got real sick an' died—Gramper, you don't think Risty *could* die, do you?"

"He could," Gramper said, "an' sometime he *will*. But I'll give my bond it won't be now—or anytime real soon, Jack Spratt!"

Fortune Smiles

To add to the excitement of the big race there was that ride on the steam-cars and the glimpse of the big city of Louisville. After it there was the two-hour ride on the mule car out to the track, and the way those children's tongues did wag the whole endurin' time was a caution, the grownups said.

Already, though it was still early in the morning, a big crowd was gathering. By midday there were more folks there than any of them had ever seen together in all their lives, Gramper said. He guessed there must be ten thousand, or would be, before the afternoon was over, and the others all agreed with him.

They trooped in through the free gate into the infield and settled themselves, real comfortable, on the grass. Polly's little sister was sleeping just as snug as if she'd been home in her own trundle bed, and Mrs. Andy took pride in that.

Mister Andy gave a knowing look at the track and said it would be fast. He didn't doubt but what the horse that won the Derby might set up a new mark for the mile and a half, he remarked as he gave them a good-by nod and headed for the barns. Jackie and Blue Jay begged to go with him but he said, no, they couldn't do that, only trainers who could show their badges would be let in today.

A man standing near Gramper said, "I hear several of the horses entered in the big race won't be starters. That so?"

Gramper nodded. "So they tell me," he said, studying the card. "War Call an' Playmate an' some the others fell out for one reason or another."

"I'm from New Orleans," the man said. "Ascension's our pick—an' after that, Vagabond."

"I say McCreery, an' I know!" another man insisted.

John Spratt shook his head. "I think you're wrong; Mister Mc-Creery's just getting over distemper. His chance ain't too good today."

"Ten Broeck's a fine-lookin' colt," the man's wife said. "His trainer told me he was goin' to win."

"Sure, Bess." Her husband chuckled. "That's what all the trainers say. Every last one of 'em."

Bess pouted as she turned to Gramper. "You got a card, ole man, read us out the names of them as is goin' to start."

Gramper said, "Always glad to be obligin', Missus," and read: "Verdigris, McCreery, Enlister, Warsaw, Searcher, Ten Broeck, Chesapeake, Aristides, Bill Bruce, Bob Wooley, Vagabond, Volcano, Ascension, Gold Mine and General Buford's Baywood Colt."

"Thirteen colts an' two fillies," the man commented glancing at the program in Gramper's hand.

"That's right, Mister," Gramper said as he turned to Jackie, suggesting that he and Polly and Blue Jay go see if they couldn't find themselves some four-leaf clovers for luck. He'd noticed a likely-looking patch, he said, right over there in the field.

The children scampered off at once, each choosing a plot. Jackie, to his great satisfaction, found a four-leaf right off.

"Good for you!" A boy who looked to be about a year or two older than himself, spoke to him. This boy, standing on the seat of one of the wagons, had been watching the search with interest. He had a nice friendly smile, Jackie thought. And he had a mighty good place to watch the race, too.

Jackie said, "I aim to put it in my shoe. I want my luck for Risty—Aristides, I mean."

The other boy said, "But Chesapeake's going to win. *Everybody* says he is!"

"Most folks think so," Jackie acknowledged, "but *I* don't. I think Risty's goin' to win, for *sure*."

The boy said, "Do tell, now!" and asked Jackie his name. Jackie told him and said, "What's yours?"

"Matt J. Winn," the boy answered, and added, "this is the first race I ever saw, but I aim to see all the other Derbies from now on for the next hundred years."

Jackie said he aimed to do that very same thing and the two shook hands on it, very solemnly.

Jackie went on back to his own group then and showed them all the four-leaf clover. Both Polly and Blue Jay had found some, too, but theirs weren't as big as Jackie's.

They ate their lunch now and Ma urged them all to stretch out and try to catch a little shut-eye, but Jackie said, "I ain't a bit sleepy, Ma," and then, for about the dozenth time asked Gramper how much longer it would be.

Gramper pulled his big silver turnip-watch out of his pocket and said, "Another hour, Young Spratt," and Jackie sighed.

Pa remarked that Andy'd told him Mister Mack had given orders for Chesapeake to stay back till the others had set the pace. When they reached the turn for home, he was to charge up and gallop away from them. Mister Mack had said he believed Chesapeake had that first Kentucky Derby in the bag, Pa told them.

Polly said, "I'm with Jackie. I *used* to think Peaky was the greatest horse in the world. He's so big and strong. But there's *something* about Risty. . . ."

Jackie looked at her gratefully and thought again that, for a girl, Polly was pretty nice, after all. They were stretched out on the grass now and Ma said for them all to shut their peepers. Jackie tried to, but his wouldn't stay shut.

Blue Jay gave him a little nudge and pointed to the crowd over yonder by the grandstand. Jackie sat up and looked where he was pointing and he saw Whispery Joe. He nodded mutely to Blue Jay and the two of them got up, real quiet-like, and tip-toed away from the others, who all had their eyes closed. They crossed the track and sneaked under the fence.

As they neared the grandstand they dodged under people's elbows and squirmed like little chipmunks through the pack of folks. They were beside Whispery now and he was smiling down at them.

Joe looked mighty grand, Jackie thought, in his checkered suit with a scarlet neckerchief around his throat and his peaked cap with a wild rose stuck in it. Beside him stood Em'ly in a yellow satin dress, all bustled out at the back in the latest fashion.

Whispery said, "And now, it's proud indeed I am, to see my two young friends and to know that they'll be witnessing the coming-true of that fortune I told for the little red horse. That mile and a half will be but a bit of bittock to Aristides. I say so and I am an Irish Traveller who knows more about horses than any other man in all the world."

"I sez Chesapeake! He's goin' to win, for sure!" a nearby man shouted wrathfully.

Someone in the crowd laughed then and Joe said, "Do you want to make something of it, my friend? I am also the world's greatest rassler and will allow you to taste the dust with much pleasure."

Em'ly said, "Come now, Joe, no fightin'. We don't want to end up in the jail-house!" and pulled him away. Jackie was right sorry, for he would have dearly loved to see Whispery make that man eat the dust.

He and Blue Jay wandered on over to the booths under the grandstand where fried chicken and crispy fish and country ham were being sold.

"Come buy! Come buy! Come buy!" The cheerful shout came from half-a-hundred throats and eager customers pushed up close, flinging down their two-bit pieces and snatching goodies off the loaded trays.

Jackie didn't have any money but Blue Jay had a pocketful of coppers and treated him to a sack of taffy. Everywhere the jolly venders were busy at their set-up stands cracking jokes and urging folks to sample their tasty wares.

Jackie and Blue Jay thought today was the mostest fun of any day in all their lives. They just stood there watching that crowd and time slipped by mighty fast. When at last they wiggled their way through the mob the first race was already being run and they missed seeing it.

Somebody shouted that Bonaventure had won the dash of a mile-and-a-quarter and they joined in with all the cheering.

When they finally got back to the infield Ma had a scolding word for them but they were too excited to hear it. Pa had already gone to sit with Colonel Lewis Clark in his box as he had been invited to do. Jackie could see him way over there, sitting up tall and proud beside Colonel Clark and Mister Mack and Mister Welch. He could squint up his eyes and see their tall white beaver hats shining in the sun. A group of pretty ladies with parasols and silken frocks was in the box, too, but Jackie scarcely noticed them though he heard Ma make some remark about fine feathers making fine birds.

The bugle was sounding now, playing "Boots and Saddles" like it had when they'd seen the Phoenix Hotel Stakes in Lexington. But this time it sounded even happier and more beauti-

ful. It sounded like an angel trump, Jackie thought, although he wasn't quite sure what that might be.

The fifteen thoroughbreds were dancing out onto the track in single file. Jackie's eyes saw just *one* horse—and that horse was Risty. His chestnut coat was gleaming and he was tossing his head and picking his way daintily onto the oval, following the scarlet-coated boy on the lead-pony.

The horses were parading now, passing the Ladies' Enclosure and the Judge's Stand, stepping off the long distance to the far-stretch for the start. Jackie's eyes glanced for a moment at the other contenders. Blue and white silks, that was Verdigris. Red with a white sash and red and white cap, that must be McCreery, Gramper said, studying the program. That next one was the filly, Gold Mine. Her boy wore green with a red cap.

Peaky *did* look fine, Jackie had to admit. He was bigger than Risty and much more powerfully made. He'd won that big race

He scrambled up a fence post and could see fine.

in Lexington not so long ago and shown some mighty fast form in his training.

Even from here Jackie could see how bright and gay the Mc-Grath colors looked. The jockeys, Oliver Lewis and Bobby Swin, both wore green coats and orange belts which showed up well against the dazzling blue sky and the brown earth of the track. Jackie couldn't really see Risty's fine red velvet saddle pad but he knew it was there, and that gave him a good feel in his heart. As the horses neared the post, that heart of Jackie's beat faster and faster. He squinted up his eyes trying to see what was happening way over there. He stood tip-toe, holding his breath.

A gentleman, Colonel Johnson from Nashville, somebody said he was, stood out there in the middle of the track with a flag which he would drop when the horses were all lined up and ready for the go-signal.

Seemed like it was mighty hard to get them all quiet at once.

A man near them had a spy-glass held up to his eye. He said it was Bob Wooley who was cutting up now. A minute ago it had been Searcher, or maybe Vagabond. It was hard to tell t'other from which, he said.

Jackie could see there was a boy with a drum standing up close to Colonel Johnson. Gramper said they were to give both signals, the flag and the drum-beat, to make sure.

Now was the moment. Now! Now! Now!

The rat-tat-tat of the drum came on the instant that the flag fell. The two figures leaped aside as the horses sprang forward.

For an instant Jackie couldn't see and then he scrambled up on a fence post and *could* see fine. Volcano was ahead, then Verdigris, but close behind *him* was Risty. That green and orange *was* Risty. Surely it was. It had to be!

The others were bunched and Chesapeake was back among them. Well, that was like they said Mister Mack wanted it. Risty and the others were just setting the pace for him.

They had covered the first half mile and Peaky was still in the ruck. Risty was moving up—moving into second place!

They were driving into the stretch.

Jackie smiled at Gramper and Gramper nodded. The horses were in the backstretch now and, as they reached the mile Risty lapped Volcano. Now he was in front of him! He was in the lead! He surely was!

But Volcano was pounding after him. Maybe he'd reach him. Maybe he'd *pass* him!

Jackie couldn't keep his eyes on those two rushing horses a single second more. He raised them to that box over there. He saw Mister Mack wave to Oliver and knew that meant, "Go on, Boy! Go on!"

Jackie saw Oliver give a little nod then, as he loosed his pull on Risty's bridle. It was too late now for Chesapeake to make his stretch run. Verdigris seemed safe for third place. McCreery was tiring. So was Searcher. So were all the others.

The crowd was roaring now, "Volcano!" . . . "Aristides!" . . . "Come on! Come on!"

They were driving into the stretch, only a quarter mile from home.

Volcano had gained a little now. He was making his last gallant challenge. But Risty was thundering on ahead, Jackie saw.

He was winning, winning, winning!

He had *won!*

Jackie and nine thousand, nine hundred and ninety-nine other folks split their throats with shouting. The others were all shouting, "Aristides!" But Young Spratt was shouting, "Risty! Risty! Risty! *My* Risty!"

FROM

The Magnificent Barb

DANA FARALLA

Kevin Fitzgerald rode his mount with great dignity. Actually it was a mule. But he always pretended it was some splendid steed, like the Godolphin Barb, a famous 18th century racing stallion. Kevin had seen a picture of the Barb, a magnificent dark bay standing 15 hands high, every inch full of beauty and grace and strength. What intrigued him most was that the Barb had a magical foot. The left hind foot was a dazzling white, a sure sign of the noblest of steeds. Then one day as the Irish horse traders come riding into town, Kevin spies a huge dark bay stallion—with the magical one white foot! The horse looks terribly thin and abused. But the boy recognizes in him the spirit of the Magnificent Barb and proves it when his owner, Taig M'Dunnagh, lets him ride the Srigo, as the traders call him. Now Kevin is trying to persuade his father, Ivor, to buy the horse for him.

Horse Trading

IN ALL the excitement the Barb was quite overlooked by everyone. But finally Kevin inveigled Ivor to come out to the stable yard.

"Would ye be callin' it a horse?" Ivor said in amusement. "Sure an' it's thin enough to be the wraith o' the Banshee herself."

His curiosity was piqued, nevertheless, and he surveyed the Barb with the trained eye of the veterinarian. His comments were terse and brusque, "Half starved. Galls. Capped elbow. The traders must ha' got him in the dark o' night. What do they aim to do with him? He wouldn't last a week in the fields. He's all used up."

"He's not meant for the fields."

"No, that he isn't. The collar and harness have well nigh killed him—body and spirit. A case like this ought to be punished as a crime."

"We'll never let him wear a collar again," Kevin said earnestly. "We have the jennet and the mule for the fields. The Barb takes to the saddle and bridle as though he were born with them."

"We've no means to buy him, Kevin," said Ivor kindly but firmly. "And even if we did, we're not making a mistake again. Ziki was enough."

"But we wouldn't be making a mistake," persisted Kevin. "Look at his head. Look at his shoulders and the sloping pasterns."

"I've looked. He's well set-up, but he's on his last leg. He's all tuckered out."

"When I ride him he comes alive. And if he had plenty of care and food and rest—"

"I can't buy a horse to hospitalize him," Ivor interrupted.

Kevin's eyes were dark with desperation. The Barb seemed to sense the boy's dejection and nuzzled his cheek.

"I see ye ha' set your heart on him, and if the traders are looking for a rest home for him, I'll gladly let the creature stay," Ivor offered in compromise. "But I can't buy him. Ye ought to know that without the asking. And it's nothing I ha' to trade, except Derry, an' her only for a horse that is sound and well."

"Lusmore already tried to trade Derry," said Kevin disconsolately. "The traders wouldn't have her."

"So that's what he's been up to this morning!"

"I thought you knew. I thought it was going to be a surprise. I thought that was why you kept me home digging up yams."

"Sure an' I'd like to ha' given ye a surprise, but that I couldn't," said Ivor uncomfortably. "'Tis sorry I am to disap-

"*I can't buy a horse to hospitalize him.*"

point ye, but some day ye'll ha' a yearling all your own. 'Tis better that way."

Kevin made no reply. Ivor's vague promise was small comfort. It was the Barb he wanted and no other. He had, he reasoned, not asked for too much. He had not asked for Fleet Foot or any of the other thoroughbreds in the Rand Stables. He had asked only for a horse that no one else wanted—a horse that had been misused, neglected, starved.

"I'll put some ointment on those galls," Ivor said, "and when you ride him back to the traders, tell them that I'd like permission to treat the capped elbow tomorrow morning—if they haven't sold the horse by then." He realized that he had said the wrong thing and added quickly, "They'll not sell him so soon, lad. 'Tis no bargain they offer."

"Taig M'Dunnagh said there is a buyer for every horse. He said the Barb would be sold before sundown tonight."

"That's traders' talk," said Ivor mildly.

"Taig said he'd lay odds that the Barb would be stabled at the Rand plantation."

"If John Rand buys him it will be only out o' kindness to the horse. He'd ha' no use for the creature. What does he say on it? He's seen the horse."

"We didn't talk about the Barb. We just talked about Orin and the piebald."

"I'll wager that Taig M'Dunnagh never spoke to him about the horse. He'd be insulting him if he did."

Involuntarily Kevin winced, and then resentment flared within him. But he knew that it was useless to tell his father about the magical white foot. Ivor had no belief in the Barb's potentialities. Ivor would have to see the horse sound and well before he put any credence in the efficacy of a magical foot.

"I don't mean to belittle the horse, Kevin," Ivor said awkwardly. "But he's in a sorry state, and Taig M'Dunnagh would ha' to be right handy with the blarney if he was to sell him to John Rand. 'Tis impressed I am that John Rand is no fool."

Kevin's resentment against his father had already abated, for he knew that if Ivor had the means he would buy the Barb just to assure him of a good home. He regretted his own inadequacy to transmit his belief in the horse so that it would be intelligible and convincing. It was easier for him to communicate his ideas and feelings to Lusmore, but even Lusmore had not been able to share entirely this dream. If he had, he would be there with him now defending the Barb. There was still resentment in him —not against his father but against material want. Here was a barrier against which his own will had no force. Again he was painfully conscious of the apathy and decadence that characterized Mare's Nest.

As though to preclude the sense of futility that threatened to overwhelm him, Kevin edged close to the Barb, stroking the forehead and shoulders, drawing strength and comfort in proximity. And while hope of possession was no longer strong within him, he was still alert to the joy of the present moment. All the negations of Mare's Nest could not entirely dissipate his sense of wonder in the realization that only yesterday morning the Magnificent Barb had been incorporeal, a creature of his imagination, and now he was here with him in the stable yard, warm and alive, nuzzling his cheek.

So, when he rode the Barb back to the traders' camp, he lagged behind John Rand's carriage. He wanted to prolong his joy. But when the Barb's hooves touched the road beyond Mare's Nest, Kevin was aware of a change in the horse. The Barb no longer moved as though inspired or eager. It was as though he were dead, spiritless. It was not physical exhaustion. The Barb seemed to know that this was their last ride together. And though Kevin had heretofore been able to transmit much of his buoyant optimism and exuberance to the Barb, there was no evidence now that the horse sensed his rider's wish for happiness. It seemed that it was the Barb who had power to project an emotion, for Kevin's brief joy was soon supplanted by dejection. He was bewildered and alarmed, for he had no strength or desire to struggle against this alien sadness.

Half way to the camp Niall M'Dunnagh met them on horseback. John Rand stopped the carriage, and when Niall was assured that Orin was all right he rode alongside Kevin. He and several of the traders had been searching for Orin; the piebald had been seen streaking down the road long before Ezekiel had come with the news that Orin was being taken to Mare's Nest.

At the camp Taig M'Dunnagh met them. He walked unsteadily, leaning on his hickory cane for support. He was neither erect nor assured now. It was obvious that Orin was his favorite grandchild, and he had been harassed with fears.

Orin, though pale-faced, was animated with a sense of importance. She was a heroine. Her accident would be the talk of the camp for days. She laughed when Taig embraced her and said mischievously, "Now I'll have to borrow your cane."

"Not before I have paddled ye with it," Taig replied.

Taig thanked John Rand, as Niall had done, with dignity. But John assured Taig that it was the Fitzgeralds to whom he owed gratitude—to Kevin for his good judgment and to Ivor for his skill in treating the fracture. The traders were conversant with the quarrel between Taig and Lusmore that morning, and they knew that Taig would be embarrassed to be under obligation to the Fitzgeralds. They watched Taig's reaction closely. His expression was one of imperturbability.

"'Tis a smart lad ye are, makin' business for Doc Fitzgerald," Taig said to Kevin dryly. "Ye think he's like the label on the bottle that reads: 'Good for man an' beast.'" He glanced approvingly at the expertly bandaged foot and said seriously, "The foot looks well set-up, an' 'tis grateful I am to you an' your father. How much is it we be owin' ye?"

"Nothing," said Kevin. "Nothing at all. Orin's my friend."

"I'll not be takin' advantage o' friendship," said Taig slowly. "A man does his work, an' pay he should get."

"My father said I was to ask nothing," said Kevin, dismounting from the Barb. "He's a veterinarian, not a regular doctor." Then he added defensively, "But he's better than most doctors."

"There's a loyal son," said John Rand smiling.

"Aye," said Taig. He looked thoughtfully at Kevin who was reluctantly beginning to unsaddle the Barb. Slyly Taig jabbed his hickory cane at Kevin's ribs so that the boy turned around.

"There's no need for ye to unsaddle the *Srigo*, lad."

"No?"

Taig nodded, and Kevin was about to hand the reins to Niall M'Dunnagh, when Taig said, "Ye don't want to walk the *tober* back to Mare's Nest, do ye? 'Tis a long road."

"He's welcome to ride back with me in the carriage," said John Rand.

"With all thanks to ye," said Taig, "I think the lad would rather ride the *Srigo*."

Taig looked at Kevin for confirmation, and Kevin stammered, "Yes, I would, only—well, Orin said you were leaving in the morning and—"

"Aye?" There was challenge and question in Taig's voice.

"I told myself there be a partnership—horse an' lad."

"Well, you see—" Kevin paused, and then he blurted out, "I've already said good-by to the *Srigo*. I'm not going to do it again."

" 'Tis no room ye ha' for him?" said Taig slyly. "I heard tell there be stalls for twenty at Mare's Nest."

Kevin stared at Taig incredulously, and then comprehension came like a radiant light.

"Do you mean he's mine?"

"Aye, lad. The *Srigo* is yours. An' 'tis not because your father ha' put right a bone in Orin's ankle. No, lad. From the day ye set eyes on the *Srigo* I told myself there be a partnership— horse an' lad. I'd ha' given him to ye yesterday, I was that tempted, but I thought to test ye a bit like a farrier who heats the metal for the shoe an' then bends it an' shapes it a bit. Ye ha' fight, lad. Ye don't give up easily. An' so 'tis with the *Srigo*. There be spirit in him yet, an' ye had the heart to see it."

And Kevin knew that it was Taig M'Dunnagh alone who had understood the magic of the white foot.

" 'Tis ye who must tell him there's life in him—an' often, so that he never forgets."

"Yes," said Kevin solemnly. "I'll never let him forget."

He felt tears trickle down his cheek, but he was not ashamed of them, and he did not raise his arm to wipe them off with his sleeve, for he saw that there was glistening in Taig's eyes something like tears too.

FROM

The Pacing Mustang

ERNEST THOMPSON SETON

*The story of this magnificent mustang is, like all of Seton's
stories, based on his keen observations of real animals. This
famous stallion lived out West in the early 90's in the Cur-
rumpaw region, not far from another one of Seton's famous
animals, Lobo the Wolf. The author says that the Pacer
"lived the life I have depicted and showed the stamp of her-
oism and personality more strongly by far than it has been
in the power of my pen to tell." But you will find that the
Pacing Mustang does emerge here with one of the most
powerful personalities in all horse stories.*

Jo Calone threw down his saddle on the dusty ground,
turned his horses loose, and went clanking into the ranchhouse.

"Nigh about chuck time?" he asked.

"Seventeen minutes," said the cook glancing at the Water-
bury, with the air of a train-starter, though this show of preci-
sion had never yet been justified by events.

"How's things on the Perico?" said Jo's pard.

"Hotter'n hinges," said Jo. "Cattle seem O.K.; lots of calves."

"I seen that bunch o' mustangs that waters at Antelope
Springs; couple o' colts along; one little dark one, a fair dandy;
a born pacer. I run them a mile or two, and he led the bunch,

an' never broke his pace. Cut loose, an' pushed them jest for fun, an' darned if I could make him break."

"You didn't have no reefreshments along?" said Scarth, incredulously.

"That's all right, Scarth. You had to crawl on our last bet, an' you'll get another chance soon as you're man enough."

"Chuck," shouted the cook, and the subject was dropped. Next day the scene of the roundup was changed, and the mustangs were forgotten.

A year later the same corner of New Mexico was worked over by the roundup, and again the mustang bunch was seen. The dark colt was now a black yearling, with thin, clean legs and glossy flanks; and more than one of the boys saw with his own eyes this oddity—the mustang was a born pacer.

Jo was along, and the idea now struck him that the colt was worth having. To an Easterner this thought may not seem startling or original, but in the West, where an unbroken horse is worth $5, and where an ordinary saddlehorse is worth $15 or $20, the idea of a wild mustang being desirable property does not occur to the average cowboy, for mustangs are hard to catch, and when caught are merely wild animal prisoners, perfectly useless and untamable to the last. Not a few of the cattle-owners make a point of shooting all mustangs at sight, for they are not only useless cumberers of the feeding-grounds, but commonly lead away domestic horses, which soon take to the wild life and are thenceforth lost.

"I run them a mile or two."

Wild Jo Calone knew a 'bronk right down to subsoil.' "I never seen a white that wasn't soft, nor a chestnut that wasn't nervous, nor a bay that wasn't good if broke right, nor a black that wasn't hard as nails, an' full of the old Harry. All a black bronk wants is claws to be wus'n Daniel's hull outfit of lions."

Since then a mustang is worthless vermin, and a black mustang ten times worse than worthless, Jo's pard 'didn't see no sense in Jo's wantin' to corral the yearling,' as he now seemed intent on doing. But Jo got no chance to try that year.

He was only a cow-puncher on $25 a month, and tied to hours. Like most of the boys, he always looked forward to having a ranch and an outfit of his own. His brand, the hogpen, of sinister suggestion, was already registered at Santa Fé, but of horned stock it was borne by a single old cow, so as to give him a legal right to put his brand on any maverick (or unbranded animal) he might chance to find.

Yet each fall, when paid off, Jo could not resist the temptation to go to town with the boys and have a good time 'while the stuff held out.' So that his property consisted of little more than his saddle, his bed, and his old cow. He kept on hoping to make a strike that would leave him well fixed with a fair start, and when the thought came that the Black Mustang was his mascot, he only needed a chance to 'make the try.'

The roundup circled down to the Canadian River, and back in the fall by the Don Carlos Hills, and Jo saw no more of the Pacer, though he heard of him from many quarters, for the colt, now a vigorous, young horse, rising three, was beginning to be talked of.

Antelope Springs is in the middle of a great level plain. When the water is high it spreads into a small lake with a belt of sedge around it; when it is low there is a wide flat of black mud, glistening white with alkali in places, and the spring a water-hole in the middle. It has no flow or outlet and yet is fairly good water, the only drinking-place for many miles.

This flat, or prairie as it would be called farther north, was the favorite feeding-ground of the Black Stallion, but it was also the pasture of many herds of range horses and cattle. Chiefly interested was the 'L cross F' outfit. Foster, the manager and part owner, was a man of enterprise. He believed it would pay to handle a better class of cattle and horses on the range, and one of his ventures was ten half-blooded mares, tall, clean-limbed, deer-eyed creatures, that made the scrub cow-ponies look like pitiful starvelings of some degenerate and quite different species.

One of these was kept stabled for use, but the nine, after the weaning of their colts, managed to get away and wandered off on the range.

A horse has a fine instinct for the road to the best feed, and the nine mares drifted, of course, to the prairie of Antelope Springs, twenty miles to the southward. And when, later that summer Foster went to round them up, he found the nine indeed, but with them and guarding them with an air of more than mere comradeship was a coal-black stallion, prancing around and rounding up the bunch like an expert, his jet-black coat a vivid contrast to the golden hides of his harem.

The mares were gentle, and would have been easily driven homeward but for a new and unexpected thing. The Black Stallion became greatly aroused. He seemed to inspire them too with his wildness, and flying this way and that way drove the whole band at full gallop where he would. Away they went, and the little cow-ponies that carried the men were easily left behind.

This was maddening, and both men at last drew their guns and sought a chance to drop that 'blasted stallion.' But no chance came that was not 9 to 1 of dropping one of the mares. A long day of manœuvring made no change. The Pacer, for it was he, kept his family together and disappeared among the southern sandhills. The cattlemen on their jaded ponies set out for home with the poor satisfaction of vowing vengeance for their failure on the superb cause of it.

One of the most aggravating parts of it was that one or two experiences like this would surely make the mares as wild as the mustang, and there seemed to be no way of saving them from it.

Scientists differ on the power of beauty and prowess to attract female admiration among the lower animals, but whether it is admiration or the prowess itself, it is certain that a wild animal of uncommon gifts soon wins a large following from the harems of his rivals. And the great Black Horse, with his inky mane and tail and his green-lighted eyes, ranged through all that region and added to his following from many bands till not less than a score of mares were in his 'bunch.' Most were merely humble cow-ponies turned out to range, but the nine great mares were there, a striking group by themselves. According to all reports, this bunch was always kept rounded up and guarded with such energy and jealousy that a mare, once in it, was a lost animal so far as man was concerned, and the ranchmen realized soon that they had gotten on the range a mustang that was doing them more harm than all other sources of loss put together.

II

It was December, 1893. I was new in the country, and was setting out from the ranchhouse on the Piñavetitos, to go with a wagon to the Canadian River. As I was leaving, Foster finished his remark by: "And if you get a chance to draw a bead on that accursed mustang, don't fail to drop him in his tracks."

This was the first I had heard of him, and as I rode along I gathered from Burns, my guide, the history that has been given. I was full of curiosity to see the famous three-year-old, and was not a little disappointed on the second day when we came to the prairie on Antelope Springs and saw no sign of the Pacer or his band.

But on the next day, as we crossed the Alamosa Arroyo, and were rising to the rolling prairie again, Jack Burns, who was riding on ahead, suddenly dropped flat on the neck of his horse, and swung back to me in the wagon, saying:

"Get out your rifle, here's that—stallion."

I seized my rifle, and hurried forward to a view over the prairie ridge. In the hollow below was a band of horses, and there at one end was the Great Black Mustang. He had heard some sound of our approach, and was not unsuspicious of danger. There he stood with head and tail erect, and nostrils wide, an image of horse perfection and beauty, as noble an animal as ever ranged the plains, and the mere notion of turning that magnificent creature into a mass of carrion was horrible. In spite of Jack's exhortation to 'shoot quick,' I delayed, and threw open the breach, whereupon he, always hot and hasty, swore at my slowness, growled, "Gi' me that gun," and as he seized it I turned the muzzle up, and *accidentally* the gun went off.

Instantly the herd below was all alarm, the great black leader snorted and neighed and dashed about. And the mares bunched, and away all went in a rumble of hoofs, and a cloud of dust.

The Stallion careered now on this side, now on that, and kept his eye on all and led and drove them far away. As long as I could see I watched, and never once did he break his pace.

Jack made Western remarks about me and my gun, as well as that mustang, but I rejoiced in the Pacer's strength and beauty, and not for all the mares in the bunch would I have harmed his glossy hide.

As he seized it, I turned the muzzle up.

III

There are several ways of capturing wild horses. One is by creasing—that is, grazing the animal's nape with a rifle-ball so that he is stunned long enough for hobbling.

"Yes! I seen about a hundred necks broke trying it, but I never seen a mustang creased yet," was Wild Jo's critical remark.

Sometimes, if the shape of the country abets it, the herd can be driven into a corral; sometimes with extra fine mounts they can be run down, but by far the commonest way, paradoxical as it may seem, is to *walk* them down.

The fame of the Stallion that never was known to gallop was spreading. Extraordinary stories were told of his gait, his speed, and his wind, and when old Montgomery of the 'triangle-bar' outfit came out plump at Well's Hotel in Clayton, and in presence of witnesses said he'd give one thousand dollars cash for him safe in a box-car, providing the stories were true, a dozen young cow-punchers were eager to cut loose and win the purse, as soon as present engagements were up. But Wild Jo had had his eye on this very deal for quite a while; there was no time to lose, so ignoring present contracts he rustled all night to raise the necessary equipment for the game.

By straining his already overstrained credit, and taxing the already overtaxed generosity of his friends, he got together an expedition consisting of twenty good saddle-horses, a mess-wagon, and a fortnight's stuff for three men—himself, his 'pard,' Charley, and the cook.

Then they set out from Clayton, with the avowed intention of walking down the wonderfully swift wild horse. The third day they arrived at Antelope Springs, and as it was about noon they were not surprised to see the black Pacer marching down to drink with all his band behind him. Jo kept out of sight until the wild horses each and all had drunk their fill, for a thirsty animal always travels better than one laden with water.

"The great black leader snorted and neighed and dashed about. And the mares bunched, and away all went in a rumble of hoofs, and a cloud of dust."

—The Pacing Mustang

Jo then rode quietly forward. The Pacer took alarm at half a mile, and led his band away out of sight on the soapweed mesa to the southeast. Jo followed at a gallop till he once more sighted them, then came back and instructed the cook, who was also teamster, to make for Alamosa Arroyo in the south. Then away to the southeast he went after the mustangs. After a mile or two he once more sighted them, and walked his horse quietly till so near that they again took alarm and circled away to the south. An hour's trot, not on the trail, but cutting across to where they ought to go, brought Jo again in close sight. Again he walked quietly toward the herd, and again there was the alarm and flight. And so they passed the afternoon, but circled ever more and more to the south, so that when the sun was low they were, as Jo had expected, not far from Alamosa Arroyo. The band was again close at hand, and Jo, after starting them off, rode to the wagon, while his pard, who had been taking it easy, took up the slow chase on a fresh horse.

After supper the wagon moved on to the upper ford of the Alamosa, as arranged, and there camped for the night.

Meanwhile, Charley followed the herd. They had not run so far as at first, for their pursuer made no sign of attack, and they were getting used to his company. They were more easily found, as the shadows fell, on account of a snow-white mare that was in the bunch. A young moon in the sky now gave some help, and relying on his horse to choose the path, Charley kept him quietly walking after the herd, represented by that ghost-white mare, till they were lost in the night. He then got off, unsaddled and picketed his horse, and in his blanket quickly went to sleep.

At the first streak of dawn he was up, and within a short half-mile, thanks to the snowy mare, he found the band. At his approach, the shrill neigh of the Pacer bugled his troop in a flying squad. But on the first mesa they stopped, and faced about to see what this persistent follower was, and what he wanted. For a moment or so they stood against the sky to gaze, and then deciding that he knew him as well as he wished to, that black meteor flung his mane on the wind, and led off at his tireless, even swing, while the mares came streaming after.

Away they went, circling now to the west, and after several repetitions of this same play, flying, following, and overtaking, and flying again, they passed, near noon, the old Apache lookout, Buffalo Bluff. And here, on watch, was Jo. A long thin column of smoke told Charley to come to camp, and with a flashing pocket-mirror he made response.

Jo, freshly mounted, rode across, and again took up the chase, and back came Charley to camp to eat and rest, and then move on up stream.

All that day Jo followed, and managed, when it was needed, that the herd should keep the great circle, of which the wagon cut a small chord. At sundown he came to Verde Crossing, and there was Charley with a fresh horse and food, and Jo went on in the same calm, dogged way. All the evening he followed, and far into the night, for the wild herd was now getting somewhat used to the presence of the harmless strangers, and were more easily followed; moreover, they were tiring out with perpetual traveling. They were no longer in the good grass country, they were not grain-fed like the horses on their track, and above all, the slight but continuous nervous tension was surely telling. It spoiled their appetites, but made them very thirsty. They were allowed, and as far as possible encouraged, to drink deeply at every chance. The effect of large quantities of water on a running animal is well known; it tends to stiffen the limbs and spoil the wind. Jo carefully guarded his own horse against such excess, and both he and his horse were fresh when they camped that night on the trail of the jaded mustangs.

At dawn he found them easily close at hand, and though they ran at first they did not go far before they dropped into a walk. The battle seemed nearly won now, for the chief difficulty in the 'walk-down' is to keep track of the herd the first two or three days when they are fresh.

All that morning Jo kept in sight, generally in close sight, of the band. About ten o'clock, Charley relieved him near José

Peak and that day the mustangs walked only a quarter of a mile ahead with much less spirit than the day before and circled now more north again. At night Charley was supplied with a fresh horse and followed as before.

Next day the mustangs walked with heads held low, and in spite of the efforts of the Black Pacer at times they were less than a hundred yards ahead of their pursuer.

The fourth and fifth days passed the same way, and now the herd was nearly back to Antelope Springs. So far all had come out as expected. The chase had been in a great circle with the wagon following a lesser circle. The wild herd was back to its starting-point, worn out; and the hunters were back, fresh and on fresh horses. The herd was kept from drinking till late in the afternoon and then driven to the Springs to swell themselves with a perfect water gorge. Now was the chance for the skilful ropers on the grain-fed horses to close in, for the sudden heavy drink was ruination, almost paralysis, of wind and limb, and it would be easy to rope and hobble them one by one.

There was only one weak spot in the programme, the Black Stallion, the cause of the hunt, seemed made of iron, that cease- less swinging pace seemed as swift and vigorous now as on the morning when the chase began. Up and down he went rounding up the herd and urging them on by voice and example to escape. But they were played out. The old white mare that had been such help in sighting them at night, had dropped out hours ago dead beat. The half-bloods seemed to be losing all fear of the horsemen, the band was clearly in Jo's power. But the one who was the prize of all the hunt seemed just as far as ever out of reach.

Here was a puzzle. Jo's comrades knew him well and would not have been surprised to see him in a sudden rage attempt to shoot the Stallion down. But Jo had no such mind. During that long week of following he had watched the horse all day at speed and never once had he seen him gallop.

The horseman's adoration of a noble horse had grown and

grown, till now he would as soon have thought of shooting his best mount as firing on that splendid beast.

Joe even asked himself whether he would take the handsome sum that was offered for the prize. Such an animal would be a fortune in himself to sire a race of pacers for the track.

But the prize was still at large—the time had come to finish up the hunt. Jo's finest mount was caught. She was a mare of Eastern blood, but raised on the plains. She never would have come into Jo's possession but for a curious weakness. The loco is a poisonous weed that grows in these regions. Most stock will not touch it; but sometimes an animal tries it and becomes addicted to it. It acts somewhat like morphine, but the animal, though sane for long intervals, has always a passion for the herb and finally dies mad. A beast with the craze is said to be locoed. And Jo's best mount had a wild gleam in her eye that to an expert told the tale.

But she was swift and strong and Jo chose her for the grand finish of the chase. It would have been an easy matter now to rope the mares, but was no longer necessary. They could be separated from their black leader and driven home to the corral. But that leader still had the look of untamed strength. Jo, rejoicing in a worthy foe, went bounding forth to try the odds. The lasso was flung on the ground and trailed to take out every kink, and gathered as he rode into neatest coils across his left palm. Then putting on the spur the first time in that chase he rode straight for the Stallion a quarter of a mile beyond. Away he went, and away went Jo, each at his best, while the fagged-out mares scattered right and left and let them pass. Straight across the open plain the fresh horse went at its hardest gallop, and the Stallion, leading off, still kept his start and kept his famous swing.

It was incredible, and Jo put on more spur and shouted to his horse, which fairly flew, but shortened up the space between by not a single inch. For the Black One whirled across the flat and up and passed a soapweed mesa and down across a sandy treacherous plain, then over a grassy stretch where prairie dogs barked, then hid below, and on came Jo, but there to see, could he be-

lieve his eyes, the Stallion's start grown longer still, and Jo began
to curse his luck, and urge and spur his horse until the poor uncertain brute got into such a state of nervous fright, her eyes
began to roll, she wildly shook her head from side to side, no
longer picked her ground—a badger-hole received her foot and
down she went, and Jo went flying to the earth. Though badly
bruised, he gained his feet, and tried to mount his crazy beast.
But she, poor brute, was done for—her off foreleg hung loose.

There was but one thing to do. Jo loosed the cinch, put Lightfoot out of pain, and carried back the saddle to the camp. While
the Pacer steamed away till lost to view.

This was not quite defeat, for all the mares were manageable
now, and Jo and Charley drove them carefully to the 'L cross F'
corral and claimed a good reward. But Jo was more than ever
bound to own the Stallion. He had seen what stuff he was made
of, he prized him more and more, and only sought to strike some
better plan to catch him.

IV

The cook on that trip was Bates—Mr. Thomas Bates, he called
himself at the post-office where he regularly went for the letters
and remittance which never came. Old Tom Turkeytrack, the
boys called him, from his cattle-brand, which he said was on record at Denver, and which, according to his story, was also borne
by countless beef and saddle stock on the plains of the unknown
North.

When asked to join the trip as a partner, Bates made some
sarcastic remarks about horses not fetching $12 a dozen, which
had been literally true within the year, and he preferred to go on
a very meagre salary. But no one who once saw the Pacer going
had failed to catch the craze. Turkeytrack experienced the usual
change of heart. He now wanted to own that mustang. How this
was to be brought about he did not clearly see till one day there
called at the ranch that had 'secured his services,' as he put it,

one Bill Smith, more usually known as Horseshoe Billy, from his cattle-brand. While the excellent fresh beef and bread and the vile coffee, dried peaches and molasses were being consumed, he of the horseshoe remarked, in tones which percolated through a huge stop-gap of bread:

"Wall, I seen that thar Pacer to-day, nigh enough to put a plait in his tail."

"What, you didn't shoot?"

"No, but I come mighty near it."

"Don't you be led into no sich foolishness," said a 'double-bar H' cow-puncher at the other end of the table. "I calc'late that maverick 'ill carry my brand before the moon changes."

"You'll have to be pretty spry or you'll find a 'triangle dot' on his weather side when you get there."

"Where did you run acrost him?"

"Wall, it was like this; I was riding the flat by Antelope Springs and I sees a lump on the dry mud inside the rush belt. I knowed I never seen that before, so rides up, thinking it might be some of our stock, an' seen it was a horse lying plumb flat. The wind was blowing like—from him to me, so I rides up close and seen it was the Pacer, dead as a mackerel. Still, he didn't look swelled or cut, and there wa'n't no smell, an' I didn't know what to think till I seen his ear twitch off a fly and then I knowed he was sleeping. I gits down me rope and coils it, and seen it was old and pretty shaky in spots, and me saddle a single cinch, an' me pony about 700 again a 1,200 lbs. stallion, an' I sez to meself, sez I: ''Tain't no use, I'll only break me cinch and git throwed an' lose me saddle.' So I hits the saddle-horn a crack with the hondu, and I wish't you'd a seen that mustang. He lept six foot in the air an' landed on all fours and snorted like he was shunting cars. His eyes fairly bugged out an' he lighted out lickety split for California, and he orter be there about now if he kep' on like he started—and I swear he never made a break the hull trip."

The story was not quite so consecutive as given here. It was much punctuated by present engrossments, and from first to last was more or less infiltrated through the necessaries of life, for

Bill was a healthy young man without a trace of false shame. But the account was complete and everyone believed it, for Billy was known to be reliable. Of all those who heard, old Turkey-track talked the least and probably thought the most, for it gave him a new idea.

During his after-dinner pipe he studied it out and deciding that he could not go it alone, he took Horseshoe Billy into his council and the result was a partnership in a new venture to capture the Pacer; that is, the $5,000 that was now said to be the offer for him safe in a box-car.

Antelope Springs was still the usual watering-place of the Pacer. The water being low left a broad belt of dry black mud between the sedge and the spring. At two places this belt was broken by a well-marked trail made by the animals coming to drink. Horses and wild animals usually kept to these trails, though the horned cattle had no hesitation in taking a short cut through the sedge.

In the most used of these trails the two men set to work with shovels and digged a pit 15 feet long, 6 feet wide and 7 feet deep. It was a hard twenty hours work for them as it had to be completed between the Mustang's drinks, and it began to be very damp work before it was finished. With poles, brush, and earth it was then cleverly covered over and concealed. And the men went to a distance and hid in pits made for the purpose.

About noon the Pacer came, alone now since the capture of his band. The trail on the opposite side of the mud belt was little used, and old Tom, by throwing some fresh rushes across it, expected to make sure that the Stallion would enter by the other, if indeed he should by any caprice try to come by the unusual path.

What sleepless angel is it watches over and cares for the wild animals? In spite of all reasons to take the usual path, the Pacer came along the other. The suspicious-looking rushes did not stop him; he walked calmly to the water and drank. There was only one way now to prevent utter failure; when he lowered his head for the second draft which horses always take, Bates

With one mighty bound he clears the fifteen feet of ground.

and Smith quit their holes and ran swiftly toward the trail behind him, and when he raised his proud head Smith sent a revolver-shot into the ground behind him.

Away went the Pacer at his famous gait straight to the trap. Another second and he would be into it. Already he is on the trail, and already they feel they have him, but the Angel of the wild things is with him, that incomprehensible warning comes, and with one mighty bound he clears the fifteen feet of treacherous ground and spurns the earth as he fades away unharmed, never again to visit Antelope Springs by either of the beaten paths.

V

Wild Jo never lacked energy. He meant to catch that mustang, and when he learned that others were bestirring themselves for the same purpose he at once set about trying the best untried plan he knew—the plan by which the coyote catches the fleeter jackrabbit, and the mounted Indian the far swifter antelope— the old plan of the relay chase.

The Canadian River on the south, its affluent, the Piñavetitos Arroyo, on the northeast, and the Don Carlos Hills with the Ute Creek Cañon on the west, formed a sixty-mile triangle that was the range of the Pacer. It was believed that he never went outside this, and at all times Antelope Springs was his headquarters. Jo knew this country well, all the water-holes and cañon crossings as well as the ways of the Pacer.

If he could have gotten fifty good horses he could have posted them to advantage so as to cover all points, but twenty mounts and five good riders were all that proved available.

The horses, grain-fed for two weeks before, were sent on ahead; each man was instructed now to play his part and sent to his post the day before the race. On the day of the start Jo with his wagon drove to the plain of Antelope Springs and, camping far off in a little draw, waited.

At last he came, the coal-black Horse, out from the sand-hills at the south, alone as always now, and walked calmly down to the Springs and circled quite around it to sniff for any hidden foe. Then he approached where there was no trail at all and drank.

Jo watched and wished he would drink a hogshead. But the moment that he turned and sought the grass Jo spurred his steed. The Pacer heard the hoofs, then saw the running horse, and did not want a nearer view but fled away. Across the flat he went down to the south, and kept the famous swinging gait that made his start grow longer. Now through the sandy dunes he went, and steadying to an even pace he gained considerably and Jo's too-laden horse plunged through the sand and sinking fetlock deep, lost at every bound. Then came a level stretch where the runner seemed to gain, and then a long decline where Jo's horse dared not run his best, so lost again at every step.

But on they went, and Jo spared neither spur nor quirt. A mile—a mile—and another mile, and the far-off rock at Arriba loomed up ahead.

And there Jo knew fresh mounts were held, and on they dashed. But the night-black mane out level on the breeze ahead was gaining more and more.

Arriba Cañon reached at last, the watcher stood aside, for it was not wished to turn the race, and the Stallion passed—dashed down, across and up the slope, with that unbroken pace, the only one he knew.

And Jo came bounding on his foaming steed, and leaped on the waiting mount, then urged him down the slope and up upon the track, and on the upland once more drove in the spurs, and raced and raced, and raced, but not a single inch he gained.

Ga-lump, ga-lump, ga-lump with measured beat he went—an hour—an hour, and another hour—Alamosa Arroyo just ahead with fresh relays, and Jo yelled at his horse and pushed him on and on. Straight for the place the Black One made, but on the last two miles some strange foreboding turned him to the left, and Jo foresaw escape in this, and pushed his jaded mount at any cost to head him off, and hard as they had raced this was the hardest race of all, with gasps for breath and leather squeaks at every straining bound. Then cutting right across, Jo seemed to gain, and drawing his gun he fired shot after shot to toss the dust, and so turned the Stallion's head and forced him back to take the crossing to the right.

Down they went. The Stallion crossed and Jo sprang to the ground. His horse was done, for thirty miles had passed in the last stretch, and Jo himself was worn out. His eyes were burnt with flying alkali dust. He was half blind so he motioned to his 'pard' to "go ahead and keep him straight for Alamosa ford."

Out shot the rider on a strong, fresh steed, and away they went —up and down on the rolling plain—the Black Horse flecked with snowy foam. His heaving ribs and noisy breath showed what he felt—but on and on he went.

And Tom on Ginger seemed to gain, then lose and lose, when in an hour the long decline of Alamosa came. And there a freshly mounted lad took up the chase and turned it west, and on they went past towns of prairie dogs, through soapweed tracts and cactus brakes by scores, and pricked and wrenched rode on. With dust and sweat the Black was now a dappled brown, but still he stepped the same. Young Carrington, who followed, had hurt his steed by pushing at the very start, and spurred and urged him now to cut across a gulch at which the Pacer shied. Just one misstep and down they went.

The boy escaped, but the pony lies there yet, and the wild Black Horse kept on.

This was close to old Gallego's ranch where Jo himself had cut across refreshed to push the chase. Within thirty minutes he was again scorching the Pacer's trail.

Far in the west the Carlos Hills were seen, and there Jo knew fresh men and mounts were waiting, and that way the indomitable rider tried to turn the race, but by a sudden whim, of the inner warning born perhaps—the Pacer turned. Sharp to the north he went, and Jo, the skilful wrangler, rode and rode and yelled and tossed the dust with shots, but down a gulch the wild black meteor streamed and Jo could only follow. Then came the hard-

est race of all; Jo, cruel to the mustang, was crueller to his mount
and to himself. The sun was hot, the scorching plain was dim in
shimmering heat, his eyes and lips were burnt with sand and salt,
and yet the chase sped on. The only chance to win would be if he
could drive the mustang back to Big Arroyo Crossing. Now almost for the first time he saw signs of weakening in the Black.
His mane and tail were not just quite so high, and his short half
mile of start was down by more than half, but still he stayed
ahead and paced and paced and paced.

An hour and another hour, and still they went the same. But
they turned again, and night was near when big Arroyo ford was
reached—fully twenty miles. But Jo was game, he seized the waiting horse. The one he left went gasping to the stream and gorged
himself with water till he died.

Then Jo held back in hopes the foaming Black would drink.
But he was wise; he gulped a single gulp, splashed through the
stream and then passed on with Jo at speed behind him. And
when they last were seen the Black was on ahead just out of
reach and Jo's horse bounding on.

It was morning when Jo came to camp on foot. His tale was
briefly told:—eight horses dead—five men worn out—the match-
less Pacer safe and free.

"'Taint possible; it can't be done. Sorry I didn't bore his hell-
ish carcass through when I had the chance," said Jo, and gave it
up.

VI

Old Turkeytrack was cook on this trip. He had watched the
chase with as much interest as anyone, and when it failed he
grinned into the pot and said: "That mustang's mine unless
I'm a darned fool." Then falling back on Scripture for a prece-
dent, as was his habit, he still addressed the pot:

"Reckon the Philistines tried to run Samson down and they
got done up, an' would a stayed done on'y for a nat'ral weakness

on his part. An' Adam would a loafed in Eden yit on'y for a leetle failing which we all onderstand. An' it ain't $5,000 I'll take for him nuther."

Much persecution had made the Pacer wilder than ever. But it did not drive him away from Antelope Springs. That was the only drinking-place with absolutely no shelter for a mile on every side to hide an enemy. Here he came almost every day about noon, and after thoroughly spying the land approached to drink.

His had been a lonely life all winter since the capture of his harem, and of this old Turkeytrack was fully aware. The old cook's chum had a nice little brown mare which he judged would serve his ends, and taking a pair of the strongest hobbles, a spade, a spare lasso, and a stout post he mounted the mare and rode away to the famous Springs.

A few antelope skimmed over the plain before him in the early freshness of the day. Cattle were lying about in groups, and the loud, sweet song of the prairie lark was heard on every side. For the bright snowless winter of the mesas was gone and the spring-time was at hand. The grass was greening and all nature seemed turning to thoughts of love.

It was in the air, and when the little brown mare was picketed out to graze she raised her nose from time to time to pour forth a long shrill whinny that surely was her song, if song she had, of love.

Old Turkeytrack studied the wind and the lay of the land. There was the pit he had labored at, now opened and filled with water that was rank with drowned prairie dogs and mice. Here was the new trail the animals were forced to make by the pit. He selected a sedgy clump near some smooth, grassy ground, and first firmly sunk the post, then dug a hole large enough to hide in, and spread his blanket in it. He shortened up the little mare's tether, till she could scarcely move; then on the ground between he spread his open lasso, tying the long end to the post, then covered the rope with dust and grass, and went into his hiding-place.

About noon, after long waiting, the amorous whinny of the mare was answered from the high ground, away to the west, and there, black against the sky, was the famous mustang.

Down he came at that long swinging gait, but grown crafty with much pursuit, he often stopped to gaze and whinny, and got answer that surely touched his heart. Nearer he came again to call, then took alarm, and paced all around in a great circle to try the wind for his foes, and seemed in doubt. The Angel whispered "Don't go." But the brown mare called again. He circled nearer still, and neighed once more, and got reply that seemed to quell all fears, and set his heart aglow.

Nearer still he pranced, till he touched Solly's nose with his own, and finding her as responsive as he well could wish, thrust aside all thoughts of danger, and abandoned himself to the delight of conquest, until, as he pranced around, his hind legs for a moment stood within the evil circle of the rope. One deft sharp twitch, the noose flew tight, and he was caught.

A snort of terror and a bound in the air gave Tom the chance to add the double hitch. The loop flashed up the line, and snake-like bound those mighty hoofs.

Terror lent speed and double strength for a moment, but the end of the rope was reached, and down he went a captive, a hopeless prisoner at last. Old Tom's ugly, little crooked form sprang from the pit to complete the mastering of the great glorious creature whose mighty strength had proved as nothing when matched with the wits of a little old man. With snorts and desperate bounds of awful force the great beast dashed and struggled to be free; but all in vain. The rope was strong.

The second lasso was deftly swung, and the forefeet caught, and then with a skilful move the feet were drawn together, and down went the raging Pacer to lie a moment later 'hog-tied' and helpless on the ground. There he struggled till worn out, sobbing great convulsive sobs while tears ran down his cheeks.

Tom stood by and watched, but a strange revulsion of feeling came over the old cow-puncher. He trembled nervously from head to foot, as he had not done since he roped his first steer,

A snort of terror and a bound in the air.

and for a while could do nothing but gaze on his tremendous prisoner. But the feeling soon passed away. He saddled Delilah, and taking the second lasso, roped the great horse about the neck, and left the mare to hold the Stallion's head, while he put on the hobbles. This was soon done, and sure of him now old Bates was about to loose the ropes, but on a sudden thought he stopped. He had quite forgotten, and had come unprepared for something of importance. In Western law the mustang was the property of the first man to mark him with his brand; how was this to be done with the nearest branding-iron twenty miles away?

Old Tom went to his mare, took up her hoofs one at a time, and examined each shoe. Yes! one was a little loose; he pushed and pried it with the spade, and got it off. Buffalo chips and kindred fuel were plentiful about the plain, so a fire was quickly made, and he soon had one arm of the horse-shoe red hot, then holding the other wrapped in his sock he rudely sketched on the left shoulder of the helpless mustang a turkeytrack, his brand, the first time really that it had ever been used. The Pacer shuddered as the hot iron seared his flesh, but it was quickly done, and the famous Mustang Stallion was a maverick no more.

Now all there was to do was to take him home. The ropes were loosed, the mustang felt himself freed, thought he was free, and sprang to his feet only to fall as soon as he tried to take a stride. His forefeet were strongly tied together, his only possible gait a shuffling walk, or else a desperate labored bounding with feet so unnaturally held that within a few yards he was inevitably thrown each time he tried to break away. Tom on the light pony headed him off again and again, and by dint of driving, threatening, and manœuvring, contrived to force his foaming, crazy captive northward toward the Piñavetitos Cañon. But the wild horse would not drive, would not give in. With snorts of terror or of rage and maddest bounds, he tried and tried to get away. It was one long cruel fight; his glossy sides were thick with dark foam, and the foam was stained with blood. Countless hard falls and exhaustion that a long day's chase was powerless to produce were telling on him; his straining bounds first this way and then that, were not now quite so strong, and the spray he snorted as he gasped was half a spray of blood. But his captor, relentless, masterful and cool, still forced him on. Down the slope toward the cañon they had come, every yard a fight, and now they were at the head of the draw that took the trail down to the only crossing of the cañon, the northmost limit of the Pacer's ancient range.

From this the first corral and ranchhouse were in sight. The man rejoiced, but the mustang gathered his remaining strength for one more desperate dash. Up, up the grassy slope from the trail he went, defied the swinging, slashing rope and the gunshot fired in the air, in vain attempt to turn his frenzied course. Up, up and on, above the sheerest cliff he dashed then sprang away, into the vacant air, down—down—two hundred downward feet to fall, and land upon the rocks below, a lifeless wreck—but free.